"Cody..

I l...

His smile grew wr... ...t blur."

"I don't mean the actual fight—"

"Gee, was there a fight?" he asked with fake innocence.

Jane had no reason to rehash their final battle, but his sarcasm rankled. "You know there was a fight. There were constant fights, Cody. Incessant fights—"

"Punctuated by phenomenal sex."

She ignored him. "If you recall, Cody, after I left you, my father arranged to have our marriage dissolved. He sent you some papers to sign. I signed some papers. Then all the papers were filed."

"Yeah, I remember."

"Well." She took a deep breath. "Apparently they *weren't* filed."

"What do you mean, they weren't filed?"

"There's no legal record of our divorce."

"All right," he said slowly, carefully. "There's no legal record. What's the big deal?"

"The big deal is…" She attempted a smile, then gave up and forced out the words. "We're still married, Cody."

ABOUT THE AUTHOR

Judith Arnold says that like Jane Thayer, the heroine of *Married to the Man*, she was one of the brainy plain Janes in high school—and like many plain Janes, she liked to fantasize about the bad boys in her class. Writing this book—and reliving those fantasies—was great fun, even though she's now very happily married to a man who's "just bad enough to make life interesting." Judith, her husband and their two sons live in Massachusetts.

Books by Judith Arnold

HARLEQUIN SUPERROMANCE

509—THE WOMAN DOWNSTAIRS
559—FLASHFIRE
581—THE PARENT PLAN
611—ALESSANDRA & THE ARCHANGEL
634—CRY UNCLE

HARLEQUIN AMERICAN ROMANCE

482—JUST LIKE ROMEO AND JULIET
496—OH, YOU BEAUTIFUL DOLL
524—PRIVATE LIES
553—THE MARRYING TYPE

HARLEQUIN TEMPTATION

561—THE LADY IN THE MIRROR
565—TIMELESS LOVE

Judith Arnold

MARRIED TO THE MAN

Harlequin Books

TORONTO • NEW YORK • LONDON
AMSTERDAM • PARIS • SYDNEY • HAMBURG
STOCKHOLM • ATHENS • TOKYO • MILAN
MADRID • WARSAW • BUDAPEST • AUCKLAND

ISBN 0-373-70684-7

MARRIED TO THE MAN

Copyright © 1996 by Barbara Keiler.

This edition published by arrangement with Harlequin Books S.A.

® and TM are trademarks of the publisher. Trademarks indicated with
® are registered in the United States Patent and Trademark Office, the
Canadian Trade Marks Office and in other countries.

Printed in U.S.A.

MARRIED TO
THE MAN

CHAPTER ONE

JANE FOUND CODY SINCLAIR in the poolroom of a bar in New Orleans. To tell the truth, she wasn't surprised.

She hovered in the doorway of the tavern for a minute, surveying the front room, which was filled with rough-hewn tables and chairs, secluded booths and a bar that ran the length of one wall. The air was thick with smoke, chatter from the television above the bar, and the scent of stale beer and male sweat. Squinting in the murky light, she realized that she was the only woman in the place.

No, she wasn't. Closer inspection informed her that the beefy, broad-shouldered bartender pulling levers and filling pitchers with sudsy beer was a woman. A large, tattooed woman with thick hands, a crew cut and a chesty baritone laugh. Chatting it up with the two longshoreman types perched on stools across the bar from her, she seemed to be in high spirits.

Jane was *not* in high spirits. She didn't want to be here. She should have resolved the matter by mail—or better yet, had someone else handle it for her.

But despite the nerves twisting her innards into macramé, despite the clammy dampness slicking her palms, she knew there was no other way but to deal with Cody in person. She'd had to reconcile her innate cowardliness with her understanding of right and wrong, and meeting Cody face-to-face was the right thing to do. She couldn't have sent a surrogate. She couldn't have hidden behind others. If she'd been bold enough to let him overturn her life twelve years ago, she could certainly be bold enough to have a civil conversation with him now.

Twelve years. Would she still recognize him? Surely he wouldn't recognize her. Those twelve years had transformed her from a reckless, giddily romantic schoolgirl into a calm, reasonable adult. Her hair was well-groomed, her apparel well tailored, her nails well manicured. She had learned, thanks to Cody, that leading with one's heart was a good way to get one's heart broken. So she relied on her brain these days.

She scanned the dim tavern once more, took a deep breath for fortitude and tried not to gag on the second-hand smoke. The room wasn't particularly crowded— no more than a dozen men were seated at the bar. Then again, it was only six o'clock. Most potential booze-hounds were probably just leaving work about now, or else catching a bite to eat before they made the scene. She felt a few pairs of eyes on her as she headed for the bar. She would have liked to believe none of the leering customers was Cody, but he *could* be one of them. The woman she'd spoken to at the *Sentinel* had been certain Jane would find him here. "Oh, he always likes to unwind at Gussie's, down in the Quarter," she'd said. "He'd be there right now."

Which one was he? Jane wondered, curiosity mixing with dread. The paunchy gentleman near the jukebox? The glowering fellow with the suspiciously ragged scar on his cheek? The Hell's Angel in the leather vest?

"What can I do for you?" the bartender asked in a pleasant growl.

Jane opened her mouth, but no sound came out. She cleared her throat, suppressed a cough and said, "I'm looking for someone named Cody Sinclair. I was told I might find him here."

"You a friend of his?"

Jane could think of a hundred words to describe what she and Cody had once been to each other, but *friend* never would have made the list. "I'm ... an old acquaintance," she said.

"Well, now, he might be here," the bartender drawled, sizing Jane up with a long, skeptical stare. "What kinda accent you got there?"

"Boston," Jane said, then cringed in anticipation of the ridicule such an admission invited. She suspected her pristine Yankee pedigree was worth less than nothing in this Deep South delta city.

The bartender swore, but the foul word had a friendly lilt to it. "What happened? Y'all get separated from your tour group?" she teased.

Jane thought wryly that Gussie's Pool Hall and Taproom hadn't been mentioned as a must-see in any of the tourist pamphlets in the hotel's lobby. It wasn't in the finest neighborhood of the city, or the most colorful. The block on which Gussie's sat could be charitably considered one notch above a slum.

The bartender's congenial smile made Jane feel safe, though. True, two lone women could drown in all the testosterone swamping the room, but the bartender seemed like the sort of person no man in his right mind would mess with.

"Or is it Cody knew you back in the good old days?" the bartender guessed. She lit a cigarette and exhaled a blast of smoke.

Jane didn't care to debate whether the old days with Cody were all that good; she simply nodded. "Is he here?"

The bartender measured Jane with a lengthy stare, tugged her cigarette from her mouth and used her thumbnail to flick the ashes onto the floor. "Yeah, he's here."

Jane shot a furtive look around the room, eyeing the motley clientele. Then she leaned across the bar and murmured, "Which one is he?"

"You don't recognize him, huh."

Jane gazed around the room one last time. He couldn't be that one, or that one, or that angry, nasty-looking lout in the corner. He just couldn't be.

She smiled sheepishly at the bartender and confessed, "I haven't seen him in a long time."

The bartender issued a quick bark of a laugh. "He ain't any of these losers, darlin'," she said, loud enough for the losers to overhear. Jane braced herself against the bar, poised to bolt for the front door if one of the losers came at her with a knife. They all looked perfectly capable of it. But those who heard the bartender only laughed. "Cody'd be in back," she said, motioning toward an open door at the rear of the room.

Jane was relieved, not only because she honestly hadn't wanted Cody to have deteriorated that badly, but also because she was more than happy to exit the barroom. Squaring her shoulders, she followed a meandering path among the tables to the rear of the room, avoiding eye contact with the men she had to pass and acknowledging that the Cody she'd known twelve years ago might very well have turned into one of these bloated and scowling thugs and slugs. He might be right that minute throwing back Scotch after Scotch and chain-smoking in the back room. Even in high school, he'd had the potential to be either wonderful or terrifying.

Jane was thirty years old and far less susceptible to
wonder or terror than she'd been the first time she'd laid
eyes on Cody Sinclair. She reminded herself of that
more than once en route to the partially open rear door.

At the threshold, she hesitated. The room on the
other side was illuminated with a lemon yellow light, its
brightness a sharp contrast to the gloomy barroom.

She closed her eyes and prayed for strength. It took
vast quantities of courage to face the man she'd once
risked her entire existence for, the man she'd loved
blindly and senselessly, with all the caution of an eighteen-year-old idiot.

Squaring her shoulders, she nudged the door wider
and entered the poolroom. And saw him.

He had his back to her, but she would know that back
anywhere. It was a strong back, lean and supple, taper-
ing from broad, bony shoulders down to a narrow
waist. Right now it was covered by a shirt of faded blue
denim tucked into a pair of broken-in black jeans. She
would know his long, long legs anywhere, too. And his
hips. Definitely his hips.

Several other men were in the room, one of them sitting on a table and two others hovering near the pool
table, which Cody was studying intently. Slowly, me-
thodically, he chalked the tip of a cue stick and analyzed the lay of the balls on the green felt. Jane observed
the motion of his wrist as he wielded the cube of chalk,
the unexpectedly graceful play of his fingers.

Oh, yes. She would know his hands anywhere. too.

Damn, but it was hot in New Orleans. Sweat gathered at the nape of her neck and under her breasts as she
watched Cody from the doorway. The churning ceiling
fans did nothing to cool her off.

He moved in lithe, relaxed strides around the table to set up his shot. Now Jane was able to see his profile.

A sigh lodged in her throat. She hadn't wanted him to go completely to seed, but did he have to look so outrageously sexy? His jaw was just as taut and angular as she remembered it, his cheekbones just as chiseled, his eyes just as intense, just as blue, just as disturbingly beautiful with their thick fringe of lashes. His hair was the same thick, unkempt black mane spilling down past his ears and curling against the collar of his shirt.

The room felt even hotter.

This was ridiculous. She was no longer the smitten schoolgirl who'd first glimpsed Cody Sinclair at the far end of the hall—cutting class if she remembered correctly—slouching near a row of lockers with his pals, all of them dressed in denim and leather, their eyelids at half-mast. They were the "cool" kids, the boys who put more effort into looking effortless than into the important things in life, like schoolwork and discipline.

Her heart had done a somersault that day, almost thirteen years ago, when Cody had lifted his blue-topaz eyes and they'd met hers. It did a somersault today, in a downscale poolhall in the French Quarter—and he wasn't even looking at her.

He was looking at the table. "Three in the corner pocket," he said, his voice low and certain. She knew his voice even better than she knew his hands, his back, his hips and his eyes. It was the same deep, husky, unbearably sensual voice that used to whisper to her over the phone, hours after her parents had thought she was asleep, hours after they themselves had retired for the night. "Are you in bed, Jane?" Cody would ask.

"Pretend I'm there with you. Pretend I'm kissing you and touching you...."

He bent over the pool table, lined up his stick and hit the cue ball. The three dropped neatly into the corner pocket.

"Oh, man," one of the table-sitters groaned. "He's gonna wipe me out again."

"You never learn, Darryl," Cody joked, with a flash of white teeth at the man who'd complained. It was only then that Jane noticed the two ten-dollar bills wedged under a bottle of beer on the edge of the pool table.

Maybe Cody earned money playing pool, but that wasn't the profession he listed on his income tax forms. The private investigator she'd hired to track him down had informed her that Cody Sinclair was a staff photographer at the *New Orleans Sentinel*. A photojournalist.

It was easier to believe he was a hustler.

"Five in the side pocket," he announced, his tone laced with just enough arrogance to make itself felt. He chalked his stick, pursed his lips and blew the excess chalk from the tip. Oh, Lord. She'd know those lips anywhere, too.

Her thighs began to sweat beneath the cool silk of her skirt.

The cue ball nudged the five, which glided to the side pocket and dropped.

"I reckon we know whose side God's on," one of the observers muttered.

"God's got nothing to do with it," Cody argued with a sly smile which, like every other aspect of the man, Jane recognized too keenly. "This is skill, Claude. Pure, unadulterated skill."

"Nothin' about you is pure or unadulterated," Claude retorted with a laugh.

"No? Two-ball in the corner."

"Looks like the damn Yankee's gonna clean you out, Darryl," one of the other men predicted as Cody lined up to shoot the two-ball.

Suddenly he froze, frowned and straightened up. And just as she had that fateful day at Brookline High School, she felt the full, stunning impact of those cool, gorgeous blue eyes on her.

His brows dipped slightly as his gaze narrowed on her. He neither smiled nor frowned, but simply studied her as she stood paralyzed in the doorway, unable to flee, unable to bound into the room, hand outstretched, and say, "Hi, there! Remember me?"

She stayed where she was, trying to guess what he was thinking. But reading Cody Sinclair's mind had never been one of her talents.

He was probably wondering who the hell she was. Maybe he thought there was something vaguely familiar about her. Or maybe he did recognize her. Maybe, behind his inscrutable expression, he was thinking that his worst nightmare had come true: Jane Thayer, the greatest folly of his life, was back.

But she wouldn't stay long, she wanted to promise him. She had come for his signature on a piece of paper, nothing more. She had no intention of meddling in his affairs—of which, she was sure, he had many.

"Hey, Sinclair," one of the table-sitters hooted. "Looks like you got a groupie."

"Come on in, baby," the man named Claude hollered to her. "We could use some sugar in this room. Why don't you all just come on in and set here on my lap?" He patted his knee.

Back in Boston, she would have told him what he could do with his knee. In Boston, men didn't come on so brazenly to women in public bars, at least not without the expectation that a woman would suggest to them, in suitably crass and precise language, that they perform an anatomically impossible feat. Women in Boston were like that.

Hell. Her failure to put the man in his place had nothing to do with being in New Orleans. It was simply that, as long as Cody was gazing at her, she felt tongue-tied.

"Fer-get it, Claude," one of the other men said. "She's only got eyes for the damned Yankee."

"He can have her eyes. I'll take the rest of her."

Cody glanced over his shoulder at his rowdy companions. "Cut it out, guys. This isn't just any old lady you're talking to." He turned back to Jane, and his bemusement dissolved into a tentative smile. "It's my wife."

This admission was greeted with a chorus of hoots and howls. "Your wife? Cody Sinclair's in leg irons?"

"Since when you got a wife, Sinclair?"

"I'll be damned. We got ourselves a genu-wine Mrs. Sinclair here!"

"Let's drink a toast to the girl!"

"She's not a girl," Cody said in a touching show of chivalry. "She's a woman." He had picked up a slight drawl himself, she noticed. Nothing as dense and sultry as the bayou accents of his friends, but his Boston vowels seemed longer and lusher than they used to be.

She was flattered that he'd recognized her, even if it had taken him a few unnerving minutes to figure out who she was. She was less pleased that he'd introduced her as his wife. He couldn't possibly know how accurate that label was.

"Hello, Cody," she said, her voice barely louder than a whisper.

His smile growing ironic, he tossed his cue to one of his buddies and strode around the table toward her. He had the same gait he'd had in high school, long and loose-limbed, conveying a confidence that disguised a lot, although back then Jane had been perhaps the only person to realize just how vulnerable Cody was beneath his self-assured swagger.

He didn't seem the least bit vulnerable now.

"You're in the middle of a game," she pointed out as he approached her. "Why don't you finish up? I can wait." In truth, she wasn't sure she was ready to confront him, not when her heart seemed to ricochet off her ribs with each step that brought him closer.

He shrugged. "I'll win it back from them some other time," he said, gesturing toward the twenty dollars on the pool table. "Those guys can't shoot to save their lives." He drew to a halt in front of her. He sounded slightly stunned when he said, "Geez, it's really you."

She felt slightly stunned until he gathered her hands in his. Then she felt *very* stunned. "Yes," she said in a pathetically weak voice. "It's really me."

"You're looking good."

She knew better than to take the compliment seriously. He was probably thinking she looked like an uptight Boston Brahmin, a full-fledged manifestation of her elite genes. Which was what she was. "Thanks. You're looking good, too."

He seemed about to question her further, but evidently he realized they'd be better off talking where his billiard pals wouldn't be watching them as if they were the evening's entertainment. "I'll buy you a drink," he said.

"Okay."

He ushered her back into the dim, smoke-filled barroom. Perhaps she would be better able to cope fortified by something alcoholic. She really shouldn't feel so awkward—not yet, anyway. She still hadn't dropped her little bombshell on him. Once she did, once he knew the reason for her being in New Orleans . . . things were going to get extremely awkward.

He led her to a booth as far from the bar as possible and helped her onto the worn banquette. "What can I get you?" he asked.

"A glass of white wine." She didn't bother to specify the label or vintage. Gussie's seemed like the sort of establishment that specialized in wines from screw-top gallon jugs.

"I'll be right back," Cody said, then sauntered over to the bar. Once again, Jane found herself fascinated by his easy grace, his rangy physique, the way he seemed to rule a room merely by crossing from one side to the other. She thought about the twenty dollars he'd forfeited so cavalierly at the pool table. Twelve years ago, twenty dollars would have been a fortune to them. God knew, a few more dollars might have supplied the glue to hold their marriage together.

But money wasn't the only glue. Nor was emotion. Just a month ago, Jane had found, to her great regret, that there was yet another kind of glue that kept a marriage from coming apart.

How was she going to tell him? She'd rehearsed various approaches in front of the mirror at her hotel room, but practicing her lines had seemed silly. After all, she'd reminded herself as she'd changed from her wrinkled traveling clothes into the summer-weight silks she was wearing now, she and Cody were both adults. She would meet him at the newspaper office where he worked, she would explain the problem and they would resolve it. Why memorize a speech?

She hadn't known then that she *wouldn't* be meeting him at his newspaper office—and that seeing him would cause her to regress. Right now, she didn't feel like an adult. She had to fight the urge to display her driver's license so the bartender wouldn't kick her out for being underage.

Cody returned to the booth carrying a bottle of beer and a goblet of wine. He set the drinks on the table and then slid into the booth facing her. The table seemed too small all of a sudden. She wished there was about ten more feet of space between her and him.

He smiled, and she upped her wish to twenty feet.

"All right," he said, relaxing in his seat. He kept his hand on his bottle, his palm curved around the chilled brown glass, but he didn't lift it. "We ought to drink a toast or something."

"To what?" *Our divorce?* she almost blurted out. *The hurt feelings? The foolishness of our youth? Or perhaps the divine luck that let us grow up and get over it?*

"Old times." He tapped the rim of his bottle gently against her goblet, then took a long chug straight from the bottle. When he set it down, his smile was gone. His gaze hadn't budged.

"Old times," she echoed faintly, swallowing a small sip of the chardonnay and trying not to grimace at its bland taste.

"So." His tone took on an ironic edge. "I don't suppose your being here is just a coincidence."

He didn't seem quite angry, or sarcastic, or hostile. But he clearly wasn't thrilled that she'd barged back into his life. She couldn't blame him. They hadn't parted on the best of terms.

Now, there was an understatement. They'd parted on the absolute *worst* of terms, hurling accusations, spewing hatred, raging wildly at each other. It had taken Jane years to recover, and while she was sure Cody had bounced back a lot faster, he couldn't be blamed for harboring a few grudges.

And now she had to ask a favor of him. A huge favor. One she hoped he would be glad to accommodate once he heard the facts. But...

But why did he have to look so damned good?

Oh, for heaven's sake. She could handle having a drink with an attractive man. It just so happened that Mark Dennison was an attractive man, and Jane was going to be marrying him on New Year's Eve. Mark was going to make her a fine husband, which was a hell of a lot more than Cody had ever done. Mark was upstanding, ambitious, cultured...everything Cody wasn't. That was what she admired about Mark. That was why she was going to marry him once she and Cody took care of business.

She sat straighter, took another sip of the watery chardonnay and met Cody's cool smile with one of her own. "It's not a coincidence. I stopped by the *Sentinel* and one of your colleagues told me I'd find you here."

He nodded, assessing her, tracing the label of his beer bottle absently with his thumb. "You tracked me down to the *Sentinel*?"

"Yes. I found out you were a photojournalist—"

"Whoa." He chuckled and shook his head. "Give me a break, Jane. You know I can't be anything with that many syllables in it. All I do is take pictures."

"For a newspaper."

"That's right." He took another swig of beer, and when he lowered the bottle his grin was back. "How about you? How many syllables in your career?"

This was the Cody she'd known—the wise guy who could get away with his attitude because there was always a self-mocking quality to it. "Two. Or three," she amended. "It depends on whether you call me a lawyer or an attorney."

"Oho. An attorney. Well, we always knew one of us would turn out all right. I don't think there was ever much question which one of us it would be."

"Photojournalism is a fine profession," she asserted.

"Maybe. But all I do is take pictures."

Yes, this was the Cody she'd known. If anyone so much as implied that he was the least bit respectable, he'd deny it from here till Sunday. Marrying her had been respectable—but they'd tied the knot in the tackiest wedding chapel in Las Vegas, with matching bargain-basement gold rings, so it hadn't been *that* respectable.

Her memories irked her. "I didn't come here to debate semantics with you," she said.

"I'm dying to hear why you *did* come." He leaned forward, resting his elbows on the table and propping his chin in one hand. "How'd you find me at the *Sentinel*?"

"I hired a private investigator."

This news apparently took him aback. His eyebrows arched and his gaze grew quizzical. "A private investigator? That must've cost some serious bucks."

"Not really. He found you pretty quickly." And given what Jane earned as an associate at Baker, Dunn, the bill hadn't even caused a blip in her personal finances. "Apparently it's easy to find someone who isn't trying to hide. You have a social security number, a driver's license—he tracked you down without any trouble."

"Lucky for me I'm not a criminal."

"Indeed."

Silence descended briefly onto the table. Someone pumped some money into the jukebox; a Neville Brothers tune filled the air. Jane listened to the sweet, soulful singing, grateful for the lull in the conversation. She felt drained, and she hadn't even broached the reason for her visit.

"So," he said. "You're a lawyer."

"Yes."

"I could've guessed."

She smiled feebly. "I was always fairly predictable." Except for one time, one marvelous moment of lunacy when Cody Sinclair had asked her to run away with him and she'd said yes. "I wouldn't have guessed you'd be—taking pictures."

"You'd've bet on a life of crime," he joked.

"No."

He studied her intently. The music coiled around them, sad and lovely. "You expected me to wind up a nothing."

"No," she murmured. "I always knew you'd turn out fine."

He angled his head, as if not sure he believed her. He seemed on the verge of saying something, but chose instead to drink some beer. "You still live in Brook-line?"

"Boston," she told him. "I've got a condo in Back Bay."

He smiled as if he'd known all along. "Figures."

She resented his cynical tone. She shouldn't have to defend herself or her choices to him. Her condomin-ium was pretty, it was expensive, and it was hers. She wasn't going to apologize for it. "You have no right to sit in judgment of me," she said, bristling.

"Lighten up, Janey. I'm not judging you." He leaned back against the cracked upholstery of the bench. "I just remember Back Bay. Rich people lived there."

Money had always been a sore point between them— more accurately, her family's money, and Cody's sore point. But she didn't want to dwell on that. She hadn't traveled all this way to pick over the bones of their old arguments. "How have you been?" she asked, wincing inwardly at the inanity of the question.

He threw back his head and laughed. Jane noticed tiny lines crinkling the outer corners of his eyes. "I've been just swell," he answered just as inanely.

She inched toward the subject she had to discuss with him. "Are you seeing anyone?"

Again he laughed. "You walked out on me a long time ago, lady. You really think it's any of your busi-ness whether I'm seeing someone?"

As a matter of fact, it was. "I was just wondering. Are you married?" Her gaze strayed to his ringless left hand.

"No, I'm not married. How about you?"

"No." Her left hand was also ringless. She'd left her diamond solitaire back at the hotel, telling herself that the two-carat rock was an invitation to muggers in a city like New Orleans, known for its crime rate. "I'm engaged to be married," she told him.

"Well. Congratulations," he said heartily.

Unable to tell if he was mocking her, she allowed herself a tentative smile. "I mean it, Jane," he insisted. "I hope things work out for you this time."

"Thank you." She sighed with relief. "I think he and I are better suited."

"He must be rich." Cody grinned.

She acknowledged his teasing with a nod. "He's a banker. I'm a lawyer. I think we'll be able to make ends meet."

"Well." He lifted his bottle. "This is definitely worth toasting. Here's to your marriage." He took a sip and set down the bottle. He was still smiling, but his expression grew dubious. "You didn't hire a detective and track me all the way down to New Orleans just to tell me this, did you?"

"No."

"Because there's nothing between us, Jane. It was over long ago. We don't owe each other anything. I've got my life, you've got yours, and whatever that line is about the twain meeting."

"I know, but..." She faltered. He was saying the right words, unknowingly making this easier for her. Yet she was embarrassed to have to admit that a mistake had been made twelve years ago, a mistake that could have wreaked disaster in both their lives if she hadn't accidentally uncovered it a month ago. "Cody... you remember when I left, don't you?"

His smile grew wry. "It's all a distant blur."

"I don't mean the actual fight—"

"Gee, was there a fight?" he asked with fake innocence.

She had no reason to rehash their final battle, but his sarcasm rankled. This was their history he was making jokes about, a history they had lived and shared and suffered through together, no matter how successfully they'd both put it behind them. "You know there was a fight. There were constant fights, Cody. Incessant fights—"

"Punctuated by phenomenal sex."

She pursed her lips to stifle her retort. He obviously remembered the fights—and she remembered the phenomenal sex just as well. But she didn't want to talk about sex with him, phenomenal or otherwise. They'd been children then. Full of energy, full of passion and a few quarts shy of a full tank when it came to things like consideration and respect and all the other vital ingredients of a mature relationship.

Why was Cody even bringing it up? Why did he care that their sex life had been phenomenal? It was over. Long, long gone.

She collected herself, determined to keep the discussion on a higher plain. "If you recall, Cody, after I left you, my father arranged to have our marriage dissolved."

"Something like that."

"He sent you some papers to sign. I signed some papers. Then all the papers were filed."

"Yeah, I remember."

"Well." She took a deep breath. "Apparently they *weren't* filed."

He shifted almost imperceptibly in his seat. His spine seemed elastic; he drew himself straighter, taller. His insolent smile vanished, as did the mildly bored expression in his eyes. "What do you mean, they weren't filed?"

"There's no legal record of our divorce."

"All right," he said slowly, carefully. "There's no legal record. What's the big deal?"

"The big deal is…" She attempted a smile, then gave up and forced out the words. "We're still married, Cody."

CHAPTER TWO

CODY SINCLAIR WAS NO candidate for sainthood. He'd crossed the line plenty of times in his life; he'd lived high and wild. He'd come very close to messing up a woman's life a long time ago simply because he'd been a cocky, headstrong punk who had somehow become obsessed with the smartest girl in his senior class.

But never had he imagined himself an adulterer.

He was a normal, healthy red-blooded male, and in the time since the smartest girl in his senior class had marched out of his life in a welter of tears and recriminations, he'd been with a few women. Okay, a *lot* of women. Women who couldn't possibly have been the smartest girls in their classes. Women who were giggly, buxom and looking for nothing more than a good time. Women who were, in fact, the exact opposite of Jane Thayer. In the twelve years since Cody had signed a piece of paper that had supposedly freed Jane Thayer from his evil influence for the rest of her life . . .

Cripes. He'd committed adultery more times than he wanted to admit.

It was only a technicality. Just a legal document that her father—no great favorite of Cody's right from the start—had forgotten to file. None of this meant anything.

And yet.

He gazed across the table at the woman who had once driven him past the point of no return and admitted to himself that it didn't *feel* like a technicality. Even Cody had morals. And according to his own personal moral code, married people weren't supposed to mess around.

Okay. It wasn't the end of the world. Surely none of the ladies he'd known since Jane could accuse him of deceiving them. He'd been deceived, too.

He allowed himself a certain wicked satisfaction over the fact that Jane's father, of all people, had been responsible for the screwup. Cody still remembered the old man, not only from his nasty, nagging phone calls once Cody and Jane had settled in Los Angeles, but from the one time Cody had made the mistake of visiting her at her parents' house.

The Thayers had lived in a massive brick mansion on the posh side of Brookline. Cody had cruised the arc of the Thayers' driveway on his rebuilt Harley hog, climbed the front steps and pressed the doorbell, convincing himself that the fancy white pillars flanking the door didn't overwhelm him, nor did the sonorous chime he heard through the beveled sidelights framing the door, nor the elaborate landscaping of the front yard . . . nor the fact that her house was bigger than the entire apartment building where he and his mother occupied a second-floor flat. Cody remembered Mr. Thayer answering the door and glaring at him as if he was a cockroach. When Cody said, "Hi, is Jane home?" Mr. Thayer had given him a contemptuous scowl and answered, "Not to trash like you, she isn't," and slammed the door in Cody's face.

How could Cody not smile at the news that Mr. Thayer had fouled up his daughter's life even worse than Cody had? The old goat had misfiled a piece of

paper, and as a result, Jane Thayer was still married to
trash like Cody.

He wanted to laugh—except that it really wasn't
funny.

He studied Jane through the smoky blue haze hovering in the air above the table. He hadn't been lying
when he'd told her she was looking good. But then, she
had always looked good to him. Back when his friends
would never have wasted their time with any female
smaller than a C-cup, Cody had always considered Jane
the ultimate in refinement. Most of the girls he and his
buddies had socialized with in high school had been
brassy and bawdy and proud of it, with voluminous hair
and jeans that left nothing to the imagination. Jane . . .

Jane had left everything to the imagination, and
Cody's imagination had gone into overdrive.

He'd known who she was long before they'd ever exchanged a word. In those days, everyone at Brookline
High School knew who Jane Thayer was. She was the
head of the honor society, the head of the philosophy
club, the head of the Société Française, the editor of the
poetry journal, the winner of the math award. National Merit Scholar.

Jane Thayer had existed in another galaxy as far as
Cody'd been concerned. He'd been one of those kids
who excelled in industrial arts and getting sent to the
principal's office, and his orbit should never have intersected hers.

But one day it had. He'd been hanging out with a few
of his pals, working on a plan to meet at a bar on Bea-
con Street that evening if they could all get hold of fake
IDs, when suddenly he'd seen Jane coming down the
hall. Their gazes had locked.

He almost hadn't noticed her creamy skin, her straight brown hair, her tailored corduroy slacks and textured sweater. All he'd seen were her eyes, dark and mysterious, luring him with what his horny eighteen-year-old mind told him was desire. He'd felt a sharp, lusty urge to get the girl everyone would have agreed was way too good for him.

He got her, all right. Only she got him worse.

He swore under his breath. He hadn't thought about her for years. A long time ago, she'd done a number on his ego—pumped it up as big as a dirigible and then exploded it, just like the Hindenburg. But he'd gotten over it. He didn't hate her anymore.

He sure as hell didn't love her, either.

Her eyes were as dark as he remembered them, still that mystifying shade of gray that made him think of night and fog and sex. Long before he'd figured out who the strange woman standing in the poolroom doorway was, he'd been bewitched by her eyes. She still had a way of turning him on like no curvy, flirty bimbo could.

And she was his wife, this woman with the mesmerizing eyes and the wistful smile, this woman who was savvy enough to be a lawyer but still looked pure and innocent. His wife.

His beer bottle was almost empty, and he considered buying another. To do that, though, he'd have to leave the table, and he didn't feel like turning his back on Jane even for the two minutes it would take to walk to the bar and back. Instead, he watched her nurse her wine and waited for his thoughts to quit jerking him around.

"So, what's the deal?" he finally said. "You can't marry this other guy until our divorce gets straightened out?"

"That's right." Her cheeks darkened to a pretty pink. It struck him as absurd, her blushing over their botched divorce. How could she blush with Cody? He'd seen her naked. He'd done things with her that he'd never forgotten about, even if she had.

She used to blush a lot then, he recalled with a private smile. She'd even made *him* blush once or twice—and he'd always believed he'd been born too jaded to blush. But Jane had been so inexperienced, so eager to please . . . so *easy* to please. So sweet and shy and adventurous, all at the same time. So soft and warm and open to him, and . . .

"I just need your notarized signature," she was saying. He forced himself to concentrate on her words rather than her lips. "Obviously, there are no property issues at stake, no assets to divvy up. I've gotten a judge to issue a divorce decree in Boston. All you have to do is sign it and—"

"No property issues?" He didn't give a damn about her money, but why make this simple for her? Her father—and Jane, too, if he thought about it—had treated him like dirt. She'd walked out on him because he couldn't give her every little thing she wanted the instant she wanted it, the way her rich parents could. The Thayers had ruined Cody's marriage, with Jane's cooperation and gratitude. Apparently they'd ruined his divorce, too.

Cody wasn't exactly feeling benevolent toward any of them. Why not let Jane sweat a little before he solved all her problems for her?

She rearranged herself in her seat, cleared her throat and pursed her lips. "No property issues," she repeated tersely.

"But you're a fat-cat lawyer. And all I do is take pictures." He tried not to grin.

"You're a photojournalist, whether you like it or not. I'm sure the *Sentinel* pays you a good salary."

"Not anything like what you and your banker fiancé must rake in."

She let out a slow, steady breath and drummed her fingers against the table. Her nails were oval, enameled the same pink shade as her cheeks when she blushed. "My father told me—way back when—that you only married me for my money," she muttered.

"Did he say that?" Cody retorted sarcastically. Closing his eyes, he could picture Jane's father, tall and aristocratic, with a shock of silver hair and the sort of even tan old men got while playing golf at exclusive country clubs. Cody still remembered that day when Jane's father had sneered at him on the front porch. He remembered thinking that maybe some fathers were worse than no father at all.

"Cody, this isn't about money," Jane said, her voice hinting at a warning.

Maybe this wasn't about money. But it was about their failed marriage and a couple of broken hearts and Jane's father messing everything up. He'd been wrong about Cody, about the kind of person he was. If Cody had wanted money, there would have been easier ways to get it than to elope with an eighteen-year-old girl, knowing that the instant she became his, her family would cut her off from all the family wealth. Cody had married Jane for a lot of reasons, and he'd be the first to admit love was only one of them. But money? Not hardly.

If he had any decency whatsoever, he'd put his old anger back into storage where it belonged and sign the documents Jane had brought from Boston. But decency had never been his long suit. "Daddy was right that I was a no-good punk," he reminded her, his voice ominously low. "Daddy was right that I'd take you away from the big Brookline mansion and set you up in a fleabag apartment, that I'd never be able to buy you caviar, that I'd drag you way down to my level and you'd never stop regretting it. The old man was batting a thousand—except he couldn't seem to get this one little piece of paper filed properly." He took a slow sip of beer, washing down his bitterness. "Yeah, I'm after your money. You've sure got me figured out."

She stopped drumming her fingers and hid her hands in her lap. He'd made her uncomfortable, and that was just fine with him. "How much?" she asked in a tense voice.

"How much what?"

"How much money will it take for you to sign the divorce decree?"

More than uncomfortable, she was alarmed. Suspicious. Maybe a little frightened.

Damn. He'd toyed with her long enough. He ought to back off and let her be. But her eyes were doing things to him again, just the way they'd done things to him in that high school corridor so many years ago. He resented that she could still affect him. If threatening her on the economic front was the only way he could get back at her, he'd do it. Not because he would ever take a stinking penny from her, but because he couldn't stand the thought that her hair, now shorter and neater than it used to be, was still the same glossy honey brown color he remembered, the same silky texture he'd once run his fingers through. And her high, clear forehead, her sharp cheeks and narrow chin, her long, slender throat, the body he'd held in his arms every night for a few tempestuous months . . . and her mouth . . . and her eyes, those witchy, hypnotic eyes . . .

"I don't know," he said. "I'll have to think about it."

"I can't believe this," she snapped, abruptly sliding out of the booth and standing. "Fine, then, Cody. Think about it. I'll be in touch." The words came out cold and brittle, like chips of ice.

He ran his gaze down her body, decked out in an expensive-looking suit, and then back up to her face. He should have stood when she did—that would have been the polite thing to do—but the devil had gotten hold of him. Let her sweep into his world, so regal in her high-priced threads, with her high-priced job and her high-priced beau. Let her reveal what a snob she was by calling him a "photojournalist" because she could never accept that she'd spent a few red-hot months of her life married to someone who currently made his living taking pictures.

Why should he make things convenient for her? Why not let her suffer a little?

"Okay," he drawled in his adopted Southern twang. "You be in touch, Mrs. Sinclair."

He noticed a flicker of anguish pass across her face as her married name—a name she hadn't had long enough to grow into—hung in the air between them. Then she pivoted on her heel and stormed out of Gussie's.

It reminded Cody of the day she'd stormed out of their tiny apartment in Los Angeles twelve years ago. Jane Thayer was awfully good at storming out of his life.

It was her storming back into his life that had thrown him for a loop.

CLARISSA BONNERT WAS used to being stared at. Her mother was Vietnamese, her father African-American, and she had wound up with a face so strikingly beautiful that people—particularly male people—couldn't seem to look away.

In fact, she had grown tired of the attention—so tired she'd learned to disguise it. She'd seen her share of silly movies, and she'd learned from them that if a pretty woman put on a pair of large-framed eyeglasses and twisted her hair into a prim little knot at the back of her head, people—particularly male people—wouldn't notice how pretty she was, and because they didn't realize she was pretty, they could take her seriously.

She had decided she wanted to be taken seriously after her modeling career had sputtered. She still got occasional calls from the agency, but she'd never had great potential, because she was only five foot two on tiptoe, and too exotic for most jobs. Besides, the money had never been dependable. And now she was twenty-five, which was practically a senior citizen when it came to modeling.

The men she'd met during her life as a model were, not surprisingly, hung up on her looks to the exclusion of all else. She wanted to find a smart man, an established man, a gentleman. So she'd bought herself a pair of large-framed eyeglasses and a lot of bobby pins, and she'd taken courses to become a paralegal.

She much preferred working at Baker, Dunn and
Associates to posing in the blinding glare of a photographer's lights, wearing gobs of cosmetics and holding
a rigid smile and a bottle of perfume. She especially
enjoyed working for Jane Thayer, who was as smart
and deep and highly esteemed as Clarissa wished she
herself was.

She sat at her desk immediately outside Jane's office, typing up the settlement papers on Jane's latest
triumph. Jane was going to make partner soon, Clarissa knew. She was brilliant and she worked her tail off.
Sixty-hour weeks were typical for her, seventy-hour
weeks not uncommon. Clarissa liked having a work-
aholic boss, because she knew that once Jane made
partner, she would bring Clarissa up the ladder with her.
Just because Clarissa was half as smart and twice as
beautiful as Jane didn't mean she couldn't have ambitions, too.

She was skimming the text on her monitor when she
felt a shadow fall across her shoulder. Swiveling around
in her chair, she saw Mark Dennison looming above her
desk. Mark was Jane's fiancé, and he was just about the
most perfect man Clarissa had ever known.

Not that she knew him well. But he was rich, he knew
how to dress and he was a banker. He was thoughtful
enough not to judge women by anything as superficial
as the way they looked—at least, Clarissa assumed as
much, given that Jane wasn't exactly the sort of woman
who turned men's heads. Plus, Mark had looks to die
for. Maybe Clarissa was shallow for happening to notice that, but just because she wore her huge, thick-
rimmed eyeglasses didn't mean she couldn't see.

She could see Mark Dennison just fine. She could see
his height, his tidy build, the perfect symmetry of his

face, the inbred Anglo-Saxon strength of his features. Having grown up in such an ethnic hodgepodge of a family, she took comfort in people like Jane Thayer and Mark Dennison and their traceable bloodlines.

Mark smiled at Clarissa. His expression seemed mildly condescending, either because Clarissa was several social classes beneath him or because she was in a chair and he was looming a good six feet above her and forced to look down.

Even at four-thirty in the afternoon, his cheeks were clean-shaven, his shirt crisp, his suit jacket as unwrinkled as if he'd just picked it up from the dry cleaner. Clarissa fingered her own blouse, knowing it was wilted and creased under the waistband of her skirt. Her bun sagged against the nape of her neck, and she'd chewed off her lipstick hours ago. Her eyeglasses slipped down her perfectly straight nose, and she shoved them back up with her thumb. Mark Dennison looked so well-groomed and dapper, she felt self-conscious about her late-in-the-day grubbiness.

"Hello, Mr. Dennison," she said politely.

He glanced toward Jane's door, then back at Clarissa. His smile grew a smidgen bigger, questioning.

"She's not in," she said, puzzled. Surely Jane must have told him she was taking a few days off from work.

"I know." He propped his hip against the corner of Clarissa's L-shaped desk so his face wasn't quite so high above her. His smile grew even bigger, almost conspiratorial. "Actually, I came to see you."

"Me?" Her smile shrank in reverse proportion to the size of his. Mark Dennison came to Jane's office quite often, but it was always to see Jane. He had no reason in the world to see Clarissa.

Just to be sure he had no reason to see her, she pushed her glasses even higher on her nose and pursed her lips in a forbidding scowl.

"Do you know where Jane is?" Mark asked.

"Right this minute?"

"Just in general. Do you know where she went?"

"New Orleans," Clarissa said with a laugh that died in her throat when she realized Mark hadn't known.

"New Orleans," he repeated, laboring to conceal his surprise.

"She's taken a few personal days, Mr. Dennison. Didn't she tell you?"

Mark loosened his tie with a precise tug, then undid the collar button of his shirt. Perhaps he was finished with work for the day. Clarissa had heard of banker's hours; maybe bank executives really *did* stop working by midafternoon. Maybe Mark was planning to remain perched on the corner of her desk for hours, discussing his sweetheart with her.

Or else, for some reason, he was about to do a striptease.

The very thought made her roll her eyes and swivel away. Strange things were known to happen at Baker, Dunn, but Jane was never a part of them—and her fiancé would never be a part of them, either. That was why Clarissa liked Jane—and why she assumed she liked Mark. They were dependable. They were predictable. They were sensible.

On the other hand, she couldn't shake the notion that the more shirt buttons Mark popped open, the better he would look.

Shame on you, Clarissa, she scolded herself.

"I saw Jane this weekend," he said. "We attended a function at the Museum of Fine Arts, and there was a sculpture there."

Clarissa had a feeling this conversation—it was really more of a monologue—was way over her head. "A sculpture?"

"A naked woman rising from a rock. The rock was shaped somewhat like a cake. When I commented on that, Jane concluded I wanted a bachelor party."

"Do you?"

"No. That's the last thing I want. But all of a sudden, she said she had to take a few personal days and she disappeared. To New Orleans," he added, trying to disguise the fact that until Clarissa had informed him, he'd had no idea where Jane had gone. "I thought she might be planning a surprise bachelor party for me—God help me, a party where a naked woman might jump out of a cake."

"In New Orleans?" Clarissa frowned. "Why would she arrange a bachelor party for you in New Orleans?"

"To surprise me. If she did anything in Boston, I'd know about it. I have an incredible network of friends and associates. Jane knows she can't keep any secrets from me here. She wouldn't *want* to keep any secrets from me, of course. We're very open with each other."

Clarissa didn't know what to say. She only peered up at Mark through the clear-glass lenses of her spectacles.

"Except when it comes to surprise bachelor parties."

"Just because you saw a sculpture of a naked lady bursting out of a rock, I don't see why you should think Jane is planning a party for you."

"It was the way she spoke at the museum. The way I stared at the sculpture. It was the context, Clarissa. Everything in life is *context.*"

Clarissa fell silent again, unsure of how she could possibly argue about context with Mark when she had no idea what he was talking about. Jane hadn't mentioned anything about a bachelor party, though. She'd said she was going to see an old friend in New Orleans and that she wasn't sure how long she'd be gone but she'd call the office every day. And she'd told Clarissa not to discuss her whereabouts with the other associates at the firm.

Maybe it *was* a secret. Or a surprise. Or something in that context.

"The thing is—" Mark leaned closer, treating Clarissa to a whiff of his citrus after-shave "—I hate surprises." He had three dimples, she noticed: a matching pair, one per cheek, and a solitary dimple at the tip of his chin, like the dot at the bottom of an exclamation point.

He was definitely the most handsome man she had ever seen. Which was saying a lot, given that she'd worked with male models during her brief career in print ads, and given the number of men—not gentleman-types like Mark—who'd come on to her before she'd learned how to hide her beauty. Mark looked so solidly chiseled—like a man emerging from a rock. Only his context was clothed, unfortunately.

"The thing of it is, Clarissa," he went on, leaning toward her again, speaking to her with an intimacy that implied they were longtime confidants, "I can't stand not knowing what's about to happen to me. If Jane is planning a party behind my back, with naked women jumping out of cakes—buxom, voluptuous, tarty ladies with frosting clinging to them—I'd really like to know about it.''

"If she's planning anything like that," Clarissa said honestly, "I can't help you. She didn't tell me a thing."

"Oh, come on," Mark wheedled, aiming his potent dimples with precision. "You can tell me."

"Well…" Clarissa faltered. If Jane had wanted Mark to know what she was up to, she would have told him herself. Clarissa couldn't betray her boss. And anyway, the idea of Jane's plotting a surprise with naked women and cakes was so romantic. So utterly unlike the sensible woman she'd thought she knew.

"I really can't tell you anything," Clarissa demurred. "But if you'd like, the next time she calls the office, I could tell her you've been asking about her. How would that be?"

He mulled over her suggestion. "I don't want her to think I'm checking up on her."

"I wouldn't have to tell her you're checking up on her," Clarissa assured him. "She'll be calling for her messages sometime tomorrow. When she does, I can tell her you called to find out how she was or something, and you miss her and you'd love to hear her voice. All right?"

"I *would* love to hear her voice," Mark confirmed, "but what I'd really love is to find out what in tarnation she's up to. I mean, let's be real here, Clarissa. I know her voice. I don't need to hear it."

"But you just said you loved it," she argued, once again at sea.

"I do love her voice," he insisted, sounding a touch impatient. "I worship her voice. Her voice implants within me the deepest amorous passion."

"But you don't want to hear it." Clarissa was really having trouble following him. But every time he leaned toward her, every time he gave her one of his multidimple smiles, she sort of forgot the importance of figuring out what was going on.

"It's not that I don't want to hear Jane's voice. If I heard it, I wouldn't be upset. I wouldn't be satisfied, but I could live with hearing her voice if that was the way things worked out. In other words, her *voice* wouldn't do anything for me one way or another."

"But...but you just said you were amorously passionate about it."

"And you just said she's in New Orleans. What good is amorous passion when she's taken her voice with her to New Orleans?"

"Well, she couldn't exactly leave her voice here in Boston, could she?" Clarissa argued. Somehow, Mark made everything seem awfully complicated.

"Here's an idea," he persisted. "How about if I sneak into her office and poke around a little. Maybe she left a clue somewhere, a notation on her desk calendar or a credit-card slip. An order form for naked women."

"Did it ever occur to you that she might be planning a bachelor party and naked women have nothing to do with it?"

His face lit up. "Aha! Then you admit she's planning a bachelor party!"

"I didn't say that!"

"Then you admit she's hired naked women?"

"No!"

"I'll tell you what. Let me sneak into her office, and I'll see if she has."

"She hasn't! I'm the only woman she's hired this year, and I'm not naked."

"I noticed."

The man was truly exasperating. But his smile soothed her. Not many men noticed her at all when she was disguised for business. "I'm sorry, Mr. Dennison," she said. "I can't let you go into Jane's office."

"Oh, come on!" If his dimples were bullets, she'd be dead. "I'm going to be her husband. She lets me in her office all the time."

"*She* lets you in," Clarissa emphasized. "I can't."

He sighed melodramatically. "She's lucky to have you as her lion at the gate. But what am I going to do? If she hires naked women and springs them on me un-expectedly, I'll be at a serious disadvantage."

"You don't really think she's hired naked women," Clarissa scolded, grinning. "You know Jane. Jane is the most down-to-earth person I know. She doesn't do things like that."

"Jane is a lot more complex than she lets on. I wouldn't put anything past her. She's in possession of the guest list for our wedding, she knows all my friends, and just days after the subject of naked women jump-ing out of cakes gets mentioned, she vanishes. It's enough to make anyone suspicious. I'm not saying I'm a suspicious person. I'm just saying I think Jane's keeping a secret from me. And you can help me figure it out."

Clarissa laughed, aware that Mark was getting to her. "I'll tell you what, Mr. Dennison. When Jane tele-phones tomorrow, I'll hint around and see if I can find out anything about a bachelor party, okay?"

"You're sure she'll call tomorrow?"

"She said she'd call every day while she was away."

"Then we ought to meet tomorrow so you can tell me what flavor cake she's ordering for the, um, festivities. How about..." He pulled a sleek leather date book from an inner pocket of his jacket, opened it and studied a page. "Hmm. Tomorrow's pretty hectic for me. Why don't we meet after work? What time do you get off?"

"About five, five-thirty." With Jane out of town, she doubted she would be working any later than that.

"Five-thirty would be good. Do you want me to stop by here? No," he answered himself. "For all you know, she may be staying in touch with other people in the firm. If they see me showing up two days in a row, they may warn her that I've been inquiring about her, and that would spoil the surprise."

Clarissa studied him for a long, dubious minute. "I think you *want* her to be planning a surprise party."

"Oh, no, absolutely not. I hate naked women. In cakes, that is."

Unconvinced, Clarissa nodded slowly. It was always possible that Jane was planning something so big she needed the help of some of the other associates or partners to pull it off. Perhaps her old friend in New Orleans was going to help her plan a huge bachelor party on a ferry boat, with a cabaret show and a casino—and naked women in cakes, since that was what Mark seemed so determined to convince Clarissa he didn't want.

Jane Thayer wasn't flamboyant or whimsical, but who knew? She was about to get married; maybe the spirit of the occasion had filled her head with crazy ideas. Maybe Jane did have a secret side.

"If you don't want to come here, we could meet somewhere," she said.

"How about the Four Seasons Hotel? The piano bar."

"Okay." She smiled at the prospect. An after-work rendezvous with Mark signified nothing, but she liked the glamour of meeting a rich, handsome man at a swanky hotel bar. If Jane could scheme behind Mark's back, Mark and Clarissa could scheme behind Jane's. Why not? Maybe they could plot an even bigger surprise to pull on her. Naked men. Pizza. Ice cream. More naked men.

It could be fun.

"The Four Seasons, then," Mark said. "Five-thirty."

"Fine. I'll meet you there tomorrow, Mr. Dennison."

He slid off her desk and stood, shaking his trouser legs down and shrugging his jacket straight on his shoulders. With a parting smile, he said, "You know, Clarissa, I think 'Mr. Dennison' is a bit too formal at this point. You're going to be my secretary-in-law, after all. Call me Mark."

She couldn't help but smile back. "All right, Mark," she said.

"Tomorrow," he murmured, then turned and strolled out of the office.

CHAPTER THREE

WHEN JANE ARRIVED at the *Sentinel* office building the next morning, she was furious. She was steaming. She was fully prepared to bite someone's head off.

Specifically, Cody's head.

She had spent the better part of the night wrestling with the sheets in her hotel room. She wasn't sure what part of the previous day's encounter with Cody infuriated her most: his determination to extort money from her; his ability to prove that her father had been right in thinking the worst of him; or the fact that even now, when she was a mature, rational adult—a woman engaged to be married, for crying out loud!—she still found Cody Sinclair unconscionably attractive.

It was ridiculous. How could she consider a jerk like him attractive? She'd come to New Orleans in good faith, to get his signature on a piece of paper that would liberate them both. Signing the document would benefit him as much as her.

How dare he ask her for money!

Ever since she'd left him and straightened out her life, she'd managed to remain levelheaded and in control. She'd breezed through Wellesley College and jogged through Harvard Law School, always organized, always on top of things, always armed with her wits and a vast store of knowledge.

Book learning, however, was useless against Cody Sinclair. Legal statutes wouldn't guide her. She was going to have to rely solely on her wits for this mission. What if Cody demanded a hefty ransom for the divorce decree? What if serious money was involved?

What if, when she saw him, she found herself experiencing the same visceral response to him she'd felt yesterday at Gussie's? What if the back of her neck tingled and her pulse raced and her palms started to sweat the instant she glimpsed him?

She would blame it on the muggy Louisiana weather. On too much starch in the hotel sheets. On anything other than the truth: that part of what had caused her insomnia last night had been not anger but memories. Memories of Cody's kisses, his touch. Memories of things he'd made her feel, things she'd had no inkling about before she'd met him.

She had lain awake last night in the king-size bed in her luxury hotel room, remembering a different hotel, years ago, and a different kind of burning. A motel off the highway, somewhere near Buffalo.

They'd been riding for nine hours by the time they'd reached it, and they were tired and sore. Jane's skin was chapped from the sharp wind, and her blood was hot with exhilaration and panic. At dawn that morning, while her parents were still asleep, she'd left a note for them on the table in the breakfast nook, hooked her arms through the straps of the backpack she'd stuffed with as much clothing as it would hold and crept out of the house. Cody had been waiting for her at the entrance to the driveway, just as he'd said he'd be. He'd tethered his backpack frame to the rear of his motorcycle, and he held a helmet in his hands for her.

And they'd left. Just like that. The one thing no one ever would have expected of Jane Thayer, good girl, highbrow, Wellesley-bound class brain: she'd run off with Cody Sinclair, straight C-minus class punk... irresistible class hunk.

By the time they'd reached the Buffalo suburbs, they were ready to collapse. They'd barely spoken to each other all day—riding tandem on the motorcycle made conversation impossible. Jane's rear end ached, her hands were stiff from clinging to Cody's ribs and she was farther from home than a distance that could be measured in miles. She'd done the unthinkable. She'd followed her heart. She'd accepted Cody's invitation to throw off her old life and make a new life with him.

She was frightened beyond words—but she didn't regret what she'd done.

Weary and breathless, they took a room at the motel. They tumbled down onto the bed, desperate for sleep. But they were even more desperate for something else.

"I've never done this before," she whispered to Cody.

"That's all right."

"I'm scared."

"Of what?"

Of your leaving me, she wanted to say. *Of winding up with nothing.*

"Oh, Janey, Janey..." His voice soothed her. So did his hands as they gently smoothed her hair away from her cheeks. "I'm going to marry you. I told you. We'll go to Nevada. They've got chapels there, and—"

"No. That's not why I'm scared." *I'm scared to think I made a mistake in loving you. I've given up everything, and I'm scared of what I'll be left with.* "Will it hurt?" she asked, her body already warming to him, responding to his caresses.

"I won't hurt you," he promised, running his hands down her body, slow and sweet, and then brushing her lips with his. "I'll never ever hurt you...."

He hadn't hurt her then, she remembered, waiting impatiently for the elevator to arrive at the lobby of the *Sentinel* building. The pain had come later.

Twelve years later, he was still hurting her, trying to blackmail her, of all things. Trying to rip her off. Trying to take an awkward mistake and turn a profit on it. She could have reached the fifth-floor City room on the power of her rage alone.

The elevator door slid open, and she decided she was better off hoarding her energy for the battle that awaited her once she confronted Cody. She boarded the car with a middle-aged woman wearing a cloying perfume and a young man chomping on spearmint chewing gum. Ignoring their clashing aromas, she used the ride upstairs to compose herself. She couldn't let Cody get the better of her again. Today she would be in charge. She would intimidate him with legal jargon. She would issue subtle threats. She would get the situation resolved and go home to her nice, tranquil, even-keeled life in Boston.

The door slid open at the fifth floor, and she stepped off, grateful for the unscented air. Just beyond the elevator alcove lay the bustling City room, where yesterday a helpful colleague of Cody's had suggested that Jane would probably find him at Gussie's.

The same woman was seated at the desk nearest the door this morning. She appeared to be in her thirties, with flawless mahogany skin and her hair woven into dozens of narrow braids. Jane arranged her face into a smile and approached the woman's desk.

The woman recognized Jane. "Well, hi there, darlin'! Did you find Cody yesterday?"

"As a matter of fact, I did," Jane said, eyeing the steaming mug of coffee on the woman's desk and feeling a pang of envy. The three cups she'd consumed at the hotel hadn't been enough. She needed a few more gallons of the stuff to get her brain to focus properly.

"Well, then, what can I do for you today?" the woman asked, her drawl so thick it took Jane a minute to translate her words into English.

"I'm looking for Cody again," she admitted, her smile turning sheepish. "Is he in yet?"

"Oh, he's in, all right. In trouble, I reckon." The woman laughed.

There was a God, after all—and he was punishing Cody. Jane grinned. "What kind of trouble?"

"I don't exactly know. He got called into the City editor's office about fifteen minutes ago. The company lawyer was in there, too. It's always bad news when a lawyer comes down from those penthouse offices upstairs."

"Maybe Cody broke a few laws," Jane said hopefully.

"I can't say it would surprise me." The woman sipped her coffee, then angled her head toward a glass-enclosed office at the far end of the vast, noisy newsroom. "They're in there, thrashing it out. Looks like Cody hasn't gotten the cuffs slapped on him yet."

Too bad. It would be a lot easier for Jane to beat the hell out of him if he were manacled.

Honestly. Where did these violent yearnings come from? Jane was a pacifist. She didn't beat people up.

Cody Sinclair brought out urges she'd rather not acknowledge.

She cast the coffee mug one final, wistful look, then thanked the woman and edged away from her desk. The City room was a fluorescent-lit expanse of desks, each equipped with a word processor, a telephone and a swivel chair. Only a few desks were occupied, although many people swarmed among them, looking frenzied. She tuned them out and concentrated on the trio in the glass-walled office.

Cody apparently didn't believe in the virtues of a professional wardrobe. He had on a pair of blue jeans faded almost to white, scuffed sneakers and a pocket T-shirt of burgundy cotton. His hair was a tumble of dense black waves; his posture showed no sign that he was under siege. The other two men in the room—both wearing summer-weight suits, Jane observed—looked a great deal more exasperated than Cody.

But his steel-hard expression didn't fool her. She knew he didn't take well to being chewed out by people in suits—or by anyone, for that matter. The cooler he appeared, the more likely he was boiling inside. She recalled the way he used to withdraw into himself when he got into trouble at school. He'd always seemed passive, unperturbed, but she knew he was only husbanding his anger, stockpiling it. He resisted anyone who tried to impose rules on him. Cody loathed all rules but his own.

Whatever was going on in that office, whatever mood he was in once he emerged, Jane ordered herself to remain composed. The calmer she was, the better her chances of calming Cody down enough to sign the papers she had tucked inside her purse. Surely there was a notary somewhere in the vicinity. They'd go, take care of business and be done with it. If Cody had other problems to deal with, he might just be willing to do whatever it took to get rid of Jane.

The door to the office opened, but she couldn't hear Cody's parting words above the general din in the City room. He backed out of the door, his arms at his sides and his chin thrust forward. And then he turned, slowly closing the door, and saw Jane.

That he hadn't slammed the door was a good sign. That his mouth tightened into a grim line at the sight of her was a bad sign. His laser-sharp eyes locked onto her from across the room, zeroing in on her like heat-seeking missiles.

Definitely a bad sign.

He shoved his hair back from his brow and ambled toward her in his familiar loose-limbed way. A muscle ticked at the edge of his jaw. Without taking his eyes off her, he deftly sidestepped desks, avoided the people rushing past him, ignored an occasional shout of greeting until he was only inches away.

"Good morning," she said, resorting to inanity, as she had last night. Clearly it wasn't a good morning for him.

"Let's get out of here," he muttered, taking her arm and steering her through the maze of desks to the elevator alcove. She was surprised he hadn't snapped at her or at least indulged in sarcasm.

She was even more surprised by his touch. She hadn't expected him to resort to chivalrous gestures with her. More important, she hadn't expected to feel the jolt of sensation his touch caused, not only in her arm but someplace deeper, someplace inside her where Cody didn't belong.

Unnerved, she bit her lip to keep from demanding that he remove his hand from her, which would only embarrass them both. When the elevator arrived, she let Cody usher her into the car. Once the door slid shut on them, he released her.

It took all her strength not to sag against the wall. The car descended so swiftly she felt her stomach lurch. Too little caffeine and too much Cody had her feeling queasy.

On the ground floor, he took her elbow once more and crossed the echoing lobby to a coffee shop. Jane's hopes rose, then sank at the idea that Cody needed what she needed, that they should have anything—even if it was only a yearning for coffee—in common.

They found a booth and sat. Jane tried not to fidget. She would have thought she'd be eager to launch right into a discussion of the divorce decree, but her curiosity about Cody's meeting eclipsed everything else.

His eyes glinted like twin mirrors, reflecting the world without offering a hint of what was behind them. His hands rested on the table, strong and broad, his knuckles forming hard ridges that sloped into thick, callused fingers. They were hands one would expect to see gripping the handlebars of a motorcycle, not operating a camera.

Her curiosity expanded to encompass Cody's entire life. "How did you wind up as a photojournalist?" she blurted out.

A waitress came to their table, carrying a carafe of coffee. "Hi, there, Cody," she murmured, acknowledging his slight nod and filling two ceramic mugs. "Can I get y'all something to eat?"

Cody glanced questioningly at Jane. "Just the coffee is fine," she said.

"We're set, then," he told the waitress, who sent a bright smile of farewell his way before returning to the counter. Cody turned back to Jane, frowning. "I hate that word, photojournalist."

"Why?"

"It sounds too…" He groped for the right phrase and came up empty.

"Too professional," she guessed.

Amusement flickered across his face and then vanished, leaving the frown unchanged. "Too arty," he corrected her. "Too intellectual."

"What's wrong with being intellectual?"

"It's not my style. You know that."

What Jane knew was that Cody took satisfaction in denying how smart he was. Intellectual, to him, implied snobbishness, bookishness, pomposity. To Jane, it implied only the willingness to use one's brain.

"What I do is very simple. My editor shouts, 'Sinclair, get your butt over to Esplanade Avenue, there's a body over there,' and I grab my gear and go and take pictures of the body. One of those pictures gets printed in the next day's *Sentinel,* and that's it."

"That sounds like the job description of a photojournalist," she teased.

Another flicker of amusement crossed his face, eroding his tension. "A photojournalist has a perspective," he explained. "He's got a point of view, an ax to grind. He goes to Esplanade Avenue and takes pictures of the body, and he's thinking his pictures will make people consider the city's terrible crime rate, or man's inhumanity to man, or the tragedy of violence in society. I just go and click the shutter."

"No point of view? No involvement?"

"None whatsoever," Cody confirmed, sounding boastful.

"How did you wind up doing this? I never would have imagined you taking pictures. You didn't even own a camera when I knew you."

"It was just one of those things," he said vaguely.

"Nobody becomes a photographer out of thin air. You were an auto mechanic, Cody."

"I was a mechanic because that was the job I was able to scare up," he said dryly. "I could have worked at a garage or I could have worked at a burger joint. The pay was better at the garage. It wasn't good enough for you, of course, but—"

"I didn't care about the money, Cody," she argued, then groaned inwardly. She didn't want to dredge up all the old fights—especially the fights about money.

Apparently, he did. "You left me because I couldn't support you in luxury."

"I didn't want luxury, Cody. All I wanted was to take some college courses. In the evenings. I was willing to work during the day, but if I could have just taken some night classes—"

"Which cost money. Lots of money. Money we didn't have. By the time we got to L.A., we had, what? A few hundred bucks between us? Enough to pay two months' rent on that godawful flat. And there you were, the Crown Princess of Brookline, saying you wanted to go to college."

"I gave up Wellesley College to marry you," she retorted, hating Cody for dragging her back to the past, hating herself for letting him.

"But Daddy sent you money so you could go back home and be a Wellesley girl, after all."

"Stop it." She ground her teeth together, then took a long, bracing sip of coffee. It scalded her tongue with its heat. But better for her tongue to be scalded than to utter words that couldn't be retracted.

She could have lived without Wellesley College. She could have lived without money. What she couldn't live without was her ambition. All she'd wanted was to take a class or two, to keep alive the possibility that she wouldn't have to work as a counter girl at a convenience store for the rest of her life. All she'd wanted was to take one small step toward a college degree.

Cody had argued then, just as he argued now, that it was all about money. But Jane had always suspected that it was really about his need not to be overshadowed by her. She hadn't cared if he never went any further in his formal education. But she'd wanted a college diploma. It had been her goal for as long as she could remember. And Cody had wanted to be the most valuable thing in her life, the *only* valuable thing in her life.

He'd been jealous. That was how she'd seen it, anyway.

But what did it matter? That was all ancient history.

"So," she said, once her tongue and her temper had cooled off, "how did you wind up taking pictures?"

He shrugged, as if it had been a fluke. "I helped this guy out on the freeway one day, a few months after you left," he told her. "He had a fat-cat car, a Jaguar. He'd pulled onto the shoulder and was freaking out because steam was coming out from under the hood. I fixed things up for him, kept him from pouring cold water into a hot radiator, gave him some antifreeze, that sort of thing. The guy wanted to pay me, but I wouldn't take money from him. So he gave me a camera."

"Really? Just like that?" Perhaps it *had* been a fluke.

"A Nikon—a damned expensive piece of equipment, though I didn't know that at the time. He said it had belonged to his wife, and they were in the middle of a nasty divorce, and it would serve her right for leaving her stuff in his car. I could relate to his emotional state of mind, so I took the camera."

Jane laughed. It was an odd story, yet she believed it. The people she'd met during her brief stay in Southern California had been awfully quirky. The Cody she'd known then definitely wouldn't have accepted money from a stranger in payment for some roadside assistance, but he would have accepted a camera from a comrade in the trenches.

"Did you take photography lessons?"

"Nah, I figured the thing out on my own. I worked at the garage during the day, and then in the evening I hung out, shooting rolls of film. Shooting scenery was never as interesting as shooting people, action, stuff going down. I guess I got good at it. I wound up getting hired by a neighborhood weekly that paid me peanuts, but someone there taught me how to use a darkroom." He shrugged again, as if the course of his life puzzled him. "Auto engines were getting kind of old. I got tired of having grease under my fingernails all the time, so I stuck with the camera work. I freelanced in Phoenix for a while, got a job up in Denver, and now this gig at the *Sentinel*. They like the way I shoot crime scenes—I don't have a point of view."

"So why are you in legal trouble?"

Cody's eyes narrowed slightly. "What makes you think I'm in legal trouble?"

"You were talking to the newspaper's lawyer when I arrived this morning."

He opened his mouth and then shut it, evidently figuring there was no point in asking her how she knew. Instead, he took a long sip of coffee and settled back in his seat. "Some clown has filed a suit against the newspaper because of me."

"Why? What did you do?"

He gave her a measuring look, then drank some more coffee. By the time he lowered his cup, he'd apparently reached the conclusion that it was all right to confide in her. "A couple of weeks ago, my editor told me to get my butt over to Esplanade Avenue because there was a body there. I shot a few rolls, developed them, and the paper ran a picture that showed a lot of rubberneckers hanging out around the crime scene, because it was the best of the bunch. It caught the whole mood of the scene, you know? Blood, gore and gawkers."

Jane nodded.

"Anyway, one of the gawkers in the background was a gentleman from La Place—that's about thirty miles west of here. A Baptist minister, a real nice guy. And there he was, standing in a doorway, gawking at the blood and gore, and in the picture his arm was draped around a hooker's backside. Well, it seems some of his parishioners saw that picture. One of those parishioners happened to be his wife. Next thing he knew, this real nice minister was fired and his wife gave him the boot. So he did the American thing—he hired a lawyer and sued for damages."

"That's absurd!" Jane exclaimed. "He was the one who destroyed his marriage by consorting with a hooker. He was the one who jeopardized his career. He has no grounds for a suit."

"He claims the *Sentinel* ran that photo deliberately to humiliate him."

"How could the *Sentinel* have done it deliberately? You had no idea he was a minister when you ran the photo, did you?"

Cody didn't answer. He met her gaze for a moment, then began fiddling with his teaspoon. His lips quirked into an enigmatic smile.

"You *did* know he was a minister?"

"Well, let's just say there was a feature story in the Sunday Living section about how some area churches contribute to their communities. One of the churches profiled just happened to be a Baptist congregation in La Place."

"You *knew* this guy was a minister?" she repeated, bristling.

This time Cody returned her indignant stare. "Yeah, I knew. I knew he'd presented himself as a regular pillar of the community, a moral leader and all that. And there I was, taking pictures of this body on Esplanade, and who should wander into the frame but the pillar himself, with his hand curved around the fanny of a hooker. It wasn't like I'd set out to expose the guy. But hey, if he exposes himself, why shouldn't I take his picture? He was there, in public, at a crime scene. The picture the *Sentinel* ran told more than one story. Why not?"

Jane subsided. Her first reaction had been that of a lawyer, furious because Cody had provoked the minister so flagrantly. But her second reaction, the fairer one, was that of a woman who despised hypocrisy. "I think you *are* a photojournalist, if you're taking pictures that tell stories."

"I was just doing my job," he protested.

"And that day your job made the world realize what a two-faced slime the minister was." She clicked back into her lawyer mindset and analyzed his plight. "Did your editor realize the minister was in the picture?"

"Yeah, his butt's on the line, too. He played innocent with the company brass, claims he didn't see the Rev in the frame, but he knew it as well as I did."

"So. You've ruined this minister's life—"

"He ruined his own life," Cody interrupted.

"Okay. He's ruined his own life and you recorded the ruination for posterity. How much is he suing for?"

"Five million dollars, but he'll take whatever he can get. The newspaper is looking at me as someone who's going to cost them a whole lot of money."

"The paper isn't going to fight him?"

Cody shook his head. "They just want to settle and get this fine, upstanding man of the cloth out of their hair."

Jane sighed. She understood the advantages to reaching settlements outside of court, even when a case was so blatantly absurd. "It's really just a nuisance suit."

"Yeah. The guy's a nuisance, all right."

"Too bad the *Sentinel* doesn't want to try its luck in court. They'd win it in a walk."

"You think so?" Cody smiled hopefully.

She returned his smile. "If there was any justice in the world, sure. It'll never come to that, though. That's the thing about nuisance suits. It's too much of a nuisance to fight them."

"But if you were the lawyer on this case and you had the time to fight him in court, you'd squash him, wouldn't you?"

Her smile grew. "It would be fun to try."

Cody lapsed into thought again, contemplating her, his gaze penetrating. She wondered what he was staring at, what he was actually seeing. Disconcerted, she hid behind her cup, taking a long sip of coffee. It had cooled down a bit, but its chicory flavor was still much too strong. She tried not to wince at the bitter aftertaste.

"You don't like Louisiana-style coffee," he surmised.

"It's not bad," she said, determined not to appear weak before she'd even entered into battle with him. "But it's strong enough to put hair on your chest."

"It hasn't put any on mine," he noted with a laugh.

She was visited by an unbidden memory of his chest, sleek and sinewy and devoid of hair. She remembered the arch of his ribs, his streamlined muscles, the way his nipples used to tighten into hard nubs when she kissed them.

Damn. She was blushing again—and here in a well-lit coffee shop, her blushing was certain to be more noticeable than it had been last night in the gloomy bar. It bothered her that Cody could rattle her so easily. It bothered her even more that he could see how rattled she was. No matter how serenely she sat, how reasonably she spoke, her face gave her away.

His smile changed into something both shy and seductive. "You know, Jane, you're the smartest person I've ever met. And you know as well as I do that Reverend Bob is just shaking the *Sentinel*'s tree, hoping some fruit will fall."

"Reverend Bob?"

"The Most Reverend Robert J. Stanhope."

She struggled not to let Cody's smile get to her, and looked away from his bright eyes to his strong, thick fingers, curved snugly around his cup of coffee. In her most lawyerly voice, she said, "I'm sure the *Sentinel—*"

"The *Sentinel* is running for cover. The *Sentinel* wants to report the news, not become the news. The *Sentinel* thinks that embarrassing a man of the cloth could backfire on them."

"And you obviously think embarrassing a man of the cloth is sound business practice."

He snorted and shook his head. "Settling with him turns my stomach."

"They aren't making you contribute to the settlement, are they?"

He shook his head again, his lip curling in anger. "They said they'd cover all the costs, but in the meantime, my editor's running scared, and he says I have to be more careful when I'm shooting. That was his word—*careful*. You know what that means, don't you?"

"It means he wants to protect himself."

"It means he wants me to censor myself."

She couldn't blame Cody for being furious, even if his fury sounded suspiciously like a point of view. People who merely took pictures didn't worry about censorship. Photojournalists did.

She kept that observation to herself, however. His boss's capitulation annoyed her as much as it did him. But there wasn't a thing she could do about it. And she had problems of her own.

"Look, Cody—just let the newspaper settle with the minister. In a few months, everyone will forget all about it, and then you can stop being careful."

"I don't know how to be careful," he reminded her.

That was true. She couldn't recall a single incident in her life with Cody where he'd been careful, except in the

most basic way—his insistence that they both wear hel-
mets on his motorcycle, for instance. When it came to
big things—such as pursuing a girl totally unsuited to
him, running away with her and defying her family...
Well, *careful* did not describe Cody.

That was why it was so important for her to exercise
the utmost care with *him*. If he was reckless enough to
want to jeopardize his career by contradicting the
newspaper's legal counsel, he could be reckless in any
of a number of ways that might affect Jane. "Cody,
about our divorce—"

"I don't want money," he said abruptly. His eyes
dimmed to a muted blue. "Never did, never will."

"Are you sure? Because last night—"

"Last night I felt like giving you a hard time."

She sighed. He could have given her a hard time
without going to so much trouble. The fact that she'd
spent the night dreaming about him instead of her fiancé back in Boston proved that money was the least of
her challenges when it came to Cody Sinclair.

"I'm not going to sign your papers," Cody remarked casually, as if he was commenting on the muggy
morning outside the air-conditioned building.

As his words sank in, Jane sat straighter, shaking off
her bittersweet sentimentality. "You've got to sign. For
your own sake, if not for mine."

His grin was back, more mischievous than ever.
"Why have I got to sign?"

"You might meet someone and want to marry her."

"I'm not the one with a fancy wedding in the works,"
he reminded her, obviously relishing the opportunity to
give her another hard time. "Let's face it, Jane—I've
already been married once, and it didn't work for me. I
can't imagine I'll repeat that mistake any time soon."

She wished she could believe he was kidding, but that would be a dangerous assumption. With Cody, one never knew what he was up to, or why. Chances were, he himself had no idea.

But if he didn't sign the papers—dear Lord. He *had* to.

"You say you don't want money, but I'll make it worth your while," she said, swallowing her anxiety. Last night, she'd been ready to throttle him because he wanted her money. This morning, she was beginning to realize that giving Cody money to sign the papers might be the ultimate bargain. "How much is it worth to you?"

"How much is it worth to *you?*" he shot back.

He knew damned well how much it was worth to her. She couldn't marry Mark without a legal divorce. Cody was simply tormenting her for the fun of it. She would rather not have to buy his cooperation, but she suspected that cash was the quickest way to his heart— maybe the only way.

His smile widened, emphasizing the hollows of his cheeks, the sturdy line of his jaw, the dazzling radiance of his eyes. "You really, really want to get this divorce deal done, huh."

"You'd be doing it for both of us. Right now you may think it isn't necessary, but someday. . . if you find a woman and fall in love . . ."

"I tried that once, too."

She didn't know if he was referring to her. She didn't *want* to know. "Please. I'm begging you." God help her—Cody had reduced her to groveling.

"All right. I'll sign your damned piece of paper. But not for money."

A different kind of anxiety seized her. What, other than money, did she have that he might want? She doubted he had any desire for her gratitude or goodwill. If he was looking for something else ...

She felt herself blushing again. She—Jane Thayer, poised attorney, successful professional—was blushing like an inexperienced girl on the cusp of puberty. She wished she could just get up and leave and let him rot in this hot, steamy, decadent city where ministers cavorted with hookers and dead bodies lay on Esplanade Avenue until people like Cody took their pictures.

She couldn't walk away, though. Not until he signed her damned piece of paper.

"Help me with this lawsuit," he said, smiling still, but deadly serious. "Help me convince the *Sentinel* that the bloodsucking Reverend doesn't deserve a dime. Help me get the suits off my back. Then I'll sign your paper."

Panic welled up within her. Paying him money would have been a cinch compared to this. How on earth could she help him with a lawsuit that his newspaper was prepared to handle? She wasn't licensed to practice in Louisiana—and if she were, she would probably follow the same course as the *Sentinel*'s lawyer. Nuisance suits were obnoxious and unfair, but usually they weren't worth the time and effort it took to fight them.

"I can't," she said quietly. "I'm not recognized by the bar here, and—"

"You don't have to be recognized by the bar. All you've got to do is convince Reverend Bob to drop his suit. You can do that, can't you?"

"No. I'm in no position to convince him of anything."

"You're a lawyer," Cody said, brimming with confidence in her. "You're smart. You're educated. You can do it."

She almost protested again. She couldn't get involved in his legal problems with a minister and the *Sentinel*. It might take days just to arrange a meeting with the Reverend, and she didn't have days. She had to go home, get back to work, get on with her life.

She had to be free of Cody, once and for all.

And if she didn't get him to sign the papers, she would never be free.

"All right," she heard herself say. "I'll see what I can do. No promises, Cody—"

"No promises?"

"I'll try. That's my best offer."

He reached across the table and gave her hand a squeeze. "I knew I could count on you," he said, leaving her with the distinct impression that he'd just manipulated her with the finesse of a master.

But then, he had always had enormous powers of persuasion. She might be twelve years older and infinitely wiser, but she still didn't know how to protect herself from a man like Cody.

CHAPTER FOUR

THE CAR—AN OLD, NOISY, Datsun ZX—rode so low to the ground, Jane could almost feel loose gravel battering the soles of her shoes. The bucket seat positioned her body like an astronaut's, semireclined. The air-conditioning apparently didn't work, so Cody had rolled down both windows. Furnace-hot air swept into the car, blasting against her face.

She was too old to be riding around in a hot rod. Too demure to be chasing after a delinquent minister and trying to get him to drop a lawsuit. Too mature to be gazing at Cody as he drove and remembering what it had felt like to ride on his motorcycle with him, her arms anchoring her to him as the powerful engine roared between her legs.

She was too *engaged* to be remembering such things.

"Whatever happened to that motorcycle of yours?" she asked, her tone deceptively nonchalant.

He shot her a quick look, although she couldn't see his eyes behind the dark lenses of his sunglasses. "Do you really want to know?"

She considered, then shook her head. Discussing the past was only going to cause trouble. "Come to think of it, no, I don't."

His low chuckle convinced her that backing off from that subject was the right thing to do.

They had left the *Sentinel* building twenty minutes
ago, after Cody had collected his photography gear and
a sheet of proofs of the shots he'd taken that day on
Esplanade Avenue. Some of the photos were more incriminating than the one the newspaper ultimately ran,
although Jane doubted that pointing out to the Most
Reverend Robert J. Stanhope that things could have
been worse was going to convince him to drop his suit.

She'd examined the proofs before leaving the building. In several of them, the corpse was barely visible.
For all Cody's insistence that he wasn't a photojournalist, he'd accomplished something awfully close to art
in his photographs of the onlookers, capturing their
horror, their shock and their lurid curiosity—to say
nothing of capturing Reverend Bob's tasteless lust. In
one picture, the minister's hand seemed to be cupping
the prostitute's breast. In another, he leered outrageously. In yet another, he had his hand planted on the
prostitute's butt. As far as Jane was concerned, Stanhope's greatest sin wasn't consorting with a prostitute;
it was showing so little respect for the murder victim
lying just a few feet from where he and his companion
were pawing each other.

The man had already been humiliated to the point of
losing his job and his wife. It was a long shot, but Jane
hoped the threat of even greater humiliation might per-
suade him to back off. If he ever hoped to salvage his
career, surely he wouldn't want to have all of Cody's
pictures made public.

They were half the distance to La Place. Cody didn't
know where Stanhope was currently residing; Stanhope's lawyer had refused to reveal his client's whereabouts because he didn't want the newspaper contacting
Stanhope behind his back. Cody had mumbled some-

thing about how the lawyer was probably afraid that if
he knew where Stanhope was, he'd hunt the bastard
down and beat the stuffing out of him. Jane had
wrested a guarantee from Cody that if they did find
Stanhope, he would keep his fists to himself.

She didn't hold out much hope of finding the minister, though. They'd gotten his home address out of the
La Place telephone directory, but since his wife had
kicked him out of the house, the likelihood of finding
him there was less than zero. Still, if his wife was vin-
dictive, she might tell them where they could find her
estranged husband.

Jane and Cody also had the address of the Zion
Baptist Church, where Stanhope had been employed
until his picture had appeared in the *Sentinel*. The
church was their destination. Jane believed it might be
easier to pry information from people with whom
Stanhope worked than from the man's aggrieved wife.

The air gusting through the open windows smelled
musky. Strip malls and fast-food joints lined the highway, landscaped with wisteria and magnolia trees and
the occasional palm. The buildings sprawled much more
here than in the greater Boston area; pastel stucco
seemed to be the facade of choice. It was remarkably
different from the cozy, Colonial brick that predomi-
nated back home.

"Do you like living in New Orleans?" she asked
Cody.

He shrugged. "Yeah. Especially in the winter. I don't
miss those New England blizzards at all."

"But it's so hot here."

"You get used to it."

For some reason, it irked her to think Cody would
prefer New Orleans to Boston. "One of your pool hall

friends called you a damned Yankee," she said, remembering the jibes of his pals at Gussie's last night.

Cody laughed. "I'd rather be called a damned Yankee than a Southern cracker. They were just giving me a hard time because I was winning." His grin faded slightly and his gaze remained on the road ahead when he added, "There isn't anything for me in Boston. I've got no reason to go back."

Jane eyed him curiously. "What about your mother?"

He snorted. "My mother did her best, Janey, but come on. She wasn't exactly maternal. And she isn't in Brookline anymore."

Jane recalled thinking Cody's mother was exotic. The few times they'd met, she had insisted that Jane call her Debbie rather than Ms. Sinclair. She'd been in her midthirties then, ridiculously young compared to Jane's mother. Cody had been the product of a high school romance that had apparently gone to pieces the instant he'd made his presence felt. He had never met his father, and he'd essentially raised himself while his mother attempted, with less than stellar success, to grow up. Jane had considered Debbie funny and snappy and utterly irresponsible. She'd been on welfare a couple of times, and was working nights waiting tables when Cody met Jane. He used to invite Jane to his apartment in the evenings, when his mother was at work.

She'd never gone to his house when his mother was out, though. It wasn't that she hadn't trusted Cody. Given what he'd learned from his mother's experience, he knew better than to knock a classmate up accidentally. But Jane was a good girl, and good girls didn't go to boys' homes unchaperoned.

"How about your parents?" Cody asked. "They still living in Brookline?"

She shook her head. "My father had some health problems a few years ago—arthritis, mostly. He's all right, but he had to retire. He and my mother live in Hawaii now. The weather is better for him there."

"So the mansion in Brookline—"

"My parents' house, you mean?" She'd never have thought of it as a mansion. It was comfortable, spacious, perhaps too big for a family of three, but it was hardly a mansion. "They sold it."

"I can't picture your parents in Hawaii. They were such dyed-in-the-wool Bostonians."

"They miss the city. They try to visit at least once a year. They spent a month in town at Easter, and they'll be back for the wedding."

"Ah. The wedding." Cody's voice was heavy with sarcasm.

Jane resented how easily he could put her on the defensive. "Just because you don't think you'll ever get married again doesn't mean you have to sneer at other people's weddings. It happens that I'm in love with Mark, and—"

"Mark? His name is Mark?"

"What's wrong with that?"

Cody shot her a quick look. His smile seemed inexplicably triumphant. "Nothing's wrong with it. All I said was 'His name is Mark?'"

She bristled. "Mark Dennison."

"Mark Dennison. It sounds like the kind of name a rich banker would have."

If any other person needled her like this, she would be able to keep her cool. But not with Cody, not after he'd coerced her into helping him negotiate a truce with

Stanhope. Cody had always had a knack for making her behave uncharacteristically, and losing her temper was definitely out of character.

"Mark is a fine man, Cody. We enjoy each other's company, and *he* doesn't drive me crazy. If you're jealous, live with it."

"Jealous?" He hooted. "Why should I be jealous?"

"Because he's rich. Because he's a banker. Because—" she put steel in her voice "—he's marrying me."

"Not if I don't sign your papers, he isn't."

"You *will* sign them, Cody."

"What makes you so sure of that?"

"You've got a good heart." Anyone else would have been touched by the remark, but she suspected Cody would take it as an insult—which was pretty much as she'd intended it.

"My heart," he retorted, "is none of your business."

"And mine is none of yours."

"Great. Terrific." He pressed harder on the gas pedal, causing the small car to lurch forward. It was as if he couldn't wait to get this errand over with and bid Jane goodbye. That was certainly how *she* felt about the whole thing.

A few uncomfortable minutes passed in silence, and then he headed off the highway and into La Place. It seemed like the sort of town that would spring up at the edge of a lake where several major highways intersected. For that matter, it seemed to Jane like the sort of place that would be called La Place. She observed nothing outstanding about it, nothing unique, nothing but streets and buildings and cars. And tropical heat.

Cody drove as if he knew where he was going. He cruised down a major roadway, past bowling alleys and strip malls and into a densely settled section of town. "There it is," he said, aiming the car at a large, whitewashed clapboard church standing on one corner of a quiet intersection. He steered up a short driveway and into the parking lot next to the church.

As soon as he turned off the engine, she climbed out of the car, eager to remove herself from the hot vinyl bucket seat, which had been sticking to the backs of her legs through her nylons. Cody took a minute to roll up the windows and lock the car—which would be even hotter by the time she had to resume her place on that fiery seat. The asphalt felt gummy beneath her shoes; humidity drenched the air.

Once Cody was certain his camera wasn't visible through the hatchback window, he straightened up and eyed Jane. "Do you want to do the talking or should I?" he asked.

"I will." She was surprised he was giving her an option. It indicated that he was unsure of how to handle the situation. Maybe—if she wasn't reading too much into his simple question—what he was really saying was that he had faith in her legal skills.

She gave him the don't-worry-about-a-thing smile she always gave clients before a particularly difficult case, smoothed her blouse into the waistband of her skirt, and started across the lot to a side door in the church building. She doubted a service would be in progress at a quarter to twelve on a weekday, but if there was one, she didn't want to interrupt it by marching directly into the chapel.

"Do we have a plan?" Cody asked, falling into step beside her.

"The plan is for me to find out where Stanhope is and for you to keep your lip zipped."

"You're an outsider," he pointed out. "These folks are Southerners. You might not speak the same language."

"I've been in this city for less than twenty-four hours, Cody, and I already know I don't speak the same language. How long did it take you before you could understand what they were saying?"

He grinned—not a cocky smile but a thankful one. Evidently he appreciated her effort to loosen him up. He reached around her to open the side door, and she returned his grin, even though she was just as apprehensive as he was about how things would go.

The church was air-conditioned. Jane stood for a moment in the back hall, savoring the cool atmosphere as she gazed around her. The corridor was brightly lit, with a linoleum floor, a bulletin board carrying messages and schedules, and several doors lining the wall. Jane started toward the first open door, Cody at her heels.

Peering inside, she found a plump woman of late middle age seated at a long table, cutting block letters out of colorful construction paper. At the sight of Jane and Cody in the doorway, she lowered her scissors and beamed. She lifted a pair of glasses that hung on a chain around her neck and settled them on her pudgy nose. "Can I help y'all?" she asked.

"We won't take a minute," Jane promised, eyeing the mess of construction paper scattered across the table. "I can see you're busy."

"It's for the preschool," the woman explained, proudly gathering up the letters. "We're starting the summer program next week, and the playroom isn't ready yet. Some of these letters are downright hard to cut. You ever try to cut out a *B*?"

"No," Jane conceded. Behind her, Cody stood rigid, his impatience almost palpable. But she knew better than to rush right into an interrogation. If the woman wanted to chatter about the difficulties of the letter *B*, Jane would let her chatter. "I bet the *G* would be pretty hard, too."

"Not as hard as the *B*. It's the enclosures, you see. Not that *G* is easy—but I think my *G* came out just fine, if you'll forgive a little immodesty." She held up a bright yellow *G*. "Those curves are tricky, I'll grant you, but *B*'s the worst. *Q*'s a close second. Now—" she finished collecting the letters into a neat pile and gave Jane and Cody her full attention "—what can I do for you lovely people? Y'all new in town? Interested in joining Zion? I know most folks around here are Catholics, but we're open to everyone, whatever your inclination. I'm Mrs. Davis, the head teacher in the preschool."

Jane smiled. "Actually, Mrs. Davis, I just wanted to ask you a question about the pastor here."

A shadow flickered across Mrs. Davis's face, but she recovered quickly. "The Reverend Joe Jeffrey Hammond. He's a fine, fine minister. Not a speck of dust on that man's soul, I tell you."

"Your previous pastor," Jane clarified. "Robert J. Stanhope."

Mrs. Davis practically spat. Her dumpling cheeks grew crimson and she shook her head briskly, causing her silver-blond curls to quiver. "Now, I don't wish to speak ill of anyone, but...that *man*—" she clearly considered him a lower species "—is no longer here, and there's not a member of the congregation who misses him."

Jane felt Cody's tension increase, generating heat along her spine. She noticed the slight alteration in his stance, the clenching of his fist against his thigh, the changed rhythm of his respiration. He was probably dying to unzip his lip and join the woman in a chorus of vituperation against Stanhope.

While Jane could appreciate the sentiment, she wanted to keep the discussion calm and low-key. "We're not exactly big fans of Reverend Stanhope—"

"Don't you use that word when you're talking about him. There's nothing the least bit reverend about him. That—that *man* sold his soul to the devil for an afternoon of delight. He ought to be ashamed of himself."

"He certainly ought to be," Jane quickly agreed. If Stanhope had had any shame, he wouldn't have dared to bring a suit against Cody and the *Sentinel*. And if he hadn't brought suit, Cody would have been holding Jane's divorce decree ransom for money instead of for legal expertise. "Right now, Mrs. Davis," she continued in her most ingratiating voice, "we're looking for Mr. Stanhope. I was wondering if anyone here at Zion Baptist Church might know where he is."

"He's burning in hell," Mrs. Davis declared.

"Someone got to him before I did?" Cody piped up, sounding both hopeful and disappointed.

Jane had the good grace to look shocked. "Did he pass away?"

"Don't I wish." Mrs. Davis began fidgeting with a kelly green construction-paper *M*. "No, he's still alive in body. His spirit is what's burning."

"Do you know where we can find him?" Jane persevered, filtering her own growing impatience out of her voice.

Mrs. Davis turned from Jane to Cody, then back to Jane. "Is he going to commit an act of violence on Mr. Stanhope? Because as much as I condemn him, I don't advocate violence. I believe in leaving the punishment to God."

Jane shot Cody a fierce look. He held up his hands in mock surrender. "I won't touch a hair on Stanhope's head," he swore, sounding dreadfully insincere to Jane. "I just want to talk to him."

"Because before Satan took ahold of him, he was a good and true man of God."

"We just want to talk to him," Jane echoed Cody.

"About what?"

Jane sized up Mrs. Davis and decided that the less she knew, the better. "It's a personal matter."

"You aren't another of those ladies of the night, are you? Oh, my Lord!" Mrs. Davis's cheeks grew even rosier, and her eyes grew round and bugged out of her face slightly, like pale green grapes. "Oh, my Lord! I'm talking to a prostitute!"

"I'm not a prostitute!" Jane said starchily. "I'm a lawyer."

"Isn't it the same thing?" Cody whispered so only Jane could hear. She jerked her foot back, kicking his shin with the heel of her shoe.

For Mrs. Davis, however, she kept her smile, even though her cheeks were beginning to ache. "Is there anyone here who might be able to tell us where Mr. Stanhope is?"

"Nobody even speaks his name around here," Mrs. Davis informed her.

"Do you think his wife would know?"

"Ah, that dear woman. The sorrow she's endured! There's some folks around here who get to ruminating on how come that—that *man* had to step out on her. But I can guess. He probably was looking for perversions, things a properly bred woman won't do. Things you'd have to pay a woman an awful lot of money to do. Imagine the horror that dear Mary Stanhope must have felt to discover her husband—that *man*—took money from their family accounts. Heaven knows, maybe it was money she'd set aside for the children's education—and that *man* took it and spent it on a prostitute. Imagine how she must have felt."

Jane dutifully shook her head and clicked her tongue. "I'd like to think she'd be willing to help us find her husband, then," she murmured. "We might be able to straighten things out."

"Our only goal is to make his life miserable," Cody added. She was tempted to kick his shin again.

She thanked Mrs. Davis, instead. "We'll see if Mrs. Stanhope knows her husband's whereabouts."

"Y'all do that. And you know, folks, if you'd like to enroll your children in our preschool here, it's an excellent program. And the tuition is mighty reasonable. And you don't have to be Baptist. Our doors are open to everyone. I just know your children will fit right in. I reckon, a young couple like you all, your children must be just the right age for our preschool. We take them as young as three all the way up to six, if they aren't ready for kindergarten yet. I know this would be the perfect program for your young ones...." When at last Mrs. Davis paused to catch her breath, Jane and Cody made their getaway.

The midday heat staggered Jane as she stepped out of the pleasantly cool building. "Honest to God," she muttered, "where did that lady ever get the idea that we had children?"

Cody snorted. "She obviously wasn't firing on all cylinders."

The truth was, more than just Mrs. Davis's misconception of Jane's relationship with Cody was bothering her. Crossing the parking lot to Cody's car, she felt her blood grow as overheated as the air around her. By the time Cody had her door unlocked and she lowered herself cautiously onto the sizzling vinyl seat, she could almost feel steam rising from her scalp.

It wasn't until Cody had climbed in behind the wheel and was jamming his key into the ignition that her discomfort shaped itself into words. "You think I'm a prostitute," she snapped.

Instead of turning on the engine, Cody twisted in his seat to stare at her. His eyes were dancing, but his mouth resisted a smile. His forehead glistened with sweat. "That was supposed to be a joke," he said.

"It wasn't funny."

"Oh, come on. You ought to be used to that stuff. Lawyers get insulted all the time."

"I don't care about lawyers. We're talking about *you* insulting *me*."

"Like it really matters."

That was the most exasperating part of all: it *did* matter to Jane. It shouldn't, but it did. The legal profession was often the butt of jokes—and frequently lawyers were the ones telling jokes on themselves. But when Cody had teased her a few minutes ago...

Damn it! She didn't want his taunts to bother her. She didn't want him to have any effect on her at all.

He seemed to recognize her uneasiness. Something softened in his eyes, shading them, thawing them. "All right," he said quietly. "Why don't we just go back to town and do the paperwork?"

"The paperwork?" She searched his face, unsure of what he was getting at. "Our divorce decree?"

"Yeah." He gnawed on his lower lip, gazed out the windshield, tapped his fingers against the steering wheel and then turned back to her. "I shouldn't have asked you to do this. It isn't working out."

"Working out?" He was right, of course—he shouldn't have gotten her involved in his professional problems. But the way he was dismissing her made her feel as if he didn't think she was up to the challenge. And damn it, she was. "What do you mean, working out? What has to be worked out? You forced me to help you—"

"And now maybe I'm feeling guilty about it. I never had to force you to do anything in the past, Janey. I shouldn't have forced you this time, either." He let out a long breath. "If you want to finalize the divorce, let's just do it. I'll take care of this other stuff myself."

She stared at him, waiting for relief to wash over her, cool and soothing. Not a hint of sarcasm undermined his words; not a hint of mischief glittered in his eyes. He was serious. He would sign the papers, and she would be able to go back to Boston. She would be able to return to her office, resume her wedding plans, and live secure in the knowledge that Cody Sinclair would never be able to disrupt her life again.

She would be free.

"I promised you I would help," she heard herself murmur.

"Actually, no, you didn't. You told me you weren't going to promise me anything. What do you say, Janey? You want to go back to town and get it over with?"

She opened her mouth and then shut it. Why couldn't she say yes? Why couldn't she take what he was so generously offering?

She wasn't used to contrition from Cody. She wasn't sure she trusted him. He must have an ulterior motive. He must be angling for something else from her. "How much money will I have to pay?" she asked warily.

"How much does a notary charge? If there's a fee, we'll split it."

Then he *didn't* want to extort a fortune from her. He was prepared to give her exactly what she had come for.

Again she tried to force out a yes. Again, the word wouldn't come.

She tore her gaze from his face, and it settled lower, on his torso. His shirt draped his body in an unintentionally sensual way, tracing the breadth of his shoulders and hinting at the sleek contours of his chest. His long legs extended beneath the steering wheel, the denim faded to white at the knees and along the seams of his jeans. Despite the car's compact size, he looked comfortable in the driver's seat. If not for his hands, she would believe him totally at peace with his offer.

But his hands weren't peaceful. He flexed and flattened them, drummed the wheel with his fingers, skimmed its arc with his palms. His hands told her what his words didn't: that he was nervous, worried about what she might answer.

She was nervous, too, and very worried. "Would it be easier for you if I left?" she asked, lifting her gaze only as far as his chin.

He slid one restless hand from the steering wheel and tucked it under her jaw, guiding her face upward until she had no choice but to stare into his eyes. His hand was warm but not hot, strong but not overpowering. There was nothing the least bit erotic in his touch, yet it jolted her, caused her breath to catch, caused her heart to beat just a little bit faster. Twelve years after her debacle with Cody, one year after she'd met Mark Dennison, one month after she'd agreed to marry him, she still couldn't fight her reflexive response to Cody Sinclair.

She hated him for that.

"I'd rather you stayed," he said.

His eyes were unbearably blue, his fingers gentle yet decisive, caressing the sensitive skin of her throat. His tone was earnest.

She really hated him.

"I'll stay," she said.

A MECHANIC AT A LOCAL service station gave Cody directions to the Stanhope house. It probably would have been easier to go back into the church to get directions from Mrs. Davis, but Cody had had enough of her nonsense about Jane's and his supposed children. He didn't want to have to listen to all that again.

Not true. He'd been afraid that if he went back into the church, by the time he came out Jane would have changed her mind and told him she had decided to go back to Boston.

He was truly baffled. He knew she wanted to be done with him, and he sure as hell wanted to be done with her. He didn't need the Crown Princess of Brookline back in his life. She'd been trouble enough the first time around. He'd vowed to himself, that wretched morning when she'd hurled her final accusations and epithets at him and slammed out of the apartment, that he would never take her back. Not if she asked. Not if she pleaded. Not if she crawled to him, begging.

Well, here she was. Not asking, pleading or crawling but volunteering to help him. Why?

Why had he felt such a surge of joy when she'd said she would stay? Why had the velvety softness of her skin made him want to haul her over the gear stick and into his lap? Why did he want her?

Too many questions and no time for answers. They'd arrived at the oversexed minister's home.

It was a modest, well-maintained ranch house, gray-shingled with a brown-tiled roof. The lawn was a couple of weeks past its last mowing, but it didn't look bad. Curtains framed the windows; a dogwood near the slate front walk still held a few late blossoms. A child's bicycle lay on its side by the garage door.

Cody stared at the bicycle for a long minute. It was one thing to cheat on your wife, but it was another thing to cheat on your kids, to destroy their world. Given his own sorry childhood, Cody had no tolerance for parents who screwed up and made their kids suffer for it.

He steered onto the driveway, killed the engine and glanced at Jane. She, too, was staring at the bicycle. Probably thinking the same thing he'd been thinking.

"You want me to zip my lip again?" he asked. He felt strangely deferential toward her, grateful she hadn't grabbed the opportunity to hurry back to Boston. He didn't like feeling grateful to anyone—especially Jane Thayer.

All right, maybe *gratitude* wasn't the right word. *Admiration* came closer. He admired her courage. Refusing to quit this mission when she had the chance proved she had grit, almost as much as eloping with him had proved it twelve years ago.

"I'd like you to zip it even tighter than before," she murmured.

"No lawyer cracks, huh."

"No cracks, period. This woman is going through hell."

"This woman," he pointed out, just to be contrary, "might be part of the reason why Reverend Bob took up with a hooker."

Jane simmered. Cody grinned, feeling a little less deferential.

He didn't bother to lock the car when they got out. They were parked off the street in a pleasant, middle-class residential neighborhood, and he doubted anyone would have the nerve to break into a car parked on a minister's private property. His camera bag was stashed under an old blanket in back, so it wasn't as if he was flaunting his wares for passing burglars.

"I thought churches provided their ministers with a house on church property," Jane remarked as she joined Cody on the front walk.

"Some do. Others give them a housing allowance." He shrugged. "Maybe once Reverend Bob got his ass kicked out of the church, they took away his house, too."

"That wouldn't be fair to his family. They'd be left homeless."

"You're really bleeding for this lady, aren't you?"

Jane glanced at him. She was a good six inches shorter than him, but her shoes had slight heels on them, and she'd always had perfect posture. As he recalled, she'd been the ideal size when they were horizontal.

Now, where did that thought come from? Just because they were talking about prostitutes, married men and wronged women, just because the way the overhead sun struck Jane's hair made it come alive with red highlights, like glowing coals that one light breath could ignite into flames, just because he'd always had a particular weakness for the curve of her lower lip...

She climbed the concrete steps to the front porch. "Yes," she said, pressing the doorbell. "I'm bleeding for her."

Before he could speak, the inner door swung open and a slight, pale woman peered out at them through the screen. She couldn't have been much older than Jane and himself. Dressed in a gray cotton housedress that was a size too big for her, she looked lost in the folds of fabric. Her eyes were small and narrow, her mouth pinched in displeasure. "Yes?" she asked suspiciously.

"Mrs. Stanhope?" Jane greeted her.

The woman's face was drawn forward toward a pointy little chin. She reminded Cody of a hamster. "Who wants to know?" she asked.

"My name is Jane Thayer. I'm a lawyer. This is my client, Cody Sinclair."

Her client? Cody rolled his eyes but obediently said nothing. Clients were supposed to do what their lawyers told them to do.

"I don't need a lawyer," Mrs. Stanhope declared, growing more leery by the second.

"I know you don't, Mrs. Stanhope. We're here because Mr. Sinclair has a legal problem he needs to resolve with your... with the Reverend Stanhope."

"That bastard," Mrs. Stanhope said with a sudden burst of spirit. Her cheeks gained color and her rodent eyes beaded with tears. "Seems like a lot of people have legal problems with him. Take a number and wait your turn."

"All we really need to know is where Mr. Stanhope is currently residing. He isn't living here, is he?"

"No, he isn't living here. So help me, if he sets foot inside this house, he might just be a soprano by the time he leaves," she threatened. Cody decided he liked her.

"Would you by any chance have his new address?"

"I'll tell you, it would do my heart good to hear that his new address is a cardboard box in a doorway. That man is evil."

"Amen," Cody murmured.

Mrs. Stanhope turned her attention to him. "Did he double-cross you, too? Did he wound you to your very soul?"

Jane shot Cody a warning look. But the lady was asking him a question and he was too polite not to reply. "He hasn't wounded me to my very soul yet, but he's trying, Mrs. Stanhope. All I want is to do my part in turning him into a soprano." From the corner of his eye he noticed Jane's leg move slightly, as if she was revving up to kick him again. He deftly inched out of the line of fire. "Can you help us out, Mrs. Stanhope?"

The woman sighed, looking genuinely rueful. "I surely wish I could. But I don't talk to Robert. His lawyer phones my lawyer, and my lawyer phones his lawyer, and I reckon it's all going to cost me a pretty penny in legal fees by the time all the lawyers are done phoning each other. Not that it won't be worth every penny to see that man fry in hell. I do wish I could help you, Mr. Sinclair. An enemy of Robert's is a friend of mine.

But I just don't know where he's gone to. You all might ask his lawyer."

"That's already been tried," Jane interjected. "He wasn't forthcoming."

"Well ... my best guess is, Robert's in some motel somewhere. A cheap one. God willing, a vermin-infested one. The church is helping me with expenses, but they aren't sending that foul man a nickel. And my lawyer had me freeze all our bank accounts so Robert can't get his filthy fingers on any more of our money than he's already taken. I reckon he's staying some-place very inexpensive."

"Thank you very much, Mrs. Stanhope. We won't take any more of your time," Jane said, just as Cody was about to list some of the vermin-infested places Reverend Bob might be camping out. But once again, the lawyer was taking the lead and he—the client—was reduced to following. He echoed Jane's thanks to the minister's spiteful wife, and they walked back to the car.

"I wonder how the kid is taking it," Jane commented. "Or kids, as the case may be."

"They don't seem to be moping around the house."

"In the middle of a weekday? Of course not. They would be at school right now."

"Which," Cody pointed out, opening the car door for her, "would imply that they aren't moping around the house. They're probably happy to see the dirt bag gone."

Jane hesitated in the open doorway, her hand resting against the chrome trim, her smoky brown eyes quizzi-cal. "Why are you doing this, Cody?"

"Doing what?"

"Opening the door for me. You never used to do that sort of thing in the old days."

She looked so perplexed, he had to take a moment to think through his answer. In the old days, when he was eighteen, he hadn't known a hell of a lot about good manners. His mother sure hadn't drilled him in the niceties, and his buddies would have hooted him off the block if they'd ever caught him doing something chivalrous.

He'd grown up, though. He wasn't eighteen anymore. He knew a few things now he hadn't known then—for instance, that when a well-bred woman with dangerous eyes and lips as soft and pink as the heart of a rose was standing beside a door, he'd be a fool not to open it for her. And Cody had never been a fool. Not then, and certainly not now.

He couldn't say that, though. He couldn't let her know how her eyes still enchanted him. He couldn't let her know how her lips enticed him. She'd done him an enormous favor by refusing to flee when she had the chance. He wasn't sure why she'd agreed to stick this Stanhope thing out to the end, but she had, and he wasn't about to let her change her mind.

A joke was called for. "In case you forgot, sweetheart, the Harley didn't have doors."

Her smile was tentative yet brave. "I haven't forgotten," she admitted.

God. Even in the soupy summer heat she smelled fresh, like lavender. The sun streamed through her hair, searching for more red highlights, and the smooth, silky arch of her throat beckoned him as it had earlier. If she couldn't think of anything better to do, he might just take her to see the old Harley. And then he'd take her to see his bed.

For old times' sake, why not? A walk down memory lane—although "walking" wasn't exactly the verb he had in mind. That she was engaged to marry a rich banker named Mark didn't matter to Cody. He wasn't looking for love. Just a little loving with a woman who happened to be his wife at the moment.

"So, what do we do now?" he asked.

To her credit, she didn't evade his gaze. He knew he must be sending all sorts of messages with his eyes. He knew he was standing a bit too close to her. But she didn't shrink from him, didn't retreat an inch. "I need to call my office back in Boston," she said. "And in all honesty, I'm kind of hungry."

"So am I." He wasn't talking about food, though.

"Okay, we'll get some lunch and I'll make my call."

"And then?"

"We'll go see a prostitute."

He laughed. She smiled. Damn, but she was a cool customer; her eyes continued to spar with his, an invisible tussle in the heated air between them. Her chin was tilted slightly as she angled her face to see him, and her fingers fluttered anxiously against the chrome, but she held her own. She was tough.

At those rare moments during the past twelve years when he'd spared a thought for her, he'd found himself wondering why he'd ever bothered to marry Jane Thayer. At this rare moment, he knew exactly why he'd married her.

CHAPTER FIVE

As MARK SAW IT, the best thing about being engaged was that a man already spoken for had a certain kind of immunity. He could look at another woman, befriend her, even desire her—and yet not feel constrained to act on his desire. Furthermore, he was under no obligation to make a good impression on the lady in question. He could appreciate a woman's particular attributes and not have to activate all the usual responses. He could make a fool of himself and not have to listen to her reproach him all night long for his foolishness.

An engaged man was safe. The risks he took wouldn't hurt him. It was like riding a roller coaster—you could indulge in death-defying thrills without having to die.

As soon as Clarissa Bonnert strolled into the piano bar off the lobby at the Four Seasons Hotel, Mark felt the roller coaster lurch.

How odd that he'd never really noticed Clarissa before he and Jane had decided to get married. He'd thought of Clarissa only as a tiny, dowdy young lady who dressed quietly and whose spectacles were wider than her face. He had never actually thought of her as a woman.

She was different—he'd noticed that much about her. She was, to put it delicately, not white. Her skin was a smooth, dusky shade that, under the right circumstances, could make a grown man of any race salivate.

And her eyes, behind those ridiculous eyeglasses, were large and intriguingly dark, angling above her pronounced cheekbones. If only she'd invest in contact lenses and fashion herself a new hairstyle, she could probably captivate her share of gentleman callers.

There was a time, Mark wasn't ashamed to admit, when young secretaries had comprised a great deal of his social life. When he'd found himself facing his thirty-fifth birthday, however, he'd realized that it was time for him to settle down. And secretaries weren't the sort of woman a man of his stature settled down with.

So he'd chosen to settle down with Jane Thayer, a decision he didn't regret. He had to admit he was unnerved about her mysterious disappearance—to New Orleans, of all places. Perhaps if he hadn't made that comment about the statue at the Museum of Fine Arts, if he hadn't pointed out that it looked like a stripper climbing out of a cake...

Jane hadn't seemed offended, though. Merely thoughtful. Ruminative. She'd stared hard at the sculpture and pressed her lips together, trapped in her own secret thoughts.

That Jane had secrets unnerved him.

That he suddenly realized he wanted a stag party with naked ladies bursting from cakes unnerved him even more.

It was like Jane to do what she believed would make those around her happy. It *wasn't* like her to run off to New Orleans without telling him why. And it wasn't like Mark to tingle with anticipation, particularly anticipation about women, naked women, beautiful, buxom women he wasn't engaged to.

Clarissa wasn't overly buxom, although given her petite stature, even small breasts looked generous on her. In truth, he'd never been aware of the size of her bust before. But when he spotted her conversing with the host, who pointed toward Mark's table, he suddenly found himself thinking about every detail of her in a way he'd never thought about her before.

It was just a roller-coaster ride, he told himself as she sauntered through the atmospherically lit lounge toward him. It was just a transient thrill to appreciate the exotic woman in black satin trousers, a turquoise satin blazer and a beguilingly lacy black blouse, her hair flowing down her back in a torrent of black curls and her eyelids dusted with a hint of turquoise to match the blazer.

He rose to his feet as she neared the small, candlelit table where he'd been waiting for her. It took great quantities of willpower not to reach out and whip off her eyeglasses to see if the transformation from caterpillar to butterfly could be improved upon. It took equal amounts of willpower not to take her by the elbow and usher her out of the lounge, straight to the check-in desk to see if a room might be available.

Of course, he was engaged. He would never act on such urges.

"My, my," he murmured as he helped her into the chair facing his. "It would seem that they've loosened up the dress code at Baker, Dunn."

She smiled at him as he resumed his own seat. "I didn't come here straight from work. I was so rumpled after eight hours at the word processor, I decided to stop home and freshen up. And anyway—" she leaned forward conspiratorially "—I didn't think a drab old suit would look right in a place like this."

Mark was wearing a drab old suit. Well, not that old; he'd picked it up at the Armani boutique on Newbury

Street a year ago. But sitting across the small table from Clarissa reminded him of yet another benefit of being engaged. When he was with Jane, he never had to feel apologetic about a year-old suit. In fact, Jane fit him as comfortably as an old suit. Comfort—that was what marriage was all about.

Clarissa didn't seem critical of his appearance. And oddly enough, he rather enjoyed the twinge of discomfort she caused him, the edgy eagerness she stirred within him, like a rapid, stomach-churning dip on the roller coaster. He could indulge the temptation to flirt, because it wasn't serious. It meant nothing. He could plummet at breakneck speed without killing himself; his seat belt was securely fastened, and the car was never going to leave the track.

Clarissa looked slightly edgy, too. Perhaps a compliment would put her at ease.

"You look magnificent."

"Oh, no I don't," she said quickly, adjusting her eyeglasses on her dainty nose.

"You ought to wear your hair down more often."

"It's a mess. It's so frizzy. I should cut it all off."

"Oh, no," he insisted, even though he sensed a certain mechanical quality in her responses to his compliments. "You must never cut it off. Promise me you won't."

She peered at him. Her lenses didn't distort her eyes at all. They were large and lovely. And it occurred to him that her lenses weren't lenses. They were plain glass.

He considered questioning her about them, but he refrained. Surely she had a reason to hide herself like the prim librarian of cliché. Letting down her hair made her almost lethally pretty. Without the eyeglasses, she would decimate men's libidos like a heat-seeking missile.

The woman was a stunner. Why had he never noticed before? And what was he going to do now that he *had* noticed?

Nothing, of course. He was engaged. He didn't consort with secretaries anymore. He was mature, settled, betrothed.

"I'll have a vodka and tonic," she said to the waiter who had arrived at their table. Mark noticed that the poor fellow appeared dumbstruck at the sight of her.

He grinned. He was not going to be dumbstruck. If Clarissa could be daring, if she could let down her hair and order hard liquor, he could enjoy the loops and swoops of the ride. "I'll have a Hennessy on ice," he said.

The waiter nodded and backed away, unable to take his eyes from Clarissa until he was nearly at the bar.

At the other end of the lounge, the pianist played a medley of songs from *The Phantom of the Opera*. Mark relaxed in his seat, his eyes on the ravishing lady before him. A thin gold chain circled her neck, winking as the candlelight skipped along the links.

"I'm amazed you didn't have a date for this evening," he remarked.

She gave him a bashful smile. She'd never seemed particularly bashful at the office. Jane wouldn't tolerate timidity in an assistant. "I don't date much."

"No? If you wore your hair down more often, and took off those glasses—" there, he'd said it "—you could probably book your calendar with dates for every night of the year."

She shrugged. "Most of the men I meet are just trying to get into my pants." So much for being bashful.

He chuckled. "Men are obnoxious, aren't they."

If he'd said that to Jane, she would have heartily concurred. Clarissa only giggled.

The waiter reappeared at their table with their drinks and a plate of sliced melon and grapes. Clarissa looked surprised, then pleased. She plucked a grape from its stem with her long, white nails, and popped it into her mouth. "What a treat! Thanks for ordering this!"

He hadn't ordered it, but elegant bars often provided nibbles to accompany drinks. Perhaps Clarissa didn't frequent elegant bars. On a secretary's salary— even a good one—she probably couldn't afford to. If men realized what she looked like, she would no doubt receive countless invitations to meet for drinks at establishments like this.

After which, the host of the evening would try to get into her pants. No doubt that was why she was willing to meet here with Mark. She knew that, as a man already spoken for, he had no designs on her.

He took a sip of the mellow Scotch, then once again settled back in his seat. "So," he said, enjoying enormously the sight of Clarissa munching on grapes, "did my runaway fiancée check in today?"

With a grape in her mouth, Clarissa nodded. Mark watched her chew, swallow and then verbalize her answer. "She phoned this afternoon. I'm sorry, Mr. Dennison, but I couldn't get a thing out of her."

"Mark," he corrected her.

"Mark." She took a sip of her drink, then gave him another bashful smile. "I really struck out. The only information I could squeeze out of her was that she isn't sure when she'll be coming home. She said things were taking longer than she'd expected."

"Things?" That sounded suspicious. *Things* could mean a party with strippers jumping out of cakes. Or it could mean a party with...Lord help him, a Mardi Gras theme or some such thing, everyone in masks and grotesque jewelry, gobbling up gumbo or chitlins or whatever it was they ate in the bayou. "What things?" he asked cautiously.

"I don't know. I couldn't just come right out and ask her."

Why couldn't she? Jane might have confided in Clarissa. No woman would plot a surprise party without confiding in another woman. That was the idea of surprise parties, wasn't it? To have something to whisper about with a friend.

"What did you say to her?"

"I asked her how she was doing, and she said fair to middling. I asked her when she might be back in the office, and she said by next Monday for sure."

"Next Monday? That's five days away! What the hell is she doing down there?"

Clarissa looked panicked, and Mark backed off, not wanting to take out his frustration on her. It wasn't her fault that Jane—solid, dependable Jane—had raced off on some harebrained caper. Clarissa was doing the best she could, after all.

"Do you know what I love most about Jane?" he said.

Clarissa's smile shimmered. "Jane's wonderful," she said simply.

How could he add to that? "Well, yes. She is."

"I mean," Clarissa said, fueling herself with another sip of her drink, "she's everything I wish I could be. She's smart and she's pretty—"

"You're pretty," he said, stating the obvious.

Clarissa rolled her eyes behind her phony eyeglasses. "Jane's refined. She's pretty the way an apple tree in bloom is pretty. She's the kind of pretty that makes you feel all warm inside."

He hadn't expected such poetry to spill forth from Clarissa, but he couldn't find much to argue with in her description of Jane's clean, straightforward beauty. Jane wasn't flamboyant. She didn't turn heads. Yet there was a balance to her, a purity. Unlike Clarissa, Jane's plain beauty was soothing.

"But more important than that," Clarissa continued, "she's smart. I mean *real* smart. I've sat in on meetings—I shouldn't tell you this." She cut herself off with another giggle.

"Oh, come on," he goaded her. "You can tell me."

"Well . . . it's just, there'll be Mr. Dunn or someone, one of the senior partners, and he's supposed to be as wise as Solomon, and he'll miss something in a case. And Jane will 'clarify' it. That's what she always says when one of the senior partners is blowing an argument—'Let me just clarify that.' She's too diplomatic to say, 'You're blowing it big, you dim bulb.' She just says, 'May I clarify that?' And then she presents the argument the way it should be presented. It's amazing."

"That's my Jane," Mark agreed. "She's amazing, all right."

"I mean, she's a genius. She's always right on the money with her arguments. You just know there's an incredible brain in her skull. I respect her so much."

"So do I," Mark said, then sighed. Sometimes, he thought traitorously, a man wanted a woman he didn't respect quite so much. "But I'll tell you what I like best about her. Her predictability."

Clarissa wrinkled her nose. "Yuck! I hope you never told her that. She'd be really insulted if you did."

If his comment had surprised her, hers surprised him more. "Why would she be insulted?"

"*Predictable!* That's so boring. Jane isn't boring."

"I don't think predictability is boring," he countered, warming to the debate. "I like predictability. Let's say I go into... oh, for example, the Armani boutique on Newbury Street. I know that whatever I buy there will be of a predictable quality. That's why I shop there. I know what I'm getting, and I know it will be good."

"Jane isn't a shirt," Clarissa pointed out, her voice tinged with indignation. "She isn't something you go into a store and buy."

"You know what I mean. With Jane, I know who she is. I know what's going on between us. That's what I adore about her—the sense that she's solid and unwavering and won't throw me any curves." He paused. "That's why I'm anxious about Jane's popping off to New Orleans and her refusal to pinpoint when she's going to return." Admitting that he was troubled by Jane's behavior should have embarrassed him. He hardly knew Clarissa, after all. She was simply someone whose desk he passed on his way to Jane's office.

Yet confessing his dissatisfaction to her seemed quite natural. Probably because there was nothing personal between them, not even an actual friendship. The only thing that united him and Clarissa was their attempt to figure out what Jane was up to and whether or not it involved females of the nude persuasion.

"Hasn't she ever surprised you?" Clarissa asked. "Hasn't she ever done anything you wouldn't expect?"

"You know Jane. What do you think?"

She twisted a plump green grape from its stem and tossed it into her mouth. As she chewed, she pondered his question. After washing down the grape with a sip of her vodka and tonic, she said, "I think Jane's kind of . . . complicated. Still water runs deep and all that. I think she's perfectly capable of doing something wild and crazy if she feels like it."

"She never feels like it. She's not a wild-and-crazy type."

Clarissa's mysterious smile troubled him as much as Jane's unexplained jaunt to New Orleans did. "I think you're wrong about that, Mark," Clarissa insisted, her smile intensifying. "I think there's a wild-and-crazy side to Jane. And I think there's a wild-and-crazy side to you, too. I think everyone is capable of cutting loose sometimes."

"Nonsense."

Instead of refuting him, she laughed.

As a rule, Mark didn't like being laughed at. But when Clarissa laughed, when her almond-shaped eyes danced with humor and her even white teeth formed a crescent against her smooth, tawny skin, he realized that being laughed at wasn't so bad if Clarissa Bonnert was doing the laughing.

"Name one wild-and-crazy thing you think I'm capable of," he challenged her. "One wild-and-crazy thing you think I'd actually enjoy."

"I think . . ." She studied him intently, her angular cheeks scored with dimples. "I think you'd enjoy going to the North End and walking down the street eating a calzone."

"I never eat sidewalk food."

"Everybody should eat sidewalk food sometimes. You ought to try it, Mark."

"What a preposterous idea." But suddenly he was laughing, too. If Jane could be unpredictable, why couldn't he? If Clarissa could let down her hair, why shouldn't he?

"A calzone, eh?"

"Do you know what a calzone is?"

"Sort of like a pizza?" he guessed.

"A turnover made of pizza crust, stuffed with cheese and sauce and other stuff. It's messy and it's delicious, and if you had a single adventurous bone in your body, you'd walk down a street in the North End in that fancy suit of yours, slobbering melted cheese from a calzone all over yourself."

"I will if you take off your glasses," he challenged her.

She blinked, her long lashes quivering. Then she squared her shoulders. "You're on," she said, pulling them off.

He steeled himself against an onrush of shock. Dear Lord, the woman was phenomenal. Her face ought to be licensed. No wonder she kept her hair up and hid behind the fake glasses most of the time. Unencumbered, she could make a healthy man keel over from the impact of her beauty.

She tucked her glasses into her purse and smiled. He swallowed a groan. "Shall we?" she asked.

"Shall we what?" His voice came out choked.

"Go to the North End and eat calzones on the street."

As long as they were out of doors and he had an ample supply of oxygen, he might survive being in the presence of such a sorceress. And perhaps, with a little

cheese-and-tomato sauce smeared on her face, she
might not be quite as hazardous to his hormonal health.

And anyway, he was engaged to be married. Nothing
was going to happen between him and Clarissa, now or
ever. He was safe. This was just an amusement park
ride.

"Definitely," he said, rising and extending his hand
to her. "Calzones it is."

"HEY, JANE, I'M downstairs in the lobby. You ready to
go find our favorite hooker?" Cody's voice came
through the phone.

"What a way you have of expressing yourself," she
muttered, twirling the coiled wire around her index finger and gazing at the unsigned documents she'd removed from her purse when she'd gotten back to the
hotel. They lay on the night table, mocking her, reminding her that all she really wanted to do was get
them signed and fly home to Boston.

Yet there she was, in her room overlooking Canal
Street and New Orleans's bustling downtown district,
preparing to traipse through the French Quarter in
search of Reverend Bob's professional squeeze.

She'd spent the past few hours alone in her room,
trying to unscramble her brain. When she and Cody had
gotten back from La Place, they'd stopped by the City
room at the *Sentinel,* where Cody's editor ordered him
to do a shoot near the Tulane University campus. Apparently, some goofball fraternity pledges had spray-
painted their Greek letters all over a rival fraternity's
house, and students were threatening mayhem. The
possibility of a full-fledged riot presented an excellent
photo-op, and the editor wanted Cody on the scene.

Jane had quickly suggested that he go to the campus. They could resume their search for the scandalous minister later. After all, the odds of their finding the hooker who'd been Stanhope's companion in Cody's fateful snapshot would be greater in the evening than in the middle of the afternoon.

The truth, though, was that Jane had needed to get away from Cody for a while. She'd needed to figure out why in God's name she hadn't accepted his offer to sign the divorce decree, no favors requested, no money extorted, no strings attached. If she had, she would have been done with him. Right now, she would be packing her bags, checking out of the hotel and heading back to her job, her fiancé and her life.

But like a fool, she'd agreed to help Cody. And instead of packing up and leaving New Orleans, she'd spent the afternoon showering, checking in with Clarissa at the office, munching on an overpriced sandwich from room service and berating herself for having passed up the opportunity to be done with Cody Sinclair, once and for all.

She owed him her assistance, she told herself. She owed him something for her father's failure to sever their relationship properly twelve years ago. She owed Cody for the fact that she'd walked out on him, even though ending their impetuous marriage had been in his best interests as much as hers.

But that debt wasn't the real reason she'd refused the escape he'd offered. It was part of the reason—perhaps a large part of it. But Jane had always been too honest with herself to deny the obvious.

Her relationship with him wasn't quite done. Divorce or no divorce, seeing him had revealed to her that something more than a legal mistake still connected her to him, and signing a piece of paper wasn't going to be enough to sever the connection.

It didn't matter that she was older and supposedly wiser. It didn't matter that she was engaged to marry Mark Dennison. It didn't matter that years ago, when she and Cody had been young and reckless, there had been more bad times than good between them. He symbolized a stage in her life when she still had options, when she was young enough to be totally irresponsible, when all that mattered were her raging hormones and her equally raging emotions. He embodied the one thing no one would ever have suspected Jane of: irrationality.

He was her first love, damn it.

Every woman had a Cody in her life, and no matter how completely she outgrew her first love, he would always be there, a memory, a flame that refused to gutter and die. He would remind her of a time when all that mattered was to satisfy an unthinking surge of love and need and desire, without regard to practical considerations. Cody had been freedom. He'd been fearlessness. He'd been . . .

"Foolishness," she said to her reflection in the mirror. She'd changed from her neat business apparel of that morning to a silk tank top and a pair of culottes. Hiking the streets of the French Quarter and interrogating prostitutes didn't require a suit.

Sighing, she reached for her purse and her room key. She couldn't back out now—but she could put aside all those juvenile thoughts about first love. And she could slap Cody's hand away if he tried to cup her chin again. As long as he didn't touch her, as long as he didn't smile his wry little smile at her and beam his too-blue eyes at her, and—when he knew she was pushed to her limit—

behave with a kindness and empathy she had trouble resisting...

She would get through this. By the time it was done, she would also be done—done with Cody, for good and forever.

She rode the elevator down to the lobby and crossed to the bank of house phones near the registration desk. Cody slouched indolently against the wall, still dressed in his faded jeans, sneakers and T-shirt, although he'd tossed a charcoal gray lightweight jacket over his shoulder. He looked out of place in the elegant lobby. He also looked unconscionably sexy.

Jane suppressed a moan of disgust. He looked unconscionable. Not sexy, though. Not the least bit sexy.

Yet her pulse gave a little hiccup, just as it had at the pool hall last night. Just as it had when she'd glimpsed him through the glass-walled office of the City room that morning. Just as it had when he'd brushed his hand along the underside of her throat and offered to sign her papers.

She didn't need this. She didn't want it. She wanted...maturity. Clearheadedness. Invincibility.

"Let's go," she said crisply, sliding the strap of her purse over her shoulder. "Where's your car?"

He pointed at his feet. "In the underground garage. We can walk to the Quarter from here. Or we can get a cab if you're too tired to walk. Parking in that part of town's a bitch."

"We'll walk," she said. Maybe she could burn off some of her nervous energy with a nice, brisk hike.

They strode across the lobby to the hotel's canopied entrance. The driveway before them was filled with cabs and bellhops pushing brass-trimmed luggage carts. Cody shrugged into his jacket and shoved his hands into

his jeans pockets, a welcome sign that he had no intention of taking her arm.

He hadn't shaved since morning, Jane noted. He
looked scruffier than usual, his hair wind-tossed, his
jaw darkened with a five-o'clock shadow. His jacket
was wrinkled; he probably kept it stashed in the City
room or the back of his car, available when he needed
it. Though why he would need it to chat with prostitutes was beyond her.

Maybe he'd brought it along because the city had
cooled since they'd parted ways that afternoon. The
sidewalks bustled with pedestrians leaving work, and
the early evening sky had taken on a pink glaze.

Courtesy compelled her to make conversation. "How
were things at Tulane?"

He snorted. "It was just a bunch of spoiled rich kids
having conniptions. You'd think they'd have something better to do with their time than spray-painting
buildings."

She tried not to take his comment personally. She
might have been a rich kid when he'd first met her, but
she wasn't spoiled, and students at Wellesley hadn't
wasted time spray-painting the ivy-covered Gothic
buildings. "Have you ever thought about going to college?" she asked.

He sent her a quick, skeptical look. "Why would I
want to do that?"

"For the mental stimulation."

He let out a laugh. "I get all the mental stimulation I
can handle by reading the *Sentinel* and walking the
streets." They reached a corner and waited for the light
to change. Jane gazed at the buildings in the next block.
They were dark brick, with arched doorways and tiled
roofs. The upper floors featured narrow balconies

trimmed with baroque wrought-iron railings. The street looked like a stage set for *A Streetcar Named Desire*.

"This is charming," she said as they crossed the road.

He glanced at her again. His smile had lost its cynical flavor. "Not exactly like Quincy Market," he remarked, naming a plaza of fashionable shops and eateries in the heart of Boston.

"But the two are kind of similar. All the people, the shops, the atmosphere. I mean, Quincy Market is the epitome of New England, and this is exactly what you'd expect New Orleans to be. But it's still just overpriced shops." The ground floors of the buildings held boutiques full of gaudy jewelry, expensive art, eye-catching hand-painted masks and outrageous clothing. "Clarissa would look stunning in that," she murmured, admiring a painted silk shawl-size scarf displayed in one of the windows.

"Who's Clarissa?"

"My secretary. She's beautiful—and turquoise is definitely her color."

"You'd look stunning in it, too," he said, abruptly ducking into the boutique.

Jane chased him inside. "Cody, we didn't come here to shop."

"I'm not shopping." But he pulled the scarf from its rack in the window and searched for a price tag. Jane tried to snatch the tag and read it for herself, but he lifted the scarf out of her reach and carried it to the counter, where an elderly woman observed them in silence. "I'll take this," he said, handing the woman a credit card. "Just snip the tag, would you? The lady will wear it."

"*Cody.*" His presumption infuriated her. His generosity infuriated her even more. "I won't wear it."

"Sure you will."

"It's much too expensive—"

"How expensive is too expensive?"

Anything Cody might buy for her would be too expensive. She didn't want him to spend his money on her. As a matter of fact, she'd been certain *he* was after *her* money.

Before she could refuse the gift, he was signing the charge slip, shoving it into his wallet and draping the scarf around her shoulders. The silk was cool and luxurious, and the vibrant color dazzled her. "There you go," he said. "A souvenir."

"I don't know what to say." That was a lie. She knew damned well what to say: *I don't want this.*

"'Thanks' would work for me."

"Cody..." She'd meant to sound stern, but her voice came out oddly breathless, dissolving into a sigh as he rearranged the silk on her shoulders, settling the fabric over her bare shoulders. That a rough-and-tumble guy, educated by the streets and living by his wits, could behave with such tenderness—especially toward a woman who wanted nothing more than a divorce from him—disarmed her.

His gaze intensified as he examined her. "Looks good," he said simply.

She lowered her gaze, unable to look into his vivid blue eyes when she was surrounded by such vivid blue silk. "Thank you," she managed to say.

"You're welcome." He smoothed a fold in the cloth near her collarbone, then grinned and sauntered out of the store, leaving her no choice but to follow.

He was several doors down before she finally caught up with him. The spell his generosity had cast on her was beginning to wear off, and suspicion took its place. "Why did you do that?" she asked.

He grinned smugly. "Why shouldn't I do it? Haven't you ever done something that made no sense, just for the hell of it? Oh, yeah," he answered himself, his smile growing ironic. "You married me."

"I gave more thought to marrying you than you did to buying this," she said, wagging one end of the scarf at him.

"And after thinking about it, you went ahead and married me, anyway. A lot of good all that thinking did you." He slowed down as they neared the next corner. Across the street, a musician played slow, sultry jazz on a saxophone. Jane dug into her purse, pulled out a dollar bill and, as soon as they'd crossed, tossed it into the hat at the musician's feet. If Cody could throw money away, so could she. Her gesture made more sense than his, too. She was supporting an artist. All he was doing was making her feel indebted to him.

The pedestrian traffic had slowed during the course of their stroll. The people milling around on the sidewalks now appeared to be people out for the evening rather than workers hurrying home from their jobs. Couples ambled along the sidewalk, hand in hand. Singles eyed each other with blatant interest. A voluptuous woman in a sequined bustier and a miniskirt as tight as a girdle lurked in a doorway, surveying the possibilities.

"Is that a prostitute?" Jane whispered, reminded of the purpose of their outing.

"Well, it isn't the Queen of England." Cody veered toward the woman, and Jane once again had to jog to keep up.

The woman in the doorway gazed at him with obvious interest until she realized Jane was with him. Her eyebrows rose slightly as she linked the two in her mind. She tossed her head of big hair and straightened up. Her cleavage glistened with perspiration above the low-cut top.

"I'm wondering if you can help us," Cody said. Jane had done most of the talking when they'd met with Mrs. Stanhope and the preschool teacher at the church, but she was sure Cody could handle an interview with a prostitute better than she could.

The woman flicked the tip of her tongue over her rouged lips. "Well, now, honey, I'm sure I can. Any kind of help you want." Her voice was low and mellifluous. "Not that y'all look like you need much help, but I can make it good for you both. Y'all like that? The three of us could have ourselves a real nice party."

Jane felt her cheeks grow hot. Cody only laughed. "I'm looking for someone," he corrected her. "I'm looking for a particular hooker—"

"And y'all found her, darlin'. I'm the best there is on this street. Why don't you all come on in, I'll get us a room and we can start having ourselves some fun?"

Jane wanted to bolt, but Cody only laughed harder. From an inner pocket of his jacket he pulled a photograph of Stanhope and his playmate, enlarged and then cropped. "I'm looking for *her*," he explained.

The prostitute stared at the picture and curled her lip. "What do y'all want with her? Anything you want, baby, I can take care of it. Both of you," she added, including Jane in her sales pitch. "Y'all like sugar? I'll give you some sugar, darlin'. Men, women—I'm an equal-opportunity lover."

"We're not looking for love, sweetheart," Cody clarified, jabbing his finger at the photograph. "We're looking for this lady. Actually, we're looking for the man. You wouldn't happen to recognize him, would you?"

The prostitute studied the photo more closely. "Him, I don't know. Her... Yeah, I've seen her around. You aren't a cop, are you?"

"A private citizen. I just have a few questions for the man, but I'm having a little trouble tracking him down. Who's the lady? Do you know her name?"

"Goes by Suzie. She only does business with regulars, though. You won't find her on the street."

"Any idea where she hangs out?"

"You could try La Luna. That's a tavern down off Esplanade. I've seen her there sometimes."

"Thanks." Cody pocketed the photograph.

"I could do you better," the woman insisted.

"Maybe someday we'll give you a try. Thanks again," he said, sending the prostitute one of his killer smiles and then taking Jane's hand.

She should have appreciated his touch—and she did. Under the circumstances, she wanted it very clear that neither she nor Cody was in the market for paid companionship. And yet... after listening to the woman's innuendoes, Jane found the warmth of Cody's hand less than comforting. His warm, strong grip made her think of the woman's hushed promise to make it good, to have a party. Cody had told her he wasn't looking for love, and neither was Jane, and yet...

She didn't want to be thinking about love just because Cody was holding her hand. But she wasn't going to telegraph how rattled she was by yanking free of his clasp. She was going to remain as composed as he was and pretend the prostitute's words had planted absolutely no ideas in her fertile mind.

Cody turned the corner. Another street musician was playing his heart out, this one with an electric guitar and portable amplifier. Cody didn't allow Jane the time to toss money into his open guitar case. He was heading up the block toward a building where a blue neon crescent moon hung above a door. The words La Luna flashed on and off in the curve of the crescent.

Cody led Jane into the tavern. It was several degrees classier than Gussie's, with red brick walls, terra-cotta tiles on the floor, polished oak tables and brass fixtures. A blues singer wailed from a jukebox at the rear of the bar. The room smelled not of beer and cigarettes, but of roasting meat and hickory smoke.

"Do you suppose Reverend Bob came here looking for God?" Cody asked, surveying the patrons. They were better dressed than the thugs at Gussie's. The two bartenders looked chic and cheerful as they took orders and mixed drinks.

"Reverend Bob came here looking for Suzie," said Jane.

"Maybe it was the same thing to him. God and sex. They're both transcendent, don't you think?"

"Do we really have to discuss religion?"

"We could discuss sex instead," he suggested, shooting her a sly look.

Once more she felt her cheeks sizzle. It was downright embarrassing how easily she blushed. "I don't see the woman in question here," she muttered.

"Maybe she'll come in later. Why don't we grab a bite to eat and see if she shows up?"

"All right."

He escorted Jane to a table that offered them an unobstructed view of the door. A waitress came over, lugging a blackboard with the day's sandwiches and snacks listed on it. Cody ordered Cajun catfish on a roll; Jane asked for a plate of fried prawns. When Cody requested a beer, she did, too. White wine seemed far too effete under the circumstances.

The waitress lugged the blackboard away, leaving them to stare at each other. "Is this our first date?" Cody asked, grinning.

She bit her lip and struggled for control. She didn't like his insinuations. She didn't like that he'd spent money on the scarf for her, and she didn't like that he'd taken her hand after turning down the prostitute's offer. She didn't like the fact that she was enjoying herself.

"This can't be a date," she said, to remind herself as much as him. "I'm engaged."

"You're also married."

Good point. She sighed, crossed her legs and folded her hands in her lap. Why couldn't Cody have gone to pot over the past twelve years? Why couldn't he have lost half his hair and gained fifty pounds? Why couldn't he at least have come to the conclusion that Ivy League-educated prigs weren't his type? Even when Jane had run off with him, she'd always wondered what Cody had seen in her—other than her wealth.

"We never did go on a date, did we?" he mused aloud.

"No."

"Why?" It wasn't a rhetorical question. He looked genuinely bewildered.

"You never had any money," she recalled. "And my parents would never have let me go out with you."

"You could have snuck out behind their backs."

"I did, once."

His smile stroked her nerve endings. She crossed her legs more tightly, but no amount of twisting herself into a defensive posture could keep the memories from flooding in.

She and Cody hadn't had to go out on dates like normal high school lovebirds. Theirs had been a relationship too intense for the usual puppy-love protocol. They used to rendezvous at the end of the math hall during lunch period and exchange looks, exchange secrets. They used to meet after school when Jane's parents thought she was at a friend's house doing homework. They would ride Cody's motorcycle out to the Chestnut Hill Reservoir, find a secluded patch of grass where Cody would unroll the blanket he kept strapped to the bike's seat, and they would neck. Cody would seduce her with deep, intoxicating kisses that caused her flesh to tremble and her body to burn. He would stroke her, make her breasts ache, make her thighs clench. He would press his hand between her legs until she was moaning—but when she told him to stop he would. "I can't go all the way," she'd whisper. "You know I can't, Cody. It would be wrong."

"It wouldn't be wrong," he'd murmur, kissing her again, moving his hands against the seam of her slacks. "I love you, Janey."

"How can you love me? We're so different."

"That's what I love most about you."

"There are so many girls who go all the way, Cody. You could be with them."

"I want to be with you," he would insist, easing away from her and groaning at his uncomfortable arousal. "I must be crazy, but I want to be with you."

They both must have been crazy, she thought with a grim smile. Crazy enough to believe they really loved each other. Crazy enough to get married so they could have guilt-free sex.

The waitress's arrival with their orders interrupted her thoughts. She realized that Cody had been staring at her, observing her while she reminisced. She deflected her uneasiness by taking a sip of beer.

"Why did your father screw up the paperwork?" Cody asked. His tone was so casual, he might have been asking her opinion of the beer.

She knew better than to toss off a glib answer. Cody was asking a question she herself had asked countless times since discovering the mistake a month ago. "I'm not sure," she conceded.

"You don't think it was some sort of Freudian thing, like he secretly wanted us married?"

Jane had to laugh at that. Her father had loathed Cody. "As I said, I'm not sure. Things were so...I guess the word would be *tumultuous*. There was so much anger and distrust between my parents and me when I went home. I couldn't talk to them about anything. All I wanted was to pack up and leave for college so I wouldn't have to live with them."

"They were angry? I thought they'd have been relieved to have you back."

"They were relieved but angry. I was just angry."

"At me?"

"At everyone. Mostly at myself." She bit into one of her prawns. It was delicious, the batter spicy and the meat succulent. She allowed herself to savor it before returning to Cody's question. "My father was so stressed out—and it was my fault, mostly. He was feeling terrible, and I felt responsible for it. My mother was always taking him to the doctor to get tranquilizers because he was so strung out. When I think back on it, I wonder whether maybe he was so upset about my running away, he just couldn't think straight."

"Was that when he started having health problems?"

"I guess it was around then. His back kept going into spasm. They found arthritic swelling in his hips and along his spine. It got bad enough that he needs a cane now, and he can't tolerate cold weather."

"Bummer," Cody murmured.

She doubted his sincerity. "You hated my father."

"I hated him twelve years ago." He bit into his sandwich. "I don't hate him now."

Jane leaned back in her chair and studied Cody. "Why are you being so nice to me?" she asked, her misgivings hovering painfully close to the surface.

He chuckled and took a swig of beer. "Oh, geez—was I being nice? I'll try to stop."

"I mean it, Cody. What do you want from me? I already said I'd help you deal with Stanhope. What else do you want?"

"You don't think I'd be nice unless I wanted something from you?"

"No," she answered bluntly.

He mulled over her accusation, then shrugged, not bothering to deny it. "I guess I do want something from you, Janey," he admitted in a quiet voice. He leaned across the table and touched the edge of her scarf. His fingers slid along the edge of the silk, slow and seductive, filling her mind with the image of those fingers on her skin. Before she could shrink from him—or lean into his caress—he sat back in his chair and shrugged. "I want something, but I'm not sure what it is. I'll let

you know when I figure it out." His gaze drifted past
her, and he set down his beer. "But I'll have to figure it
out later," he said. "It looks like our friend Suzie's
made the scene."

CHAPTER SIX

JUST IN THE NICK OF TIME, he thought, tossing down his sandwich and focusing on the blond woman who'd sashayed into the bar. Compared to the hooker he'd talked to out on the street, she was almost discreet; she wore a low-cut blouse tucked into a billowing skirt just sheer enough to reveal the silhouette of her legs. She looked less like a prostitute than simply a woman on the make.

Whatever she was, however she looked, he was glad to have her to focus on. Things were getting too intense between him and Jane. He was playing with fire—which wasn't anything new for him, but it wasn't going to do either of them any good.

Besides which, Jane Thayer had always been one person he hated to lie to. And when he told her he didn't know what he wanted from her, that was an outright lie. He knew damned well what he wanted from her: a long, hot night between the sheets, just to prove to himself that sex with her wasn't as spectacular as he'd remembered.

Or else to prove that it was. Either way would be all right with him.

He shouldn't have bought her the scarf. He didn't mind that she'd failed to kiss his feet in gratitude—hell, watching her get all steamed about it had been half the fun. But seeing it on her made him wish he could see her in it and nothing else.

What was it about her that reduced him to the slobbering adolescent he'd been when he first met her? What strange magic did she possess? Why hadn't she taken him up on his offer to finish the paperwork and get the divorce over with? She'd always been the more sensible of the two of them, and getting the divorce over with would have been the sensible way to go.

Suzie was walking to a table near the bar. Cody fought to keep his mind on her. She had full hips, he noticed, lush curves, pouty lips, mascara-darkened eyes.

He'd take Jane over her in an instant.

"I'll be right back," he said, rising from his chair and crossing to Suzie's table. He moved slowly, cautiously, not wanting to spook her. When he neared her and she peered up at him, he acknowledged that she wasn't the sort of woman who would spook easily. Her eyes were cold, her skin glazed with makeup. Several strands of glass beads, the kind people threw around during Mardi Gras, circled her neck.

"Suzie?" he asked.

"Who wants to know?"

"I've got a couple of questions for you."

"I don't know anything," she said, turning away.

"I'm not a cop," he assured her. "Can I sit for a minute?" Before she could object, he settled into a seat across the table from her. Behind him, he heard the scrape of chair legs along the tiles. He turned in his seat and saw that Jane had decided to join them.

He probably could have handled this better without her—particularly because she was seated so close to him he could smell her herbal shampoo through the aromas emanating from the kitchen beyond the bar. She was seated so close that when he moved his arm his wrist brushed the silk edge of her scarf. She was seated so close, he flashed on a picture of them riding his bike, her arms tight around him, her body pressed to his back, her crotch nestled right up close against his butt, and he realized that he didn't want to be handling anything but Jane.

Exercising enormous willpower, he concentrated on Suzie. "I've got a picture of you with one of your clients," he said, digging into his pocket and pulling out the photograph.

She looked at the photograph and snorted. "Yeah, that's me, all right. Not my best side, though. Who took this picture? He got my bad side."

"I took it," Cody confessed, then added, "but you don't have a bad side, Suzie. You look great from every angle."

She eyed him skeptically. "And who might you be?" she drawled.

"Cody Sinclair. I'm with the *Sentinel*."

"The newspaper?" This seemed to impress her. She nodded and glanced at Jane. "You with the newspaper, too?"

"I'm with him," Jane said succinctly.

"Well, don't get in a sweat about it, darlin'. I won't touch him." She sniffed and swiveled back to Cody. "If it's all the same to you, Mr. Cody Sinclair of the *Sentinel,* I'm here to drum up some action. So I'd appreciate it if you stated your business and removed those cute little buns from that chair."

He ignored her attitude. "Actually, what I'm interested in is the guy you're with in the picture."

She pursed her lips and folded her arms across her chest, looking sort of like an R-rated schoolmarm. "I don't discuss my friends with strangers. Especially strangers from the *Sentinel*."

"I'm not a stranger," he said. "I've told you who I am. And I'm not here on newspaper business. It's just... I think this is a guy I used to know, and I'd like to find him if I can."

"What for?"

Cody scrambled for a believable excuse. "He saved my soul. He was a religious man, and he prayed with me and saved me from eternal damnation."

She leveled her gaze at Cody, still schoolmarmish despite her mountain of blond hair and two mountains of breast. "He saved your soul, did he?"

"As much as it could have been saved at the time. And when I saw this picture and realized he was in it, I freaked out. I said, wow, that's my man! Stanhope!"

"Stanley," she said.

"Stanley?" He didn't dare to look at Jane.

"Stanley Roberts. I thought you said you knew him."

"I said he saved my soul. It was a long time ago—I guess I scrambled his name a little." *Stanley Roberts, my ass,* Cody muttered under his breath. "I'd really like to see him so I could tell him how much I appreciate what he did for me all those years ago."

Frowning, she tilted her head slightly to study him from another angle. "How do I know you're not really a cop?"

"If I was, I'd be setting you up for a bust right now, trying to get you to solicit. I'm not doing that, am I?"

"What about her?" she asked, eyeing Jane dubiously.

"I'm not a cop," Jane declared.

"You don't look like a cop. *You*..." Suzie turned her knowing gaze back to Cody. "You look like the sort of cop who'd be amenable to doing a little business on the side."

"I'm not looking for business. What I'm looking for is Stanley Roberts." He said the fake name smoothly, easily. "Any idea where he lives?"

"Now, how am I supposed to know where he lives? I only know the important things about my clients."

"What important things do you know about Stanley?" Cody asked.

She pulled a cigarette and a butane lighter from the small gold-lamé purse she held in her lap. When she put the cigarette to her lips, Cody gallantly lit it for her. She stared at him through her smoke as she exhaled. "He likes it doggie-style. That's the sort of thing that's important for me to know."

"I can imagine."

"How about you, Cody Sinclair of the *Sentinel*? Do you like it doggie-style?"

Cody wouldn't like it any style with Suzie. With Jane...

They'd done it sitting, standing, on the floor, in the shower, on the beach. They'd done it up, down and every which way, but he was almost certain they'd never done it doggie-style. Jane wouldn't have liked it. She was so inexperienced.

But willing to try. Willing to experiment. Willing to race to the edge with him. Almost willing to jump. For two months of marriage, they'd fought passionately and made love even more passionately.

Doggie-style, though? He could no longer remember. He hadn't thought about Jane Thayer for a dozen

years, but now, all of a sudden, it infuriated him that he
couldn't remember which positions they'd made love in.

"What makes you think Stan would want to see
you?" Suzie said, breaking into his thoughts.

"Why wouldn't he want to?"

She tapped her index finger on the table. It was polished half scarlet, half metallic gold. "I could give him
your name and see if he's interested."

"No, don't do that," Cody said quickly. "I want to
surprise him. Could you tell me where he lives?"

"No way. I don't give out that kind of information."

"Oh, come on. You're not giving it out. You're just
telling me so I can thank him."

She shook her head. "Sorry. Stan's a regular. I'd
never betray his trust."

Cody almost laughed. She would blab about what
position Stan preferred, but his address was off-limits.

"How much do you charge?" Jane asked.

Cody almost fell out of his seat. What was she up to?
Planning to hire Suzie for an evening's entertainment?

The prostitute turned to Jane. She seemed rejuve-
nated by the question. "A lot, darlin'. Quite a lot."

"I'm sure you're worth it, too," Jane said in her best
Boston-lawyer voice. "I'm just wondering, how much
would it cost for you to tell us where Stanley Roberts
lives? Maybe we could come to terms."

"You want to buy that information?"

"If we can agree on a reasonable price."

Cody relaxed into his chair and scrutinized Jane. She
was as smart now as she'd been then. She was still the
class brain—and a lawyer, to boot, prepared to negotiate. The scarf set off the highlights in her brown hair,
the creamy undertone of her complexion. Her throat

was as smooth as her face, he noted, and the scarf draped over the arches of her collarbones, which, of course, made him that much more aware of her collarbones.

A genius with a scarf. The most dangerous kind of woman there was.

"I'll tell you the truth, hon," Suzie was saying. "I don't know his address. I don't make house calls. He wants to see me, he beeps me on my pager, we make a date and he comes to me. I don't go to him."

"Do you expect to see him soon? Perhaps the next time you see him, you could find out his address." Sensing Suzie's hesitancy, Jane toyed with the flap of her purse. "We're willing to pay."

"How much?"

"How much is it worth?"

"A hundred dollars," she said.

"Twenty," Jane counteroffered.

"A hundred bucks is my going rate."

Cody rolled his eyes. Jane inhaled sharply, then let her breath out in a sigh as she regrouped. "That's way too much, Suzie. It's not as if we're asking you to... to..."

"To get down and shimmy with you," Suzie completed. Cody watched crimson seep into Jane's cheeks. "If you wanted to get down and shimmy, doll, it'd cost you a bit more than a hundred."

"Whatever you charge for sex is between you and your johns," Jane said, obviously struggling to keep her voice steady.

"They aren't all johns, you know," Suzie said. "Some of them are janes."

Jane glanced toward Cody, and he saw a sweet helplessness in her eyes. He doubted a tough hooker like

Suzie could trounce an equally tough lawyer like Jane. Her helplessness had some other cause—like, for instance, the fact that whenever the subject swung around to sexual matters, she got all flustered.

Cody decided to jump back into the debate. "Twenty bucks, Suzie," he said. "That's a pretty piece of change for doing nothing."

"It's not nothing. You're asking me to spy on him."

"No, we're not. We're asking you to find out where he lives so we can visit him. Twenty bucks. You could buy yourself a lot of cigarettes."

Suzie thought it over. "I don't know. Maybe."

"When are you going to see Stanley Roberts?"

"When he calls me. If I'm free."

"We'll meet you here tomorrow," Cody said with finality. "We'll have your money. See what you can find out." Refusing her the chance to prolong the negotiations, he stood, took Jane's hand and hauled her out of her chair. "Tomorrow, Suzie. Try to help us out, okay?"

Jane's hand fit perfectly in his, he noticed as they walked back to their table, where he left some money to cover the bill. He didn't want to stick around and finish their meals, because if they remained at La Luna, they'd be giving Suzie a chance to dicker some more about how much they should pay her for getting Stanhope's address. More important, Cody wanted to leave the tavern so he could get some fresh air and purge his mind of memories, of yearning, of all the things he shouldn't be thinking about when he thought about Jane.

She was engaged to be married, he reminded himself. She was in love with a Boston banker named Mark. She was living the life she'd been groomed for, the life she'd always wanted and could never have had with Cody, a life of high-class luxury, good breeding and good manners. It was a life that had nothing to do with him.

Night was descending on the city as they exited the tavern. The sky had turned a deep blue, and the guitarist on the corner played a deep, bluesy song to match. Jane turned toward the sound of the music, deftly sliding her hand from Cody's as she did.

Okay. He could take a hint. She wanted him less now than she had the day she'd walked out on him twelve years ago. Whatever her reason for not leaving New Orleans, it wasn't because she wanted to take a quick, fun detour back to the past.

Which made him wonder why, exactly, she'd agreed to stay and help him.

"Do you think Suzie's going to come through?" she asked.

He studied her in the evening shadows. The violet neon washed pink across her face, reminding him of the way she'd blushed earlier that evening. "We'll find out soon enough whether she'll come through. But let me ask you this, Janey—how come you could go one-on-one with *her* but the lady in the doorway on Bourbon Street had you turning three shades of red?"

Jane's eyes grew darker. "Suzie wasn't offering to have sex with us," she said.

"She hinted she might be interested in getting something on with me," he goaded her, just to see how she'd react.

She reacted like the Crown Princess of Brookline—prim and chilly. "Her only interest in you was that she thought you were a cop, and she was willing to make it worth your while not to arrest her."

JUDITH ARNOLD 125

"And the lady on Bourbon Street . . . ?"

"Obviously *she* didn't think you were a cop."

He chuckled. "The lady on Bourbon Street had you squirming, Jane," he said. "Did her suggestion of a threesome rub you the wrong way?"

The color in Jane's cheeks had nothing to do with the overhead lighting. "Sex," she said crisply, "is something very intimate, something private, between two people. Not between three."

"Now that's what I call being close-minded." Cody plunged his hands into his pockets to keep him from the temptation of adjusting her scarf and started ambling down the street toward the corner.

Jane caught up. She glanced furtively at him, her hand running back and forth along the edge of her scarf and putting naughty ideas back into his head. "Do you think threesomes are a good thing?" she asked.

He suppressed the urge to laugh. "We could go back to that hooker and see if she's still available."

"I didn't say *I* wanted to do that. I was only asking about you."

"Interested in my sex life, are you?"

"Forget I asked," she snapped.

He looped his arm around her and gave her a playful squeeze, nothing seductive, just a friendly embrace. It felt natural to hold her that way. She fit in the curve of his arm as well as her hand fit in his. It dawned on him that the slim contours of her body, her warm skin, the flutter of her hair against his sleeve made him feel . . . more than friendly. Much more.

The guitarist was playing his heart out. Cody got to his wallet before Jane got to her purse, and he tossed a bill into the man's case. "You're certainly throwing money around this evening, aren't you," she chided.

"You were the one who offered to pay Suzie."

"I thought someone ought to act like a professional."

"That was exactly what Suzie was doing."

"And what were you doing? That ridiculous story about how Reverend Bob saved your soul—"

"It was the first thing I could think of," he said, not taking her criticism personally. If she really thought he was ridiculous, she would have moved away from his arm. But she stayed where she was, close beside him, her pace matching his.

"It was all I could do not to laugh out loud when you told her that absurd story," she remarked.

"I guess I'm just a funny guy, huh."

She shot him a quick look, then relented with a smile. "I always thought you were pretty funny."

"Really? The last time we were together, it seemed all I ever did was make you cry." He hadn't meant to revive the touchy subject of their past just when she was beginning to relax with him. But the words slipped out and he couldn't take them back.

She lapsed into a reflective mood, but she didn't escape from the shelter of his arm. "I didn't cry that much, Cody," she disputed him. "I'm not big on crying."

"That's one of the things I always liked about you."

"You made me miserable, though."

"The feeling was mutual."

She laughed again, a soft, musical laugh. "Why on earth did we ever run off together?"

"Lust," he said simply.

"I guess that was it."

"A little lust can go a long way. I have no regrets."

"Really?" She peered up at him, wide-eyed. "Even after..."

"After you walked out on me? No. No regrets." A group of carousing teenagers swarmed the sidewalk, coming toward them. Cody tightened his arm around Jane as they sidestepped the rowdy kids. Her shoulders were just the right width, not skinny enough to seem flimsy, but not husky enough to make him think of football players. Twelve years after he'd last seen her, he was still impressed by the proportions of her body— neat, trim, wide and narrow in all the right places.

"Why?" she asked.

Why was he impressed with her body? No, that wasn't what she was asking. He groped backward to pick up the conversational thread he'd dropped. "Why do I have no regrets? I don't know. Life happens, and I've always figured my best strategy was to ride along with it. I wanted to get the hell out of Boston. Nothing good was going to happen for me there. My mother was drinking, fancy people like your family thought I was dirt, and it was time to try something new. If you hadn't come with me, I probably would have gone on my own."

"To Los Angeles?"

"If that was where I ended up, sure. I wanted to be someplace warm, someplace far away. Los Angeles fit the bill."

"So I was just an afterthought," she concluded, sounding less insulted than philosophical.

"No, Jane," he snapped. "You were the main thought. If you'd been willing to move in with me in Boston, we could have stayed. Your father probably would have come after me with a shotgun, though."

"My father isn't violent," said Jane.

"All right. He would have come after me with a lawyer and a lot of money. He *did* come after me with legal threats—and he came after you with the money. Either way, I guess he got what he wanted."

"Don't blame it on him," she protested. "If I hadn't thought our marriage was a mistake, I wouldn't have left, no matter how many college tuitions he dangled over my head. I left because it wasn't working."

"The sex was working," Cody insisted.

They were nearing Canal Street. Her hotel occupied the entire block; they were only a few feet from a revolving side door into the lobby. Jane eyed the door, then halted and turned to face Cody. "The sex wasn't enough."

"What would have been enough?" he asked, already knowing her answer. Money. Creature comforts. A fancy college education. That would have been enough.

"Maturity," she said, surprising him. "Wisdom. Understanding."

He gazed down at her, astonished by the way her intelligence still turned him on, more now than it had then. Her intelligence and her smoky eyes and the delicate line of her jaw. Her scarf, and her body inside the scarf.

He would never be able to offer her what she wanted in a marriage. But, then, he didn't want a marriage. All he wanted was Jane Thayer.

She didn't shrink from him as he lowered his mouth to hers. She didn't resist as he circled his arms around her and drew her to him. She didn't hesitate as his lips covered hers, brushed and nipped and stroked and coaxed until she opened to him.

This wasn't like their make-out sessions by the reservoir, back in high school. It wasn't like the night she'd given herself to him, or the night she'd given her hand to him in marriage. It was both less and more—less weighted down with emotion, more influenced by self-awareness. They weren't two crazy kids anymore. They were mature, and wise, and at the moment they seemed to understand each other perfectly.

He felt her hands on him, sliding under his blazer and flattening against his back. He could feel the impression of her palms and the flexing of her fingers through the cotton of his shirt. He pulled her even closer and felt the tight swells of her nipples through her shirt and his.

Twelve years had given him a bit more experience, a bit more control. If he made love to her now, he'd be better at it. He'd make her come and come until she couldn't stand it anymore. He'd make her forget about Mark the Banker, about anyone else she'd ever known. He'd make her recognize that, at least right now, she was still his wife.

He cupped his hands around her bottom and angled her to feel his arousal. "Let me come in," he whispered against her mouth. He'd meant she should invite him into her room, but if she interpreted his words in a more carnal way, that was fine, too.

She moaned, turned her head to break the kiss and hid her face against his shoulder. She was breathing raggedly; every gasp thrust her breasts into his chest. If only he wasn't standing on a street corner, he would have bent down and kissed them, closed his mouth around one of her tight little nipples and sucked until she was sobbing with pleasure. The Princess of Brookline; he could still make her his.

"Don't do this, Cody," she whispered.

He lifted one hand to her head and stroked her hair. It was silkier than the scarf. "Don't do what?"

"Seduce me."

"I thought you were seducing me," he murmured.

"Then let's both stop."

"I've got a better idea—let's neither of us stop."

She leaned back and eyed him, her expression a blend of impatience and dismay. "This isn't why I came to New Orleans."

"I know. You came to divorce me."

"And I will."

"No argument, Janey. We can go to bed together and then do the divorce."

"That's a morally repugnant idea."

Uh-oh. She was dragging out the Wellesley vocabulary now. It probably meant she was running scared.

He tried not to grin. "It isn't immoral to go to bed with the person you're married to. We're still married."

"Only because a mistake was made."

"Then let's make another mistake and go to bed," he suggested.

She wrestled with her smile. The smile won. "You were a scoundrel then and you're a scoundrel now," she complained. "The only difference is that I'm no longer attracted to scoundrels." She extricated herself from his embrace, made a feeble attempt to adjust her clothes, and then pivoted and walked to the revolving door.

Liar, he thought, watching her push the glass pane and vanish into the hotel. He'd be the first to admit he was a scoundrel. But she was lying—to him, and maybe to herself—when she said she wasn't attracted to scoundrels anymore—one particular scoundrel, in any case.

CHAPTER SEVEN

CLARISSA CHECKED HER watch: ten o'clock. Nine o'clock, New Orleans time. Jane could be calling her any minute.

Her gaze drifted to the silent telephone on her desk. She shuddered.

God, what was she going to do? What could she say to Jane? "Good morning! I've got three messages for you. Everett Baker wants you in the second chair when the Gaylord suit goes to trial. Tom Lewis wants to take you out for lunch next week. Mark Dennison wants to know what the hell you're doing in Louisiana. Oh, and by the way, I'm falling in love with him."

Dread rippled down her spine, icy and dire. How could she be falling in love with Mark Dennison? He was Jane's fiancé, for crying out loud. He loved Jane. Jane loved him. How in heaven's name could Clarissa have gotten a crush on him?

She knew how. It was that damned stroll through the North End. Watching him struggle with his calzone, watching him lick the oozing sauce from his fingers and laugh and scold Clarissa for having talked him into such an impulsive outing...watching his neat, aristocratic features convulse with laughter...watching as he loosened his tie, as he just plain loosened up...

She should never have taken off her glasses. Or let down her hair—in any sense of the term.

Four hours. They'd spent that long together. Four hours, from the moment they'd met at the hotel on the Common to the moment he'd walked her to the door of her apartment in the Fenway while a cab kept the meter running. He'd patted her shoulder—nothing romantic about it—and told her to meet him tomorrow for another update on Jane, and then he'd bounded back down the front steps to the cab and waved at her. Four hours in his company, then another twelve hours alone in her apartment reliving those four hours, replaying them over and over like a tape.

Mark had asked her about herself—*real* questions, like about how her parents had met when her father was a marine stationed in Vietnam. Clarissa had told Mark the romantic story of how her parents had fallen in love and how, after his tour of duty, her father had sent for her mother, who had loved him so much she'd left her family and her homeland and journeyed halfway around the world just to marry her American soldier. Clarissa had told Mark about the difficulties, the adjustments, the struggles she and her brothers had faced growing up mixed-race—and also the advantages. She'd explained to him what American success meant to her family and described her own determination to achieve it.

Mark had listened to her, really listened. He'd said he was glad they'd finally gotten to know each other outside the formal setting of Jane's office, because in truth he'd never met anyone like Clarissa before. He'd confessed that he lived a sheltered life, ensconced in his own caste-conscious world, and he was thrilled that she was exposing him to new things. Like calzones and flavored ices.

It was the ices that had sealed her fate. After they'd devoured their hot, gooey calzones, Mark had suggested something cold and sweet to cleanse their palates. They'd caught sight of a vendor selling ices, and Mark had bought a cup of cherry-flavored ice for her, chocolate-flavored for him. He'd insisted that she taste his chocolate ice, and she had. And then she'd insisted that he taste her cherry, and she'd lifted her spoon to his lips, and he'd licked the spoon . . .

She shuddered again.

She would simply have to quit her job. She had no other choice. Any secretary who could spend an entire night fantasizing about her boss's fiancé's tongue didn't deserve to keep her job.

Although . . . maybe she wouldn't have to quit, if she could figure out a way to cure herself of this stupid infatuation really fast—preferably before she saw Mark that evening. She reminded herself of his instructions: "When Jane calls, try to squeeze more information out of her. At least you might get her to narrow down when she's coming back. Or—if it wouldn't be too much trouble—perhaps you could go into her office and see if she left any clues there. Surely *you* can go in."

They were the words of a man devoted to his wife-to-be. All he was looking for from Clarissa was her help. It didn't matter what she thought of him. All that mattered was that he wanted her to help tighten the bond between him and Jane.

Her gaze traveled from the phone to Jane's closed door. Yes, she could go into Jane's office. She could prowl and snoop and do Mark's bidding—which, of course, would be one more bit of proof that she was stuck on him. For no one else would she even *consider* spying on her boss.

But if Clarissa did search Jane's office, she might find evidence of what Jane was doing and when she'd be coming back—and even if she didn't share the information with Mark, it would help save her from herself. Learning the specific date of Jane's return would give Clarissa something to work with. Knowing Jane was doing something special for Mark would give Clarissa a weapon to fight off her attraction to him. And if she could fight it off completely, she wouldn't have to quit her job.

Resolved, she plucked her key ring from the top drawer of her desk and located the key for Jane's office door. If Jane phoned while Clarissa was inside, she could answer the call on Jane's extension.

She had plenty to feel guilty about, but entering Jane's office shouldn't have caused such twinges of conscience. She was in and out of Jane's office all the time. Yet she felt like a trespasser as she entered the silent room. It was small, tidy, decorated with a few plants on the windowsill and a framed still life on the wall. Partners got bigger offices and nicer furniture, but Jane had arranged her standard-issue desk, chairs and credenza tastefully.

Of course she had. Jane did everything tastefully.

Her desk was clear of paperwork. Clarissa scrutinized the blotter, the pen stand, the console phone, the crystal bud vase. The desk calendar was opened to Tuesday, the day she'd left.

Timidly, Clarissa flipped back to Saturday. *Museum of Fine Arts—fund-raiser* was written in Jane's neat hand. *Eight p.m., with Mark.*

That was where they'd seen the naked-lady sculpture, Clarissa recalled with a sigh.

She turned the page to Sunday and found that page blank. On the Monday page, Jane had noted the settlement conference she'd be spending the day at, and then had written: *Confirm nine-thirty flight for Tuesday a.m.*

Well, that didn't tell Clarissa anything she hadn't already known.

A stronger pang of conscience overtook her as she slid open the top drawer of Jane's desk. Even the inside of the woman's desk was tidy and classy, her paper stacked neatly, her pens all facing the same direction. Clarissa recognized the top two folders. One held Jane's notes on the settlement she'd negotiated on Monday, and the other held notes on the Gaylord suit, which Jane had been researching for Everett Baker. A floppy disk was inserted into each file. Clarissa herself had typed all the notes onto those two disks. She wasn't going to learn anything new from them.

Below the two folders was a green-and-white legal envelope Clarissa didn't recognize. Telling herself she had to do this to save her sanity and her job, she lifted the envelope from the drawer. It was addressed to Jane at her Back Bay condo. The return address was another law firm.

This was personal. Clarissa wouldn't dare look inside the envelope, even though the seal had been broken and the flap hung open. If another lawyer had sent it to Jane at home, it had nothing to do with Baker, Dunn.

But it was in her office, wasn't it?

Clarissa chewed on her lip and considered her options. If she looked inside the envelope, she would be encroaching on Jane's privacy. Who knew why Jane would correspond with an outside attorney? Was she planning to buy some property? No, she would have

used one of Baker, Dunn's real estate specialists for
that. Ditto if she was writing a will. Maybe she was being sued—but if she was, she'd ask one of her colleagues at Baker, Dunn to defend her.

The only reason Jane would go outside Baker, Dunn
for a lawyer was if she was doing something she didn't
want anyone at the firm to know about.

And if she didn't want anyone at the firm to know
about it, she wouldn't want her secretary to know about
it, either. Clarissa jammed the envelope back into the
desk and slammed the drawer shut. The flap got caught
on the lip of the drawer and forced it back open.

A message from the gods, Clarissa decided. A sign
from above, telling her she needed to look inside the
envelope.

Maybe there was something bad about Mark in it.
Maybe Jane had been investigating him. Maybe the
contents of the envelope would destroy any misplaced
affection Clarissa felt toward the man.

She pulled the envelope from the drawer, bit her lip
and shook out the papers inside.

The top sheet was a form of some sort: *Account
#3754. Subject: Cody Sinclair.* Below that: *Age 30.* A
social security number. A street address in New Orleans, Louisiana. And a few typewritten paragraphs:
*Subject is employed as a photojournalist by the New
Orleans* Sentinel. *Subject's previous address: Denver,
Colorado. Education: None beyond high school. No
military record. No criminal record. Subject drives a
1981 Datsun 280-ZX....*

Frowning, Clarissa skimmed the page stapled to it. It
was an invoice from a private investigator.

Maybe Cody Sinclair was related to an upcoming case
of Jane's, although if he was, Clarissa would have

known about it. She'd never heard of Cody Sinclair before. Nor had she heard of any case in the firm that might involve someone from New Orleans.

She set the private investigator's report aside. The next page bore the letterhead of the law firm named on the envelope's return address. Jane scanned the letter.

Dear Ms. Thayer,
Re your inquiries concerning the proper documentation of the divorce decree in question, an extensive search has failed to produce said documentation. We have combed data bases dating back twelve years and find no such decree was ever issued through the courts....

Clarissa began to figure it out: Jane was working on a case on the side. A favor for a friend, perhaps. She must be lending her expertise to someone at the other law firm. An old classmate, maybe—those Harvard Law School alums had quite an active network. A friend of Jane's was investigating a man named Cody Sinclair, handling a messy divorce or something, and the lawyer had asked Jane for her assistance. Why Jane would agree to help on such a two-bit case puzzled Clarissa, though. She certainly didn't need the extra money.

It must be a personal favor. There was no other possible explanation.

Turning aside the lawyer's letter, Clarissa discovered that there was, indeed, another possible explanation. The last document from the envelope was a marriage certificate, dated twelve years ago and issued by the state of Nevada. It declared that a contract of marriage had been entered into, presided over by Henry Latimer, Justice of the Peace, Las Vegas, Clark County. The husband's name was Cody Sinclair.

The wife's name was Jane Thayer.

JANE STARED at the flashing message light on her telephone. She'd heard the phone ringing while she was in the shower but she hadn't bothered to answer it. She could think of only one person who'd call her at the hotel, and he was the reason she was showering.

She'd showered last night, too. A long, hot, scalding scrub. But neither last night's shower nor this morning's could wash away the lingering effects of his kiss.

Perhaps a cold shower would have worked better.

She sat cross-legged on the bed, her head propped in her hands and her gaze drifting from the blinking red light to the beautiful turquoise scarf, tossed over the arm of an easy chair. She'd dreamed about that scarf last night.

She'd dreamed about Cody.

An assortment of pungent curses filled her mouth. If there was one thing she didn't need, it was a night of Cody Sinclair dreams. She was supposed to be levelheaded and organized; her life was plotted out on a graph that most definitely did not include him. If she was so levelheaded, though, what was she doing sitting squaw-style at the center of her bed, wrapped in a hotel-supplied terry-cloth robe, gawking at the scarf Cody had given her instead of longing to get back home to Mark?

Damn Cody for kissing her that way. Damn him for stirring up memories that ought to have been left alone. Damn him for being the sexiest man she'd ever known, even twelve years after she'd left him. Damn him for leaving her a message.

Nothing to do but get on with it, she thought disconsolately, lifting the phone and dialing the hotel's extension for message retrieval. The operator at the other end informed her that, just as she'd guessed, Cody Sinclair had called. "He said that if you're free for lunch, you should meet him at the *Sentinel* building at noon."

"What if I'm not free for lunch?" Jane grumbled.

"I'm sorry, ma'am. He didn't allow for that possibility."

Well, of course he didn't. He knew the only reason she wouldn't go to the *Sentinel* building was that she didn't want to see him. Freedom had nothing to do with it.

After thanking the operator and lowering the phone, she swung her legs over the side of the bed and stood. A cup of coffee remained in the insulated pot room service had delivered an hour ago, and it was almost hot enough to drink. And it didn't taste burnt like that chicory-flavored brew she'd drunk with Cody yesterday morning.

She carried her refilled cup back to the bed, sat and dialed her personal office number in Boston. Talking shop would help unscramble her brain more effectively than an ocean of coffee and all the showers in the universe.

The phone rang twice before she heard a breathless voice. "Hello?"

Jane frowned. Clarissa Bonnert was an ace secretary; she knew the proper way to answer an office phone. "Clarissa?"

"Oh, Jane? Oh, hi!" Clarissa jabbered too brightly. "Hi, how are you?"

"Are you all right?"

"Sure, I'm fine. Why?"

"You sounded so strange when you answered."

"I was about to sneeze," Clarissa explained.

Laughter eroded Jane's scowl. "Well, then, go ahead and sneeze."

"Oh, I don't have to anymore." Clarissa still sounded oddly breathless.

"Are you coming down with something? Take a day off," Jane urged. "For heaven's sake, Clarissa—"

"No, I'm fine. Really. A hundred percent."

Jane wasn't convinced, but she saw no point in nagging her secretary. Clarissa was a big girl; she could take care of herself. "So," Jane said casually, "how are things at the office? Do you have any messages for me?"

"Oh—um—yeah. Everett Baker wants you in the second chair for the Gaylord case, and Tom Lewis wants to have lunch with you."

Jane nodded. Everett was getting on in years, but he was still sharp enough to know when he needed a young hotshot at his side in a difficult trial. And Tom Lewis liked to take Jane out for lunch once a year to celebrate the huge libel suit she'd won for him during her rookie year at Baker, Dunn. "Go ahead and set up a lunch with Tom," she told Clarissa. "Any weekday next week should be fine. And tell Everett I'll do the trial with him."

"Okay," Clarissa said, then lapsed into silence.

Jane gave her a full minute, but Clarissa didn't speak. "Were there any other messages?" she asked.

"Um . . ." Clarissa inhaled audibly and said, "Mark wants to know what you're up to."

"Mark?" Jane's frown returned, stronger than before.

"Mr. Dennison, I mean."

Jane drained her cup and grimaced as she swallowed a mouthful of tepid dregs. Setting the cup on the night table, she noticed the naked ring finger on her left hand and grimaced again, a spasm of guilt squeezing her gut. It wasn't as if she'd been wearing the ring for so long she felt peculiar without it. She and Mark had only agreed to get married a month ago.

It was a gorgeous ring, however, and her fear of getting mugged wasn't reason enough not to wear it in New Orleans. She was never afraid to wear it in Boston.

She tore her gaze from her hand and it settled, as if magnetized, on the peacock blue scarf draping the arm of the easy chair.

This time it was Clarissa's turn to break the awkward silence. "Mark—I mean, Mr. Dennison—he's, um . . ." She faltered.

"He's what?"

"He's curious about you being gone without telling him where you are, or why. You haven't called him—"

"He told you that?" Why on earth would Mark have been discussing her with Clarissa?

She could have sworn she heard Clarissa gulp before answering, "Well . . . yeah, he did."

"I see."

"Because he's worried about you," Clarissa hastened to add.

"Well, if you should talk to him again, tell him not to worry." She reached for her cup, remembered it was empty, and swore under her breath.

"He wants to know what you're up to."

"Tell him I'm visiting an old friend."

Clarissa said nothing for a moment. "A *friend?*"

Jane mentally acknowledged that Cody was no friend. Granted, before he'd kissed her last night, she'd felt almost friendly toward him. The way the two of them had talked to Suzie, negotiated, worked together without even planning beforehand what they would say, how they would approach her... That had been kind of friendly. And then their stroll afterward, when Cody had wrapped his arm around her as if they were buddies from way back...

Well, they weren't buddies, but it was easier to tell Clarissa that than anything else. "I can't understand why Mark would be pestering you about me, but yes, that's what you can tell him."

"Oh, he's not pestering me. He's been so nice, Jane. He's just worried about you—because he loves you."

Jane discerned a strange undertone in her secretary's voice. Why was Clarissa so anxious to remind Jane that she and Mark were supposed to love each other?

Supposed to? She did love Mark, she told herself. Even if kissing him was nothing like kissing Cody, even if *friend* seemed a more appropriate term than *husband,* even if Jane had spent more time in the past two days dreaming about Cody than she'd ever spent dreaming about Mark...

The thought horrified her. "Tell Mark I'll call him as soon as I get home," she said.

"Why won't you call him now?"

"It really isn't any of your business," Jane snapped, feeling rather cowardly. But she wasn't about to explain to Clarissa that many years ago, when she'd been young and foolish, she'd eloped with a high school heartthrob and had been mistaken in her belief that that marriage had been legally voided. Nor was she going to explain to Mark what a nitwit she'd been in her youth. There was no reason he had to know she'd been married once before—to a motorcycle-riding ruffian like

Cody. She knew Mark well enough to suspect that the revelation would bother him. Why should she go out of her way to upset him?

All she had to do was get the damned divorce straightened out. Mark didn't have to know about it.

"I'll call you tomorrow," Jane said abruptly, deciding that checking in with Clarissa had been a bad idea after all. Far from clearing her mind, the call had only reminded her even more vividly how very cluttered and confused her mind was.

She said a curt goodbye and hung up. Then she slid out of her bathrobe and donned her bra and a pair of panties, figuring that the sooner she got dressed, the sooner she could go downstairs and buy some more coffee.

She hesitated near the mirror above the dresser. The reflection that greeted her was plain and pale. Her underthings were a lacy white, flirty but virginal, doing little to jazz up her underendowed figure. She recalled Suzie's bounteous curves and groaned.

Why had Cody picked her, of all the girls in their senior class? Why was he picking her again, twelve years later? Surely he had his choice of women these days— buxom women, flashy women, women with dreamy cheekbones and breasts that created a cleavage without the help of intricately engineered lingerie. She could hardly believe she'd been his type back then, and she couldn't believe it now.

She strode resolutely to the closet, knelt in front of the room safe and pressed in the code she'd programmed when she'd checked into the room. When the heavy door swung open, she reached in and retrieved the hinged velvet box that held her engagement ring. She slid it on her finger. It felt huge, heavy, cold.

After closing the safe, she pulled the skirt of her suit from its hanger, along with the silk tank top. She hadn't packed expecting to spend more than a day or two in New Orleans, so she was going to have to start recycling her outfits, mixing and matching to make them look fresh.

Carrying the clothes back into the bedroom, she paused at the chair where the scarf lay. Its color was darker than Cody's eyes but just as vivid, just as intense. She lifted the silken rectangle and hung it around her shoulders. The fabric slithered across her skin, skimming her breasts above the lace of her bra, caressing her midriff.

Closing her eyes, she imagined Cody's hands skimming across her skin, stroking and caressing. And then she relived their kiss once more, feeling the hunger, the hardness of his body, his bold arousal and hers, not as obvious but no less overwhelming. It didn't matter that she was thin, that she was plain, that she was engaged.

She wanted Cody. Still.

A low moan, part fury and part longing, escaped her. Tossing the scarf onto the bed with her clothes, she stormed into the bathroom, hoping against hope that one more shower would do the trick.

HE SAW HER ENTER the City room and felt his hopes rise along with the corners of his mouth. She could have skipped lunch and he would have taken the hint. But she'd come, and just like last night, when her body had said yes even when her mouth was saying no, he sensed that she wasn't exactly averse to ending their marriage with a bang.

Then he noticed a blinding white flash in the vicinity of her left hand. She stopped at Sherry's desk to talk, and he squinted to see what the hell it was. When his own eyesight failed to tell him what was on her hand, he lifted the camera he was loading and zoomed the lens until he had a clear picture of her ring finger.

He cursed. As diamond solitaires went, that wasn't just a rock; it was the Rock of Gibraltar. And whether it was truly an engagement ring from Mark the Banker or a ruse on her part, a piece of paste jewelry she'd picked up at one of the boutiques on Canal Street, Cody knew why she was wearing it. She might just as well have donned a sandwich board reading Do Not Touch.

But the damnedest part of it was, she was still interested in him. The way she'd kissed him yesterday, the way she'd closed her arms around him and pressed her taut, trembling body to his...she'd wanted what he was offering the way a thirsty cat wanted fresh cream.

Yesterday. Obviously today was a whole different ball game. She was wearing an engagement ring, and she wasn't wearing the scarf Cody had given her. Her message came through loud and clear.

No. It came through muddy and muddled. If she hadn't wanted to see him, why had she come to the *Sentinel* building? Why had she accepted his invitation?

Lowering his camera, he snapped the lens cap into place and tucked the equipment into his old leather camera case. Then he tossed in two spare lenses and another couple of rolls of film. He lifted the strap over his shoulder, rounded his desk and sauntered across the room toward Jane, determined not to pay any attention to her damned ring.

She straightened up from Sherry's desk as he approached. "See? You know where to find him now," Sherry declared, her grin big enough to include both him and Jane. "Gettin' to be a daily thing, isn't it, Cody?"

"I'm only in town for a few days," Jane said tersely.

"And she isn't going to stop coming after me until she gets what she wants," Cody said, letting his tone imply that what she was after was a lot more exciting than his signature on a piece of paper.

His insinuation worked. Jane's cheeks flushed pink, and she stalked to the elevator alcove without another word.

"She's ticked off," Cody confided to Sherry, "but deep in her heart she's crazy about me."

"Yeah, I can tell," Sherry drawled. "Better put your ego back in its cage, Sinclair. She ain't buying."

"Twenty bucks says she is."

"I'm not one of your pool hall chums," his colleague joked. "Save your betting for them, darlin'."

With a farewell smile, Cody hurried out of the City room after Jane. She stood stiffly in the alcove, her hands closed around her purse as if she was afraid he was going to steal it and her gaze riveted to the illuminated numbers above the elevator door. It slid open, and she stepped inside without a word.

Cody got in beside her and waited until the door had shut before he spoke. "Okay, I give up. Why did you accept my invitation?"

"You know why."

"You crave my body."

"I crave your signature."

He sighed. "Last night—"

"You came close to ruining my life once, Cody. I'm not going to let you do it again."

Ruining her life, huh. She was hauling out the big guns. She must really be scared. He allowed his hopes to rise once more.

If he'd felt inclined toward logic, he would have been the first to admit that the idea of their having sex at this point in their lives was preposterous. It wasn't as if he couldn't find anyone else. It wasn't as if he wanted Jane's undying devotion till death did them part. It was just . . .

She was Jane Thayer. The unattainable. Practically royalty. And once upon a time, in a past shrouded in mists of memory, she'd been his in name, in law, in the eyes of God and the whole nine yards. Like an alcoholic who'd been on the wagon for twelve long years, he was dying for just one little taste, a sip of what he knew he shouldn't have.

Cripes. Alcohol was poison to an alcoholic. Would one little taste of Jane send Cody down the slippery slope into self-destruction?

The elevator doors opened onto the lobby, which was crowded with workers on their lunch breaks. A mob of people swarmed toward the elevator door, separating Cody from Jane. For a moment she was lost to him, and then he spotted her behind a small knot of people surging toward the elevator. He plunged his arm into their midst and snagged her wrist. The feel of her soft, velvety skin made him think one last taste of Jane would be worth destroying himself for.

He pulled her through the crowd, keeping his hand closed tightly around hers as he elbowed a path for them through the lobby to the street. "I hope you're not in a hurry," he said. "The cafés are all going to be jammed."

"I'm not under any time constraints," she said lofti-
ly. "You're the one who has a job to worry about."

"Some job," he muttered, walking with her to the
corner. The huge stone in her ring dug into the side of
his finger. Cody wondered how many exploited South
African miners it had taken to bring that enormous diamond to the surface.

Jane eyed his camera bag. "I gather they're letting
you work today."

"Yeah, I've been working real hard. I spent the
morning with a reporter who was interviewing some
lady in the Garden District who collects Fabergé eggs.
I got to take a bunch of posed pictures of her with her
glitzy little eggs. It was a real thrill."

"I imagine a photojournalist would find that sort of
assignment below him," she said, a taunting undertone shading her words.

"It has nothing to do with below me or above me,"
he retorted, then swallowed at the sexual image that
flashed across his brain, of Jane below him, above him,
either way, both ways... "It was a bore, that's all. I like
doing action shots, street scenes. Decorated eggs are a
bore. Here, let's try this place," he suggested, heading
toward a local eatery. "It doesn't look too crowded."

Before he could open the door for Jane, he was startled by the screech of an auto braking hard. He spun
around to scan the street. A spiffy white Cherokee was
at the far end of the block, creeping toward where he
and Jane stood. The Cherokee couldn't have been going faster than three miles per hour. It zigged to the left,
then zagged to the right, inching along while the other
cars on the road slammed to a halt or veered half onto
the sidewalk to avoid its loopy, woozy path. When the
car headed toward their side of the street, Cody stared

at the windshield. He couldn't see anyone behind the wheel.

Someone screamed. Pedestrians scattered. The Cherokee bumped a parked car with a metallic *thunk,* then crawled back toward the other side of the street. Someone else screamed.

Jane squeezed his hand in panic. "Oh, my God," she whispered. "Oh, my God, Cody..."

The Cherokee ricocheted off another parked car as a cab skidded out of its path, leaving tread marks half the length of the block. As if he were watching one of those ghastly slo-mo shoot-'em-up scenes in a bad movie, Cody stared in morbid fascination as the Cherokee made its leisurely way toward him and Jane. It was almost mesmerizing, those huge, all-season tires, the heavy-duty bumper, the goggle-eyed headlights rolling straight at them.

Jane's nails bit into the flesh of his palm. Jolting himself back to life, he yanked her out of the vehicle's path, pressing her to the restaurant's brick wall and shielding her with his own body, his back to her and his gaze fixed on the Cherokee. Her breath fanned his neck. Her hands clutched at his waist. Her hair brushed his ear. Feeling the swell of her breasts against his back almost completely distracted him from the bizarre drama unfolding just a few feet ahead of him on the street.

On the sidewalk, he amended as the driverless Cherokee lurched up over the curb and rolled slowly, inexorably into a fire hydrant. The sound of metal against metal ripped through the air, followed by a hiss as a geyser spurted skyward when the top of the hydrant sheared off.

More people screamed. Some people crowded into the restaurant; others streamed out of it, drawn by the

spectacle. Water sprayed like a festive fountain over the
Cherokee before raining down into the gutter.

Jane's hands relented on his waist. He glanced down,
amazed to see her fingers clinging loosely to his shirt. If
there weren't all sorts of folks chasing around, he would
have covered one of her hands with his and guided it
lower... But this was neither the time nor the place—
and Jane had made a point of implying that there never
would be a time or a place for that. So Cody did the
next best thing.

He pulled his camera out of the leather case, popped
off the lens cap, popped on the 50-mm lens, twisted it
into focus and hit the shutter. While all around him
people were screeching and howling in panic, Cody
went to work.

CHAPTER EIGHT

CODY SHOT PICTURES the way he played pool: with total concentration and total confidence.

Jane watched him as he prowled around the accident scene, completely focused on what he was doing. People rushed here and there, babbling and shouting; teenagers splashed through the flooded street; someone pried open the door of the vehicle to reveal a stunned toddler seated behind the wheel, wailing in harmony with the approaching police sirens.

In the center of all the commotion, Cody was an island of calm resolve, immune to the hysteria surrounding him.

Jane wilted against the wall of the restaurant, relieved that no on had been injured. A woman charged down the sidewalk, shrieking, "My baby! My baby!" Cody spun around and snapped pictures of her, one after another after another, as she raced toward the Jeep.

Closing her eyes, Jane thought back to the Cody she'd known in high school. Sure, he'd hung out, he'd loitered, he'd exhibited a cocky don't-give-a-damn attitude about school. But when he'd wanted something, truly wanted it, he'd turned up the intensity and shut out the world. He'd aimed, focused and captured what he was after.

That was how he'd gotten Jane.

Now he was after different prey. With quick, economical motions, he removed one lens and attached another. He strode to the front end of the Jeep, ignoring the water that lapped at his sneakers and the hems of his jeans, and resumed snapping shots—of the car, of the child in his mother's arms, of the police officers, of the scrambling, swarming onlookers.

Jane felt the same tingling sensation at the nape of her neck that she'd felt two nights ago, at Gussie's—only this time, she wasn't merely remembering the Cody he'd been. She had much more recent memories to contend with.

A police officer approached her, holding a notepad and pen, and she was forced to look away from Cody. "Did you witness the incident?" the officer asked.

She nodded. She described the Cherokee's wavering journey up the block, the fact that no driver had been visible above the steering wheel, the horror of watching the huge vehicle clip parked cars as drivers and pedestrians dove for safety, and the relief of learning that the imp who'd hijacked the car was unharmed. According to the police officer, the child's mother had left the engine idling when she'd run into a store for a quart of milk, and the toddler had somehow wriggled out of his child seat, released the brake and taken the Jeep for a little joy ride.

A fire engine arrived on the scene to shut off the hydrant. The police officer abandoned Jane, moving on to another witness. She surveyed the crowed, looking for Cody, and the loss she felt when she didn't see him was so fierce it caused her bones to ache. She wove her way among the teeming witnesses, murmuring "Excuse me," under her breath as she searched the crowd for him. At last she spotted him across the street, tak-

ing photos of several youngsters who had pulled off
their shoes and were dancing barefoot in the ankle-deep
river that gushed down the roadway.

She paused to observe him. He stood rock-still, intent on his task, his hair so black it glinted silver blue
beneath the noontime sun. His shoulders shaped the
snug-fitting cotton of his black T-shirt; his faded jeans
hinted at the contours of his thighs and calves. The
camera seemed dwarfed by his large hands. His chin was
firm, his mouth set.

A faint, miserable sigh escaped her. He was simply
too sexy. In fact, he was even sexier than before, because now he had a skill, an art. Watching him take
pictures was like watching a performance—although she
knew that if she ever told him that, he'd scoff. He
wouldn't like people thinking of him as an artist.

After a few minutes, he lowered the camera. He gazed
around him, blinking, as if awakening from a snooze.
Then he rolled his shoulders to loosen them. Tucking
the camera back into his bag, he sloshed across the
flooded street to the sidewalk where Jane stood. "Just
a couple more minutes," he told her as if she was impatient. She wasn't, though. She was transfixed by the
spectacle—particularly, the spectacle of Cody plying his
craft.

He pulled a pad and pencil from his camera bag and
walked over to where the mother was clinging to her
panicked little boy. Cody asked her something, jotted
a few notes onto his pad, spoke briefly to a few other
people and took a few more notes. Then he folded the
pad shut and stuffed it into his bag.

Jane smiled as he neared her. She reminded herself
not to make a fuss over him, but she knew her eyes must
be bright with admiration. She wished she could accept

JUDITH ARNOLD   155

what she'd just seen as a simple demonstration of a
simple man doing a simple job. But Cody had always
been complicated.

"I've got to drop this film off at the City room," he
said. "Sorry about lunch, but if this is going to make it
into tomorrow's paper..."

"Of course. Let's go drop it off. That'll give you a
chance to dry off a bit, too."

He glanced at his jeans and frowned, apparently surprised to discover they were soaked around his ankles.
He must have been so intent on his work that he hadn't
even noticed he'd been wading through several inches
of water.

"What did you ask the mother?" she inquired as they
started back to the *Sentinel* building.

"Her name, for a caption. I don't know what pictures they'll use—if any. They're so freaked out about
using any candids from me now. I mean, look at the
crowd." He gestured toward the mass of people lingering on the sidewalk near the runaway Jeep. "I got some
good stuff, but they'll probably nix it. After all, there
could be an adulterer in the crowd, just looking for an
excuse to sue the pants off the *Sentinel*."

Jane couldn't miss the sarcasm in his tone. "I'm sure
if the pictures are good—"

"The newspaper doesn't care if they're good or not.
They only care about covering their asses. They aren't
going to risk getting another lawsuit slapped on them."
He let out a weary breath.

"Once we get Reverend Bob to drop his suit, the
company lawyer is going to back off," Jane assured
him.

He shot her a quick look, and she realized what she'd
said—specifically, the word "we." The diamond ring on

her finger notwithstanding, Jane wasn't running from the battle. She was prepared to see Cody's problems through with him.

She tried to convince herself that it was only her thirst for justice that made her say "we," her indignation that Cody was facing censorship from his employers. But she knew the truth: after watching him in action, after acknowledging his potent charisma, after allowing him to star in her fantasies for two nights running, after kissing him ... Well, no divorce decree was going to get in her way. Cody needed her help, and she would help him.

Neither of them spoke during the rest of the walk to the *Sentinel* building. Their silence left that "we" hanging between them, like a rainbow-tinged bubble neither of them was willing to puncture.

They were still silent as they rode up the elevator to the fifth floor. Cody hurried ahead of Jane through the alcove and into the City room. The friendly woman with the desk by the entry was missing; indeed, most of the desks were empty. Probably everyone was at lunch.

Cody moved briskly past the vacant desks to the glass-walled office at the far end of the room. Since he hadn't told her to wait for him, Jane followed. A balding man who looked to be in his midforties sat behind a large desk in the inner office—or, more accurately, lounged, his chair tilted backward and his loafer-shod feet propped on his blotter as he skimmed a computer printout in his lap.

Without knocking, Cody swung open the door. "I've got some shots of an accident scene," he announced. "You want them or should I throw them out?"

The editor lifted his face and peered up at Cody over the rims of his reading glasses. "An accident scene?"

"A baby behind the wheel. A broken fire hydrant. Nobody was hurt."

"A broken fire hydrant?"

"Oceans of water. You want this film or should I chuck it?"

The editor looked torn as he scrutinized Cody. Clearly he knew the photographs would be fabulous, but Cody's sarcastic tone didn't seem to be sitting well with him. "You tell me, Sinclair," he drawled. "Should you chuck it?"

"Sure. I didn't want a Pulitzer prize, anyway."

The editor held his stare for a moment, then shook his head and resumed reading the printout in his lap. "Go ahead and have the film developed. Once I've had a look at the proofs, I'll be able to tell whether we're talking about a Pulitzer or the unemployment line—for you and me both."

"Thanks a hell of a lot," Cody snapped, letting the glass door whip shut.

"I can see you've got a great relationship with your boss," Jane commented, suppressing a smile. Cody still hadn't overcome his resentment of authority figures—like the teachers back at Brookline High, or Jane's father, or anyone else who tried to tell him what to do.

Cody shrugged, apparently determined not to take his frustration out on her. "Let me drop off the film and then we'll get something to eat."

They left the City room and headed down a corridor to a door labeled Photo Lab. It opened into an anteroom flanked by two darkroom doors with red light bulbs glowing above them to indicate that film was being developed inside. A young woman was seated at a desk in the anteroom; she beamed at Cody as he entered. "Hey, there! Don't tell me you're back in business!" she greeted him.

He managed an unconvincing smile, then busied himself removing the film from his camera. "I've got a roll here, but I don't know if they're going to use anything from it. Can you take care of it for me?"

"Sure thing." She scribbled something on a label and affixed it to the film canister once Cody handed it to her. "Should we be looking for anything incriminating?"

Cody groaned. "Who knows? The way things are going, I may just have to quit this job and try to make a living as a blackmailer."

"I bet you'd be good at it," she teased. "Don't worry, Cody. They aren't going to fire you."

"Nah. They'll just keep me on a short leash. Which is the same thing, as far as I'm concerned."

"You take everything too personally," the clerk said. "It's that Yankee blood, Cody. Y'all got to learn to relax."

"Get the suits off my back and I'll relax just fine. I'll be back in half an hour or so," he said, then gave the young woman a wave and ushered Jane out of the room. He sagged against the wall and let out a long breath. "I bet you and Mark have lunch dates like this all the time," he muttered.

Astonished, Jane smiled. Didn't Cody realize she was in awe of him? A leisurely lunch at a fancy restaurant was nothing compared to watching Cody do his job under the most discouraging circumstances.

"Lunch isn't important," she assured him.

He chuckled. "Maybe not to you. I'm starving." He pushed away from the wall. "How about let's hit the

vending machines in the lounge? We'll have an hour's
wait for a table at any decent restaurant."

"The vending machines sound great."

Again he chuckled. "You've never eaten from them."
He gestured toward the elevator and took a step. His
sneakers squeaked, reminding Jane that he'd been
wading through the flooded roadway, soaking his feet
just to take pictures his editor might refuse to publish.

"Do you have any dry clothes here?" she asked.

He eyed his damp jeans and shrugged dismissively,
then pressed the elevator button. "It's just water."

"Wet shoes can be so uncomfortable."

He gave her a self-mocking smile. "I'm tough. I can
handle it."

He *was* tough—not because of his wet clothes, but
because of his perseverance, his integrity, his refusal to
back down when he knew he was in the right. She didn't
dare express that thought, though. She only squeezed
into the crowded car ahead of him. He wriggled in and
the door slid shut.

Several passengers were carrying take-out snacks, and
the air was redolent with the oily aromas of fast-food
burgers and pizza. The smell was so strong Jane almost
got heartburn just from inhaling it. When the door
opened one floor up, she sprang out right behind Cody.

He led her down yet another bland, ruler-straight
hallway lined with offices and workrooms. At the end,
he shoved open a door to a small, unoccupied lounge
featuring a refrigerator, a microwave oven and an assortment of vending machines filled with soda, coffee,
wrapped sandwiches, candy bars and—thank God—
yogurt and fresh fruit. Jane pointed to a container of
yogurt and an apple.

"Geez. Health food," Cody muttered, feeding the machine coins and pressing the buttons. He bought himself a cola and a hot dog, which he zapped in the microwave for a couple of minutes.

Jane made herself comfortable on a vinyl upholstered chair. Cody gathered his steaming hot dog and icy soda and sprawled out on a matching sofa. "New Orleans is famous for its cuisine, you know," he quipped before taking a bite out of the frankfurter.

Jane stirred her yogurt and smiled tentatively. His lanky body took up the entire couch, forcing her to acknowledge how long his legs were, how broad his shoulders. His hair fell, disheveled, around his face; his eyes glittered as vividly as the diamond on her ring finger.

"Why did you wear it?" he asked as if he'd read her mind.

"The ring?" She stared at it for a moment, herself unsure why she'd put it on. With her thumb, she nudged the stone around until it was tucked into her palm, but that made the ring look like a wedding band, so she turned it back to her knuckle.

"I don't know," she said.

"Just a little reminder," he told her.

"I suppose so."

"What, did Mark rob a bank to buy it? Oh, that's right—he doesn't have to rob a bank. He owns one."

"He doesn't own a bank," Jane informed Cody. She might have objected to his snide tone, but in a way she felt she deserved his scorn. He'd guessed correctly; she had worn the ring as a reminder to them both.

But Cody was a reminder of other things, things she'd thought weren't all that important. Like passion. And brashness. And a certain reckless spirit. "I wore the ring because last night was a mistake," she explained.

"No kidding. A major mistake."

"You agree with me, then?"

"Absolutely. You shouldn't have turned me away. You should have let me come up to your room."

She shoveled some chilly, creamy yogurt into her mouth, wishing it would cool her blazing cheeks. "We've got a situation, Cody. I came down here to straighten it out, not to make it even more complicated."

"Tell me about him," Cody said, sounding as casual as a disinterested neighbor. "Tell me about this guy with the bottomless pockets."

"He's..." Jane faltered. What was there to tell? Mark was Mark: dependable, solid, as predictable as Jane herself. That was what she liked about him, but if she described him in those terms to Cody, he'd ridicule her even more. "He's good-looking."

"Now, *that's* important," Cody deadpanned.

"He's smart."

"Ah. I bet he's got a wall of diplomas, too. That's the quickest way to your heart."

"He has two diplomas, one from college and one from business school."

"I bet he reads the *Wall Street Journal*, too. And he drives a Lincoln, and—just a wild guess here—he wears Armani suits."

"Right," she said. "So what?" She tried to inject some defiance into her tone, but a laugh came out instead. "What can I say, Cody? He's my type."

Cody closed his eyes and made a snoring sound. Jane giggled. "It sounds like you haven't got any rebelliousness left. Do I get credit for that?"

Jane's smile faded. Of course Cody got credit for it—except that he hadn't done a complete job. There was still a flicker of rebelliousness in her. Maybe more than a flicker. When she gazed at Cody, when she noticed the athletic contours of his chest beneath his dark T-shirt, the way his smile lit his eyes, the way he shot his chin forward, daring her, always daring her, she wanted to rebel again. Just run away, jump on a motorcycle and head into the horizon without a backward look.

But she couldn't. She was too old. She had responsibilities. She had a career, parents who were getting on in years, a mortgage, clients. She was a grown-up now.

"I take it Mark doesn't object to marrying a divorcée," Cody half asked.

"He doesn't know," she admitted.

Cody sat up slightly and raised his eyebrows. "You didn't tell Mark the Banker about our marriage?"

She bit her lip and shook her head. "It was so long ago," she explained, "and the marriage was so short...."

"And you figured it didn't mean anything, so why mention it?"

"It meant a lot," she said fiercely. "It meant more than you'll ever know."

He sat even straighter, tossed his can into the recycling bin and brought his feet to the floor. Then he leaned forward, resting his forearms on his knees and studying her in the glaring fluorescent light of the lounge. "How much did it mean?"

"I don't want to talk about it," she muttered, sorry she'd spoken without thinking.

"How much?"

"I loved you, Cody. You know that."

"How much?"

His voice was low, lulling, dangerously seductive. She averted her eyes. "I loved you so much I couldn't think straight—and thinking straight was the only thing I knew how to do. It scared me. And I won't let it happen again."

"I don't blame you," he said, too reasonably.

She risked looking back at him. He was leaning even closer to her, so close he could reach out and gather her hand in his. He stroked her fingers, turned her hand over and traced a curving line across her palm.

Her breath caught. Her abdomen tensed. "Don't, Cody."

"Don't what? I'm just looking for your marriage line."

"My what?" She wished she didn't sound so breathless.

"One of my neighbors is a hoodoo lady. She reads palms, among other things."

"Oh?"

"She read mine once. Told me I have a long, solid marriage line. I had to laugh."

"That's my point," Jane said, trying to suppress the quiver in her voice. His fingers were callused, scraping lightly over the sensitive flesh of her palm and sending a shimmering heat up her arm. "Our marriage was so brief—and so foolish—it doesn't count."

"If it didn't count, Janey, you wouldn't be in New Orleans asking me to sign papers. Ah, now, look at this. You've got a long, solid marriage line, too. No breaks there. No divorces."

"I don't believe in palmistry." She really didn't. She just wished she could sound as sure as she felt.

"Of course not—you went to Wellesley. But you see that line there?" He stroked his finger along one of the

creases in her palm again, a soft, seductive caress that
made her pulse thrum wildly in her ears. "That's the
marriage line, right there. And yours is long and unbroken."

She laughed nervously. "Come on, Cody—you don't
believe that tripe, either."

"Maybe it is tripe," he allowed. "But my neighbor
says our fate is in our hands. And that, Janey, is something I *do* believe." He grinned, released her hand and
sat back. "I should go check my film, see whether it's
been developed yet."

"Yes," she agreed, anxious to get away from him and
regain her bearings.

He collected her trash and tossed it into the garbage
pail. They left the lounge, his sneakers still squeaking
slightly. Reaching the elevator, he pressed the button.
The elevator arrived, but it was jammed with people,
and it was going up. "We'll wait," Cody said, letting
the door slide shut.

They waited. Jane stared at the numbers. Cody
smiled at her. She stared at his damp jeans. He smiled
at her.

"This is stupid," he finally said. "It's only one flight
down. Let's take the stairs."

Jane nodded and followed him to a thick metal door
with the word Stairs stenciled on it. He opened the door
for her, and they entered a brightly lit stairwell that rose
many stories above them and extended six flights down.
Jane experienced a reflexive chill. Like many women,
she'd been raised to avoid public stairwells whenever
possible because, according to her mother, it was a
prime setting for a woman to get assaulted. Jane had
never met a woman who'd been victimized in one, but
she still felt uneasy.

No one was going to attack her here, of course. The white walls reflected light, and she had Cody with her.

He seemed to sense her hesitation. "You okay?"

"Of course," she said flippantly, marching to the stairs and starting down.

"The elevators are a zoo at certain times of day," he remarked, descending with her. His voice echoed in the narrow stairwell. "You could wait forever just to find a sliver of space in one."

"Exercise never killed anyone," she agreed, turning to him and missing her footing.

He caught her as she stumbled down the last two steps. "Whoa!" he whispered, gripping her arms and holding her upright. "What happened?"

She felt like an idiot. "Nothing. I just tripped."

"Are you sure? Did you turn your ankle or anything?" Still holding her forearms, he bent to scrutinize her feet. "You look pretty pale."

"I'm just slightly shaken up—but really, I'm fine."

He straightened and gazed into her eyes. His hands remained on her, strong yet soothing. He was as solid now as he had been shooting pictures earlier, as absorbed on the object of his focus. Only this time, that object was Jane.

Her fate was in her hands. And his. And when he bent to kiss her, it felt like fate to her.

His lips were warm, slightly sweet from the soda he'd drunk. They were strong, compelling, brushing over hers with a confidence she knew not merely from past experience, but from an understanding that this was what a kiss was supposed to be, that this was a kiss that could change her life if she let it.

She told herself she was trembling from her slight tumble down the stairs, but she didn't believe it. The small tremors that racked her soul were a result of desire. She wanted Cody's kiss. She wanted her husband.

He backed her into a corner of the landing and threaded his fingers through her hair to hold her head steady. Then he kissed her again, a slower, deeper kiss, his tongue sweeping into her mouth and stealing her breath away. She tried to remember whether his kisses had affected her so powerfully twelve years ago, but the past was overwhelmed by the present, this very instant, this kiss. Her mouth moved with his, welcoming him, uniting with his in a long-awaited reunion. She lifted her hands to his sides and felt him shudder, felt the sharp intake of his breath as her fingers curved around his ribs.

"Janey," he murmured, lifting his mouth from hers to kiss her cheeks, her brow, her temple. He grazed down to her jaw, to her throat, and she gasped as he pressed his lips to the sensitive flesh below her ear.

He slid his hands down through her hair to her shoulders, cupping them, kneading the exposed skin. Her hands moved, too, although she wasn't consciously guiding them. They were traveling an old, familiar path across the lean contours of his chest, up to his shoulders and down again, to the taut surface of his abdomen and back to the sides of his waist. Twelve years had failed to add a single molecule of fat to his physique; he was as sleekly muscled now as he'd been then.

Yet something about him had matured. He moved at a more stately tempo, no longer a frisky young kid, but instead a seasoned man, taking his time, savoring each inch of her skin the way one might savor a fine whiskey. He nipped, he paused, he tasted and sighed. He skimmed his thumb along her collarbone to the edge of

her shirt's neckline and then back again, learning the
ridges and angles of her body.

He was her husband, she thought vaguely, bringing
her hands to his back, up the sturdy column of his spine
to the fringe of black hair that covered his neck in back,
and then down to his waist, past his waist to his hips. He
was her husband, he was her fate.

He hooked his fingers around the narrow straps of
her blouse and eased them over her shoulders. This
pinned her arms at her sides; she couldn't move her
hands from his hips, and he seemed quite satisfied with
that. He rose to kiss her lips once more, and his hands
glided down over the front of her blouse to caress her
breasts. She felt a sweet pain in them as her nipples
tightened. She felt a sharper tug deep inside her, in her
heart, in her womb, a fierce magnetic pull that drew
Cody to her.

He was hard. He found her, his erection straining the
denim of his jeans, nestling into the hollow between her
thighs, and when she flexed her fingers against his but-
tocks he groaned. He squeezed her breasts as his tongue
battled with hers, and he groaned again, rocking her in
a distinct rhythm.

She could have made love with him. Right there in the
stairwell, between the fifth and sixth floors of the *Sentinel* building. Right now. She could have opened completely to him, without a moment's pause, without an
instant's regret. She wanted Cody Sinclair as much as
she had when she'd been young and impulsive and
shamefully careless. She wanted him even more.

He yanked her blouse free of the waistband of her
skirt and reached under it to touch her skin. A small cry
escaped her, barely audible except for the way it echoed in the air around them.

His hands moved higher, to her bra. He stroked over the lacy cups and then eased her breasts out of them. He chafed her nipples with his fingertips. Her body felt feverish; her legs felt weak.

Dear God, she wanted him. Unbearably. She was steaming, she was damp, her heart was beating so fast she was probably going to die in another minute, and before she died she wanted Cody inside her one last time, loving her.

Somewhere, seemingly miles above her, she heard a click and then a resounding clank. The noise cascaded down upon them like ice water, freezing them. Jane muffled her moan against Cody's shoulder.

Footsteps echoed above them; someone else must have gotten tired of waiting for the elevator and decided to use the stairs. Jane didn't know how close the person was, or how far down he intended to walk. She only knew that Cody's hands were under her blouse, cupping her breasts, and she was so aroused she could barely stand up.

Shielding her with his body, Cody eased his hands out of her bra, leaving her chilled in the absence of his touch. His breathing was harsh; when he lifted the sleeves of her blouse back up onto her shoulders, she glimpsed his eyes and saw they were cloudy. His mouth curved into a mischievous smile.

"Cody, I—"

"Shh," he said, silencing her, then tilted his head to listen to the footsteps. They heard a creak, a squeak and another resounding clank as a door opened and closed. Whoever had interrupted their passionate interlude was no longer in the stairwell.

Jane let out a long, ragged breath. She ought to be grateful for the intruder. As the fog cleared from her brain, she was forced to acknowledge the folly of what she'd just been doing, what she'd been longing for.

"Kind of like high school, huh?" he teased, adjusting his jeans now that his body had returned to normal.

She remembered Cody stealing kisses from her in the stairs by the math rooms, near the cafeteria kitchen, behind the auditorium—any place where no one would see them. She recalled one time when he'd stolen more than a kiss from her in the hallway outside the gymnasium—and who knew what would have happened if the gymnastics coach hadn't happened along?

The gymnastics coach might have saved Jane from Cody's seductive powers then, but she hadn't saved Jane from marrying him. And while someone had obviously saved her from making a complete fool of herself just now, no one could save her from what she was feeling.

She busied herself straightening out her blouse. Her hands were shaking, and the facets of her engagement ring sent out flashes of white light.

Why couldn't she be satisfied by the simple pleasure of being able to trust a man, to rely on him, to know he'd be a pillar in her life? Why, as she stared disconsolately at the engagement ring on her finger, did she feel as if something important was slipping away? She wanted Mark. She wanted marriage. She wanted what Mark could give her, what she could give him. She wanted the life they could make together.

But even as she regained her balance and cooled off, she forced herself to admit the truth: more than any of that, she wanted Cody.

CHAPTER NINE

LIKE EVERYONE ELSE in the plaza outside Faneuil Hall, Mark was transfixed by the jugglers. Clad in matching tuxedos, the man and woman tossed jokes to each other with the same agility as they tossed an array of objects back and forth: bright red cubes, black batons, silver hoops, green feather boas, witty punch lines. It was obviously a well-rehearsed act, the jokes and the juggling both dependent on precision timing. Mark was not a big fan of cutesy street performance art, but these jugglers were *good*.

He'd never actually explored the district of downtown Boston known as Quincy Market. He had assumed it was a gathering spot for tourists and the hoi polloi, an outdoor mall for people on the prowl or fools eager to part with great sums of cash at the pricy boutiques and gift shops that opened onto the plaza. In addition to the shops, the market featured numerous bars and outdoor cafés where the primary activity appeared to be ogling members of the opposite sex. Vendors sold all manner of kitsch—stenciled T-shirts, plastic flowers, phosphorescent costume jewelry—from wheeled carts and kiosks, among which were interspersed an assortment of mimes, break dancers, jazz musicians and these two spirited jugglers. Frankly, Mark couldn't pinpoint a single aspect of Quincy Market that ought to have appealed to his refined taste, yet the sights and sounds and smells exhilarated him. The corny patter of the jugglers amused him. Perhaps his taste wasn't so refined, after all.

The crowds unnerved him, though. How on earth was he going to find Clarissa in such a mob?

It had been her decision to meet him in front of the steps to Faneuil Hall—a historical landmark, the site of numerous protests against the British by colonists who counted among their ranks several of Mark's ancestors. He doubted Clarissa, with her hodgepodge ethnic background, cared one way or another about Boston's grand past. She'd probably chosen this site because it was a hangout for young professionals.

Well, Mark was a young professional, wasn't he? Perhaps he was pushing the upper limit of "young," but for heaven's sake, he was entitled to chuckle at the antics of the jugglers and enjoy the balmy June evening along with scores of other Bostonians at the end of a working day.

But how was he going to find Clarissa?

It turned out that finding her was easy. As the jugglers began a routine that involved eight golf balls and a flurry of quips about birdies and bogeys, three-quarters of the audience turned from the show en masse to stare at the lovely slip of a woman wending her way through the crowd toward Mark. He waved, she waved and many of the gawkers turned their stares to him.

His ego shouldn't have entered into it, but it did. What a thrill to have so many men gazing at him in envy! Yes, he wanted to shout, the most beautiful woman in the Faneuil Hall plaza was with him! Eat your hearts out, suckers.

He immediately chastised himself. How dare he pretend the most beautiful woman in the plaza was any-

thing more than a friend to him? And barely that.
Clarissa was willing to meet him only because she had
a kind heart and she worked for his fiancée.

His *fiancée*.

He tried to conjure up an image of Jane, but all he
could see was Clarissa, startlingly vibrant as she wove
through the throng. She had on a red shell blouse and a
short white miniskirt. Smoky nylons covered her legs,
and high-heeled sandals added a couple of inches to her
diminutive height. As she drew nearer, he noticed
through the open leather straps that her toenails were
polished.

He lifted his gaze to her face. Her eyelids were dusted
with gold powder. Her cheeks were touched with rouge,
and her exotically dark eyes were made even darker with
mascara.

Jane never wore much makeup. He'd always appreciated her clean, fresh-scrubbed look. But Clarissa—
polite, demure, chronically secretarial Clarissa—looked
downright tarty.

Mark discovered, to his astonishment, that tarty was
a serious turn-on. More of a turn-on, even, than the
prospect of a nude woman emerging from a cake.

He waited for a surge of guilt to overtake him, but it
didn't. Jane just didn't seem to be present for him in any
way. His emotions were focused solely on Clarissa—
specifically, on the discomfort haunting her eyes and
creasing her brow.

"What's wrong?" he asked.

She smiled bravely. "What makes you think something's wrong?"

The crowd returned their attention to the jugglers,
who were striving toward a finale that featured just
about every juggleable object in their possession. Mark

gathered Clarissa's hands in his and peered down into
her shimmering eyes. "You look worried."

"No. Yes," she contradicted herself, then smiled
again, a forlorn smile that made him want to close his
arms around her in a reassuring hug. It occurred to him
that perhaps her worries stemmed from Jane's mysterious trip to New Orleans, but the notion didn't linger.
Jane just wasn't a terribly significant part of this moment.

He did experience a twinge of guilt at that admission—followed by a massive tide of guilt. How long was
he going to fool himself into thinking all he wanted
from Jane's troubled secretary was the opportunity to
comfort her? How long was he going to keep telling
himself he wanted to see Clarissa only because she
might be able to clarify what Jane was up to?

Somewhere along the way—he couldn't pinpoint
precisely when—his rendezvous with Clarissa had become more about Clarissa than about Jane. This was
something he was going to have to deal with before Jane
came home.

But Jane wasn't home now. She hadn't even done
him the courtesy of telling him where she was going, or
for how long, or why. And until she came clean with
him, he didn't have to come clean with her. Fair was
fair.

"These jugglers are terrific," he commented, wishing he could make Clarissa's smile more genuine.

She nodded absently, not the least bit interested in the
jugglers. "Why don't we go get something to drink?"
she said, nodding toward one of the cafés. It had an
outdoor section, with dozens of quasi-intimate tables
crammed into a fenced area, each of the tables shielded
by a perky little parasol. It was a far cry from the pi-

ano bar at the Four Seasons, but if it would make
Clarissa happy, Mark would gladly drink cheap liquor
at a patio café with her.

He took her elbow and steered her through the milling crowd. He was aware of how many people, both
male and female, stared at Clarissa. His chest swelled
with unearned pride. Even if she wasn't his, even if he
wasn't hers, it was fun to pretend.

A line extended from a gate in the fence, and an im-
perious young fellow stood guard there, refusing anyone admittance until a table became available. "It's
worth the wait," Clarissa insisted before Mark could
comment on the inconvenience. "They've got the best
beer here. A huge selection, lots of imported beers."

As if that was supposed to impress him. But he hu-
mored her with a smile. "It sounds charming."

"If you'd rather go somewhere else . . ."

"No, this is fine," he said. Her lower lip started to
tremble. "I mean it, Clarissa. I'm actually rather par-
tial to imported beer."

Too late. Her lip went from trembling to wobbling,
and her eyes brimmed with tears. A piteous sob escaped her, and then she clapped her hand over her
mouth and turned away.

If his mother was weeping in the middle of downtown Boston, he would hug her. If his sister was weeping, he would hug her. If his cousin Frances, whom he'd
never liked and who always smelled like rotting daisies,
had burst into tears a block from Quincy Market, he
would pinch his nose and hug her. Surely consoling
Clarissa wasn't out of line.

She shrank from him when he touched her, and then
changed her mind and collapsed against him, wailing
and blubbering with profound abandon. He was flab-

bergasted that such a tiny woman could make such a huge scene. He was also amazed to realize that even with her eyes red and her cheeks tearstained, Clarissa Bonnert was incredibly pretty.

He handed her a handkerchief, and she wept copiously into it. People in the line ahead of them nudged each other and pointed at her. Action was called for.

Putting his arm snugly around her narrow shoulders, he ushered her past the onlookers to the guard at the gate. "My companion has just learned some dreadful news," he murmured, fishing in his pocket for his billfold. "She needs a drink and a nice, quiet room to pull herself together." He discreetly plucked a large bill from the wallet and slipped it into the guard's hand. "Perhaps you can find us a small, private table somewhere. Preferably indoors. Somewhere where she can have a bit of privacy."

"I'm sure I can find something," the guard said, beckoning to Mark to follow him inside the gate. A few people on line jeered in protest, but Mark ignored them and Clarissa was too far gone to hear their complaints.

In less than a minute, Mark and Clarissa were ensconced in a small, secluded room off the main tavern area. With its burgundy-satin-striped wallpaper, its fringed Victorian love seat flanked by a pair of oversized wing chairs, its oval pedestal table marred by ancient-looking nicks and scratches and its tacky cabbage-rose carpeting, it had the aura of a bordello anteroom. Mark steered Clarissa straight toward the love seat, where he would be able to sit beside her and provide a shoulder for her to bawl into. "Please ask the waiter to bring us two Courvoisiers," he requested. "And a glass of ice water for the lady."

"Yes, sir." The guard vanished. The door clicked shut, sealing Mark and Clarissa off from the rest of the world.

She emerged from her hysterics long enough to gaze around her. "Where are we?"

"In a private room."

"Oh." She hiccuped, then dabbed her cheeks with his handkerchief. "Oh, my God. This is silk," she wailed, staring in dismay at the damp rectangle.

"What's the problem? Are you allergic to silk?"

"No. It's just—it'll get stained. Silk has to be dry-cleaned, and—"

"Don't be silly. It's meant to be used." When she hesitated, he eased the wrinkled handkerchief from her hand and swabbed her cheeks with it. The worst of her caterwauling seemed to be behind her. She sniffled a few times and lowered her eyes bashfully, making him want to caress her cheeks some more. They were such delicate cheeks.

He regarded her as she struggled to regain her poise. He had never seen Jane cry, not once. He had never seen her fall apart. He admired that about her, of course, and yet... And yet, every man at least occasionally yearned for a dainty young lady to protect and comfort. Mark had persuaded himself that he wanted to marry someone he considered his equal, but perhaps he was deluding himself. Perhaps he was, in fact, an unreconstructed male chauvinist who responded to a fragile thing like Clarissa because she was so precious, so exquisite.

She took the handkerchief back from him and gave her nose a prim blow. Then she set the crumpled silk on the coffee table and crossed her legs, a maneuver that shifted her skirt a couple of inches higher. Her thighs were slim, but what truly fascinated him were her knees. Her kneecaps looked no bigger than a robin's eggs.

He heard a light tap on the door, and then it opened. A waiter entered, carrying their cognac and a glass of water for Clarissa. He set his tray down on the table, smiled nervously at Mark and disappeared.

"What is this?" Clarissa asked, eyeing the snifters warily.

"Cognac. Good for what ails you." Mark handed her one glass, then took the other for himself.

Before he tasted the cognac, he watched as she took a timid sip. Her shoulders twitched and she shuddered, then set down the glass. "Whoa. It's got quite a kick."

"Are you feeling better?"

"Yes. No." She sighed and took another sip.

"Can you tell me what all those tears were about?"

"I'm going to lose my job," she said, lifting her eyes to his for the merest second and then glancing away.

"Lose your job? You're joking!"

She shook her head grimly.

"That's ridiculous. Does Jane know about this? Is she behind it? I'll speak to her. I won't let her—"

"She doesn't know. Oh, God..." Clarissa issued a broken gasp, apparently inclined to dissolve into tears again. She opted for more cognac instead—a wise choice, Mark believed.

"Did someone else at the firm fire you? Clarissa, I'm sure that if Jane isn't behind it, she'll fight tooth and nail to keep you."

"No, she won't. You have no idea what's going on. She's not..." Clarissa gnawed on her lower lip.

"She's not what?" he asked carefully, suspecting that he was about to get a surprise. The prospect didn't please him.

Clarissa said nothing, leaving Mark to complete her sentence fragment: *She's not in any position to save Clarissa. She's not a good boss. She's not what Mark thought she was. She's not coming back to Boston.*

"What is she not?" he finally asked, unable to bear the suspense.

Clarissa sighed shakily. "I shouldn't be here with you. This is all wrong." She sniffled some more and stared at one of her magnificent knees. "You've got to understand, Mark—I adore Jane. I just adore her."

"Oh." This was more complicated than he'd thought. He deemed himself an open-minded man, but if Clarissa really preferred women to men...well, it would be a tragic loss for the male of the species. "It's not a good idea to become involved with one's employer that way, Clarissa," he said delicately.

"Oh, I'm not..." Despite her obvious distress, she giggled. "I don't adore her like *that.*"

Relief gusted through him, but he suppressed the urge to shout for joy. "If you had," he said evenly, "it would have been unrequited. Jane is as straight as a flagpole."

Clarissa sighed and shook her head. "Mark, this whole thing is such a disaster."

"I wish you would fill me in, Clarissa. What whole thing are we talking about? What happened?"

"I can't tell you. I can only say I shouldn't be here with you, and I can't work for Jane anymore."

"Oh, my." He attempted a laugh. "Jane and I are both causing you problems, then?"

"Yes," she confirmed sullenly. She glanced at him, then reached for her snifter. After a dangerously large gulp of brandy, she blurted out, "I adore you both. That's the problem."

A threesome. Jane would balk, of course. She wasn't adventurous that way. But... once again amazing himself, Mark admitted that he liked the idea of Clarissa's adoring them both. His mind liked it. His body, stirring with a sudden flush of heat in the nether regions, *definitely* liked it.

"This should not be cause for tears," he declared. "You adore Jane and you adore me. I'm sure Jane adores you. I know for a fact that I do."

Clarissa glanced at him again, curiosity softening the despair in her dark eyes. Abruptly she shook her head and lowered her gaze. "It's a bad idea."

"What's a bad idea?"

"Everything. My whole life."

"Don't be melodramatic, Clarissa. There's nothing terrible about people adoring each other."

"It's terrible when you're supposed to be marrying Jane."

She fell silent once more, her fingers fluttering nervously against the crystal bowl of her glass. Her words hung in the air, reverberating strangely until Mark was forced to speak. "What do you mean, I'm *supposed* to be marrying Jane?"

"Well you are, aren't you?"

He suddenly felt out of his depth. There were things going on here, things beyond his healthy attraction to Clarissa, beyond his straying eye. The room hummed with dangerous undercurrents. This wasn't just about threesomes and mutual adoration.

"I don't know that *supposed* has anything to do with it," he observed. "Jane and I have agreed to get married—but our wedding is scheduled for New Year's Eve, which is many months away," he added, implying that things could occur in those months, things that had

nothing to do with Jane and everything to do with the
two people in this bordello room. "Is there anything
wrong with my arrangement with Jane?"

Clarissa's failure to answer disconcerted him. Closing his eyes, he put more effort into picturing Jane. He
visualized her in one of her clever Donna Karan suits,
her brown hair in a neat, smooth pageboy around her
face, her gray eyes clear and earnest, her voice ex-
pounding on some intelligent concept. He pictured her
at his breakfast table, debating the headlines in the
Boston Globe. He pictured her emerging from the Suf-
folk County Courthouse, carrying her leather brief-
case and looking like the mistress of all she surveyed.
He imagined her poring over legal abstracts at a desk,
late at night, with only one lamp burning.

He tried to picture her in his bed but drew a blank.

"Where is this conversation heading?" he asked,
moving from disconcerted to downright anxious.

"Nowhere," Clarissa declared, setting down her glass
and uncrossing her legs. "I should go."

She started to stand. Mark sprang to his feet, determined not to let her go until she'd explained her cryptic
ramblings and her tears, until she'd told him what was
going on with Jane, until he'd held her one more time.

It happened so fast—his arm circling her, her body
turning toward him, her head tilting up and his lips
crushing down on hers. The choreography seemed pre-
ordained. If he'd given one instant of thought to it...

If he had, he would have kissed her, anyway.

The most mind-boggling part was that she kissed him
back. Fiercely. Wildly. With more of a kick than any
brandy he'd ever tasted in his life.

"We shouldn't do this," she whispered, her lips gliding against his.

"Don't worry about it," he groaned, brushing his lips across her cheeks and digging his fingers into her dense, black hair so he could angle her face toward his. He covered her mouth with his own again, coaxing and pressing until her lips parted for him.

God help him, she was magnificent! Her tongue scooted into his mouth, caressing his teeth, the roof of his mouth, thrusting and thrusting until he felt the strain against the fine lightweight wool of his trousers. Would they tear from the pressure? he wondered. Did he care?

No. Not in the least.

"Mark," she moaned, wrenching her mouth from his. "We can't do this. It's wrong." She hid her face in the hollow of his neck and touched her damp mouth to his skin. If she were a vampire, he would gladly sacrifice his entire supply of blood to her. Let her nip. Let her bite. He would go to his doom without a moment's regret.

He buried his nose in her hair; it smelled like jasmine. "I'm not married yet," he reminded her.

"You can't marry Jane."

He drew back slowly, unsure of what she was getting at. Did this kiss mean his engagement to Jane was no longer viable?

Perhaps it wasn't. Perhaps one minute of wayward passion with this woman had disqualified him from anything sacred with anyone else. He wasn't sure—but it was a decision to be contemplated calmly and rationally, not decided when Clarissa's lithe little body was snuggled up to him and her lips still rested against the warmth of his neck.

"Why can't I marry Jane?" he asked in a strange, breathless voice.

"I can't tell you. She'll have to tell you herself."

His head began to pound. He wanted his life straightened out. He had experienced too many surprises in the past several days, this kiss being the latest and most disorienting. He hated surprises; he wanted everything to proceed as intended.

He also wanted to screw the living daylights out of Clarissa Bonnert.

He struggled to regain his composure. Easing back from her, he digested her words. What did Jane have to tell him? Whatever it was, Clarissa apparently knew about it. "You've spoken to her?" he asked.

"I talk to her every day," Clarissa said, sounding evasive.

"And what did she say today? What was different from yesterday?"

"I can't discuss this with you, Mark. You'll have to ask her."

"Why did you even bring it up if you can't discuss it with me?"

"I—I can't bear to see you get hurt."

How could Jane hurt him? The very idea was preposterous. "That's quite noble of you, Clarissa—"

"I'm not noble," she retorted, storming toward the door, her lower lip once again quivering with emotion. "I don't want you to get hurt because I'm in love with you!"

Before he could stop her, she yanked the door open and raced out.

He should have chased her. Should have grabbed her and sat her down and demanded that they work this situation out like the reasonable adults they were. But he only stood motionless in the lurid red room, grin-

ning like a moonstruck fool at the news that Clarissa
Bonnert was in love with him.

HOW MUCH WOULD TWENTY dollars buy from a
hooker? Cody wondered. Would Suzie tell him what he
needed to know? Would she even show up at La Luna?

Did he care?

The bar looked the same today as it had looked
twenty-four hours ago—brick and tile and polished
brass. It smelled the same, like smoked meat and bourbon. The music was Crescent City blues, just like last
night.

Last night, though, he'd been thinking about Reverend Bob. Tonight he was thinking only of Jane. As a
matter of fact, Jane was all he'd been thinking about
since she'd left the *Sentinel* building immediately after
the incident on the stairs.

She had promised to meet him at La Luna at six, and
she'd been true to her word. She looked almost the same
as she'd looked that afternoon. Only two things had
changed: she'd added the turquoise scarf he'd given her
and she'd removed the diamond ring.

He had her exactly where he wanted her—or, if not
exactly, then damned close. Exactly where he wanted
her was naked in his arms. And after the way she'd responded to him earlier that day, he doubted he was far
from that goal.

The only problem was, where did she have him?

Before the kiss on the stairs, he'd been happy to
imagine a nostalgic roll in the hay with his soon-to-be-
ex-wife, one last fling for old times' sake and all that.
He wasn't looking for more than a night of fireworks.

But that afternoon, once she'd departed and he'd
spent a few hours going through the motions of being

a photographer at a major metropolitan newspaper, scanning his proofs from the mishap with the Jeep and arguing with his editor over which shots, if any, to use, one part of his mind clung to the notion that he wanted more than sex with Jane. He wanted his wife.

The last time he'd been with her, the last time he'd wanted her so intensely, she'd walked out on him. Just up and walked out, leaving him alone and unmoored, in more pain than he'd ever known a man could suffer. He'd been floored. Totaled. Eviscerated.

He couldn't let her do that to him again.

He wouldn't. This time he wasn't defenseless. He knew what she'd come to New Orleans for, and it wasn't anything that could be described with the words "till death do us part." The only thing they could possibly share was sex. Lots of it, with no strings attached. This time when he had her, he would go into it knowing how it would end.

The truth was, that built-in conclusion made a lot of sense to him. Getting back together with her would never work. When she was ready to leave, he would hold the door open.

She'd been waiting for him at La Luna, which meant either that she was so eager to see him she'd shown up early or that she'd had nothing better to do. Whichever it was, she seemed to have trouble meeting his gaze. Whenever he looked at her she looked down and fidgeted with the scarf, which lay loose around her neck, dropping in two tails over her breasts.

He wished he could put his hands where her scarf was. Man, but she'd felt so sweet when he'd touched her that afternoon, sweet and warm and yearning. And her sighs, her moans, the way her mouth had sought his, the way her hands had clutched him . . .

"You want something to drink?" he asked, ignoring the rough edge to his voice.

She shook her head. "Do you think Suzie will show up?"

"If she can't find someone willing to pay her more than twenty bucks, she will. Money talks."

"I should have offered her more."

"Twenty dollars is about fifteen dollars too much."

"Well, forgive me for not being more up-to-date on the going rate of prostitutes in New Orleans," Jane snapped.

Cody grinned. He liked it when her Boston-Brahmin poise cracked.

The door swung open and a couple of guys in suspenders strolled in, ties loosened, no doubt yuppies looking to wash away the effects of a day spent behind a desk. The door started to close, but one chivalrous fellow caught it and held it open for a woman entering behind them. "There's our twenty-dollar friend right now," Cody murmured.

Jane twisted in her seat. Suzie quickly spotted them; she sashayed over to their table, swinging her hips with each step. She had on another of her gauzy skirts and translucent blouses. Her silhouette did nothing for Cody, though. She was just . . . too much.

She plopped her bottom onto a chair at their table, pulled out her pack of cigarettes and handed Cody her butane lighter as if he were an old acquaintance and lighting her cigarette for her was a well-rehearsed ritual they shared. He did his part, igniting a flame for her and waiting while she took a deep double-lungful of smoke into her body.

She exhaled. Jane's nose twitched. "Well," Suzie drawled, "I'm here."

"We appreciate that," Jane said quickly. "Were you able to find out Stanley Roberts's address?"

Suzie eyed her languidly. She looked mildly miffed that Jane was charging right into the main event without any preamble, any affable chitchat. But Jane could be very direct when she wanted to be.

"I believe there's a matter of some money that has to change hands," Suzie reminded her after another deep drag on her cigarette.

Jane nodded and turned expectantly to Cody. Oh, so *he* was supposed to provide the twenty bucks, huh. Jane had set the price, but he was the one who had to foot the bill.

Not that twenty bucks made a big difference one way or another in his life. And after all, he was the one on the ropes, thanks to Reverend Bob. But still . . .

Sending Jane an annoyed look, he pulled out his wallet, removed a twenty and placed it on the table. Suzie reached for it, but he slapped his hand down over it so fast she almost singed him with her cigarette. "It's yours after you tell us where Stanley Roberts is hanging his hat."

"No money, no address."

"There's the money," he said, nodding at his hand. He really didn't want to play games with this woman. He just wanted to make sure he got what he was paying for.

Suzie gave a long-suffering sigh and pulled a scrap of paper from her compact gold purse. "There," she said, nudging the paper toward him. "It's an apartment in Metairie. I'll take my fee now."

He released the money and lifted the paper. It was a shred, barely bigger than a pencil shaving. The writing on it was microscopic. "I can hardly read this," he

complained, pinching the tiny paper between his thumb
and index finger and squinting at it.

"Here, let me," Jane offered, taking the paper from
him. She held it at an angle, at a distance, and then removed a neat leather-bound pad and a sterling-silver
pen from her purse and rewrote the address in readable
script. "Is that it?" she asked Suzie.

"That's the place. He pays one week at a time. Any
disposable income he's got, he disposes on pleasures of
the flesh."

"What a guy," Jane murmured, sharing a look with
Suzie. "Well, Cody, the man saved your soul. I guess
it's your turn to save his."

"Don't save it too much, darlin'," Suzie requested.
"I got expenses, too, and Stan's money is a sure thing
for me." She tucked the twenty-dollar bill into her itty-
bitty purse and stubbed her cigarette out in an ashtray.
"By the way, you didn't get that address from me,
honey," she said, jabbing one of her long, elaborately
enameled fingernails at the sliver of paper. "We've
never talked."

"Maybe we haven't. But if the information is bad, we
will," Cody warned, deciding he hadn't liked that moment of sisterhood between her and Jane. As if all guys
were like that. As if all guys used their disposable income to buy it doggie-style from a hooker.

"I expect a little appreciation, Mr. Sinclair. It wasn't
easy getting that for you," Suzie said. "Last night in
our hotel room, I had to sneak into Stan's wallet while
he was using the facilities. I jotted it on the telephone
pad—I had to write small so's he wouldn't notice—and
then I managed to tear off the part I wrote on while he
was otherwise occupied. There are times when a man

just isn't aware of anything else but." She and Jane exchanged another look.

"Men are aware of everything," Cody argued. "At least good men are."

"Well, I won't challenge you there. Stan's a dear man, but I don't know as he's a good one. Anyway, I went to an awful lot of trouble for you. Twenty dollars barely covers it."

"Twenty was what we agreed on," Cody reminded her coldly. "Jane, let's go check this out and see if Suzie's been straight with us."

Jane glanced apologetically at Suzie. "Thanks for helping out."

"Thanks for paying. It never ceases to amaze me what people are willing to pay for." Smiling like a cat with a full belly of cream, she stood and sauntered over to the bar, carrying her butane lighter and pulling out another cigarette. A hapless yahoo at the bar lit the cigarette for her. Cody bet she'd wind up a whole lot more than twenty dollars' richer at the end of the evening.

"Well," Jane said, lifting the scrap of paper and comparing the writing to the notes she'd jotted on her pad, "I wonder how she smuggled this out of the hotel room."

"She probably hid it in an orifice," Cody muttered.

Jane gasped and dropped the tiny paper. Her face went pale.

"Maybe she stuffed it between her toes," he amended. "Or tucked it into a hair clip or something."

"Never mind." Jane grimaced. "Do you know where that street is?"

"I can find it," he said, pushing back his chair and standing. "How about let's take a drive to Metairie?"

Jane gave a final glance at the paper and cringed, then stood and turned her back on the table. "All right, Cody," she said. "Let's take a drive."

CHAPTER TEN

"I'M SORRY," JANE SAID.

The highway was thick with rush-hour traffic. Even with the windows open, the interior of Cody's coupe was stultifyingly hot and heavy with the scent of auto exhausts.

He shot her a quick look, then shrugged. "No big deal."

She twisted in the bucket seat, unsticking her legs from the vinyl, and frowned at him. Lord. She had too much apologizing to do. After she'd fled from Cody earlier that day, she'd spent several hours rehearsing another apology she would have to make very soon: *I'm sorry, Mark, but I can't marry you. I'm not ready to settle down yet.* Sure she wasn't. She was thirty years old, about to become a partner in her law firm, hearing the first faint ticks of her biological clock marking her passage toward middle age . . . and she wasn't ready to settle down? Jane Thayer had been born ready to settle down.

I'm sorry, Mark, but I can't marry you. You don't turn me on the way Cody Sinclair does. As if sex were enough to build a marriage on. She'd believed that once and stumbled into a dreadfully poor excuse for a marriage. She and Cody might not hold the world record for matrimonial brevity, but two months was probably about the maximum for a marriage fueled by passion alone.

I'm sorry, Mark, but I can't marry you because I'm married to someone else. But by the time she got back to Boston she had only to file the divorce papers and then she wouldn't be a married woman anymore. What happened in the stairwell wasn't going to change the fact that she had come to New Orleans to get Cody's signature, and she wasn't going to leave without it.

I'm sorry, Mark, but I can't get married until I figure out how to get over Cody. That would have to do, because it was the truth. She couldn't stay married to a semivagabond photographer who despised everything that mattered to her: her genes, her yearning for stability, her Boston-area roots. She especially couldn't stay married to him because he'd given her no indication that he harbored anything for her other than a grudge, leavened by a large helping of lust. He didn't love her. He shouldn't love her. She didn't want him to love her.

But she had to do something about that grudge. Leaving him would be difficult enough when her heart still beat traitorously for him. She *would* leave him, because it was the only sane thing to do. But she had to obtain his forgiveness first. To have both Cody and Mark loathing her at the same time would simply be too much.

"I *am* sorry," she repeated.

Her emphatic tone surprised a laugh out of him. "Well, I guess twenty bucks is worth two apologies."

"Twenty bucks? Oh, you mean what you paid Suzie?"

"What *you* offered to pay her yesterday. What *I* actually paid her today. One of us is out twenty big ones, and it isn't you."

"All I had on me were traveler's cheques and a credit card," she protested. "And you didn't seem to have too much trouble walking away from twenty dollars at that pool hall the other day."

"Oh, that," he said dismissively. "I'll win it back from those guys. They're lousy players. But I'm not in the habit of handing my hard-earned cash to prostitutes."

"Well—" she didn't want to waste time on nonsense, but she felt she ought to win this skirmish before she surrendered on the big issues "—you're the one who wanted Stanhope's address."

"You want it, too. If you can't make him see the light, you won't get your divorce."

The threat sounded hollow to her. She knew that if she pushed hard enough, Cody would sign the papers. And she suspected he knew that even if the divorce wasn't still pending, she would help him with Stanhope if she could.

The divorce. That was the big issue. She took a deep breath and let it out, searching for the strength to continue. "When I said I was sorry just now—" another deep breath helped her to force out the words "—I was referring to the way our marriage ended."

He turned to stare at her. Behind him a car honked. He jerked his attention back to the road, sighed and veered onto the shoulder. Yanking on the parking brake, he switched off the engine and stared at her. "You're sorry for the way our marriage ended," he repeated, his voice low but intense, reaching her ears despite the din of traffic noise spilling through his open window.

Late-day sunlight filtered through the windshield, glazing Cody's face with a copper light that emphasized his brow, his dark lashes and cool, pale eyes. He kept his left hand draped over the steering wheel and his right hand on the gear shift, as if he intended to drive back onto the highway the minute things got uncomfortable.

They were already uncomfortable. But Jane simply couldn't leave so much unspoken any longer.

"Do we really have to have this conversation?" he asked.

"I think we do."

He weighed her claim, then conceded with a shrug. "Okay. Go ahead. I'm listening."

She twisted the slippery silk of the scarf around her finger, then uncurled it and smoothed it against her palm. "It was never about money," she said quietly, wondering if he could hear her above the traffic and perversely hoping he couldn't.

"Okay. It wasn't about money." He sounded unconvinced.

Silence lay between them, as oppressively heavy as the delta heat. Jane was dimly aware of the cars and trucks rumbling down the highway beyond the open window. What mattered was the connection between her and Cody, and at the moment that connection consisted of a wordless pall. Cody clearly would have preferred for them to skip this discussion altogether. He wasn't going to make it easy for her.

But then, he'd never made anything easy for her. Except sex. She'd been such a prude before she'd met him—and she'd reverted to her basic modesty once she'd left him. During their few months together, though, he had made it easy for her to enjoy her body and his, to welcome new experiences, new responses. With him it was still easy. She could stand in the stairway of a commercial building and behave like a wanton woman. Cody made wantonness easy.

But nothing else was easy with him. Certainly not a heart-to-heart conversation. Not baring one's soul.

"It was about control," she said.

"Control."

"I wanted to be able to control my own life."

"You wanted to go to college," he said. "And I had no problem with that except for the fact that college was expensive and we had no money. It always came back to money."

"No, it didn't."

"You were a rich girl whose parents could send you to Wellesley. I couldn't send you to Wellesley. I couldn't even send you to the local community college. We had no money."

"It wasn't up to *you* to send me anywhere," she argued. "It was *my* decision, *my* need. I *had* to go to college," she explained, watching bewilderment cloud his eyes. "Don't you see? I'd spent my entire life being a student. It was the only thing I'd ever been good at, Cody. I wasn't clever. I wasn't artistic, I wasn't athletic, I wasn't graceful or pretty. All I've ever been was smart. Getting good grades was the only thing I knew how to do."

His confusion deepened; his brow creased with a frown line. He stared at her as if she'd suddenly started speaking Swahili. "What the hell are you talking about?"

"I'm talking about who I was when we got married. Who I still am, if you want to know the truth."

"You're a lawyer," he reminded her, enunciating each word with care, obviously trying to guide her back to English.

"It's the same thing. Succeeding at law takes the same basic skill as getting straight A's. You read, you memorize, you say the right things in court and fool everyone into thinking you know what you're talking about. That's all it is."

He still looked puzzled. "I didn't marry you because you were a straight-A student," he said.

"Why *did* you marry me?" Her voice was hushed, plaintive. "I used to wonder about that all the time. Why did you marry me, Cody?"

He opened his mouth and then shut it. He scrubbed a hand through his hair and turned to gaze at the salmon pink sun as it made its final descent toward the horizon. His inability to answer would have wounded her if she hadn't already reached the conclusion he was staggering toward: that he'd had no good reason to marry her.

"It was just a stunt, wasn't it?" she guessed, straining the hurt from her voice. "Just a gag. A way to thumb your nose at the world."

"No." His voice had dropped even lower.

"A way to get back at the rich folks, right? It wasn't about me—it was about your ego."

"No."

"Then why—?"

"You were everything I wasn't."

His words stunned her. She stared at him in the fading light, watching the lines and angles of his face fall into shadow. Unable to accept the raw truth in his statement, she laughed. "I guess I was. You were tough, I was a wimp. You were daring, I was a coward. You were dexterous, I was clumsy. You were—"

"Clumsy? A coward? What are you talking about? You were beautiful. You were like . . . a rose. I lived in a world of weeds, and you were a beautiful pink rose."

"Oh, please!" She hadn't expected poetry from him. "I was at best a dandelion."

"You were brainy. You were cultured. You grew up in a world I only dreamed of, where you knew who your family was and every day for dinner you ate something from each of the basic food groups. You thought about things. You noticed things." He reached across the console and brushed a strand of hair from her cheek. "You were sexy. You're still sexy. Where did you ever get the idea that all you had going for you was your re- port card?"

His fingers left a trail of heat on her face. She still wasn't clear on why he'd married her, but she knew now why she'd married him. Not because she'd wanted to rebel. Not because she'd grown weary of living up to everyone's high expectations of her. Not because the one time she'd had the opportunity to do something wild and crazy, she couldn't bear to let it pass her by. Not even because Cody had charisma, a cockiness that bewitched her, a confidence that belied his weed-garden background.

She had married him because when he'd looked at her, he'd seen more than just a soft-spoken, well- behaved straight-A student. He'd seen a rose. He'd seen a woman.

"I didn't want to leave you," she confessed, won- dering whether that would be as true in the future as it had been in the past. "Leaving you broke my heart."

"But it made Daddy happy," Cody recalled, his dry tone failing to disguise his bitterness.

"My father had nothing to do with my leaving you."

"He was always calling on the phone and begging you to come home."

"He did want me to go back to Brookline," she admitted. "But he wasn't the reason I left. All he did was to make it possible by buying me a plane ticket."

"And working out a divorce. Although obviously he screwed up that part of it."

She didn't want them to detour into an analysis of her father's flaws. "If he hadn't arranged for the ticket," she pressed on, "I would have figured out another way to leave. I couldn't survive without an education. I loved you, but if I'd stayed I would have grown to hate you."

"So you left, and I got to hate you instead."

He said the words so quietly and calmly it took her a minute to feel their sting. "I'm sorry, Cody," she whispered, staring at the turquoise silk clenched in her fists. "I hated myself, too."

"Well, look." He drummed his fingers against the steering wheel and watched the last scarlet slice of the sun vanish below the earth. "This is all history. It doesn't matter anymore. We both got over it."

She nodded, afraid that if she spoke she might say she hadn't gotten over it yet.

"You haven't thought about me in years. And if you hadn't stumbled across the fouled-up paperwork from our supposed divorce, you wouldn't have thought about me ever again."

"That's not true."

He angled his head, trying to see her face, which she kept resolutely lowered. Cody slid his thumb under her chin and steered her gaze back to him. The sun was gone, transforming the evening light from pink to mauve, but she could see him clearly in the gloom. She could see his eyes, glowing with questions, with mystery. She could see his mouth, the mouth that had kissed her with such erotic force just hours ago. The strong, defiant chin. The long, straight nose. The midnight mane of hair.

"You thought about me?" he asked.

"Sometimes. Yes."

"Not after Mark the Banker made the scene," he guessed.

"Even then."

"Yeah?" A glint of arrogant pleasure flashed in his eyes. "How did I compare?"

"I thought a lot about our marriage before I accepted his proposal. I thought about whether to tell him I'd been married before."

"And you decided that telling him about it would be too embarrassing."

"Embarrassment had nothing to do with it, Cody. It was just that I never talked about it with anybody. Not even with my parents, really. Nobody knew I'd been married."

"What do you mean, nobody knew? Didn't you tell anybody?"

She shook her head. She hadn't even told her friends at Wellesley. On a perpetual crusade to find boyfriends, they'd traveled to mixers and parties and yammered about the guys at Harvard or Tufts or MIT. But Jane had never participated in their chatter. She'd smiled and nodded and made comments when she felt she had to, but she'd had no interest in meeting men.

"I was . . ." She struggled for the right word. "I was in mourning. My parents didn't want me to grieve. They just wanted me to put the whole thing behind me and get on with my life. It made sense. Tormenting myself over you wasn't doing me any good, so I tried to put the grief away. I didn't always succeed, but I tried." She didn't like the way he'd managed to make her feel defensive, and decided to turn the conversation around. After all, it wouldn't kill him to do a little apologizing, too. "You obviously got on with your life once I left."

"Yeah."

"You've more than just gotten on with it. You've done quite nicely."

"For a kid without an education," he muttered, putting words in her mouth. "For a kid with nothing."

"Don't tell me you had nothing. You had plenty. You had your wits and your talent and your determination. You had survival skills I'd never even imagined. If you had left me, I couldn't have survived in Los Angeles on my own."

"Sure you could have."

"I didn't even have transportation! I didn't know how to drive the Harley. I didn't know how to earn money. I was so dependent on you, Cody, it frightened me."

He opened his mouth and then shut it. She wondered what he'd been about to say: that if she'd really been so dependent on him she wouldn't have left him? That *he'd* been dependent on her?

"There ought to be a law," he murmured, sounding gentler than he had since she'd launched this conversation, "that anything you do when you're eighteen doesn't go on your permanent record. We were both stupid, Janey. The only thing is, I never thought being stupid was a tragedy. I forgave myself a long time ago. You should have, too."

"This isn't about me forgiving myself," she said, hearing her voice catch. "It's about you forgiving me."

She felt his gaze on her, as palpable as a touch. "I forgive you," he said.

She dared to look at him, and her breath lodged in her throat. The harsh lines of his face were softened by the sunset and the emotions filling the car. Behind him the cars buzzed by, but he was still and steady, his eyes reaching to her, luminous but not terribly reassuring, making her wish she'd never done what he had to forgive her for.

Then it was his turn to look away. "We ought to get ourselves over to Metairie while there's a little light left," he said, igniting the engine and glancing over his left shoulder to find a break in the flow of traffic.

She was relieved that they were abandoning the discussion, even though she hadn't accomplished what she had to. She'd gotten things off her chest, but...

She didn't believe Cody. She didn't believe he'd forgiven her.

Or maybe it was just that she still hadn't forgiven herself, after all.

FINDING REVEREND BOB'S address wasn't hard. Thinking about the good pastor was all but impossible, however. How was Cody supposed to concentrate on getting Stanhope off his back when his mind was crammed with everything Jane had just said, everything she'd gotten him to say?

Their marriage had been the last thing on his mind when he'd kissed her that afternoon. He'd been firmly in the present, eager to make love to Jane as she was now. Notions of control and hatred and forgiveness hadn't been anywhere on his agenda when he'd been kissing her, touching her, wanting her.

But maybe she was right. Maybe money wasn't what had torn them apart twelve years ago. He had memories of fights, fiery no-holds-barred combat with her in their rattrap apartment in Los Angeles, and in those memories money was always the central issue—him calling her spoiled, her accusing him of not understanding her needs, him retorting that her needs all seemed to have whopping price tags attached to them.

But maybe it wasn't just the cost of a college education that had worried him. Maybe it was that he'd been afraid of losing her. She would have gone off to school and experienced new things, things that excluded him. She would have advanced in the world, leaving him behind.

I was so dependent on you, Cody, it frightened me.

If she'd gone to college, she would have stopped being so dependent on him.

No wonder he'd forgiven himself for his share of the mistakes in their marriage. He hadn't realized how serious those mistakes were.

Damn. He had to unclutter his brain and stay focused on Stanhope. This might be the only opportunity he would ever have to confront the guy; he couldn't waste his chance by letting thoughts of his brief, bungled marriage distract him.

He veered onto the exit ramp and coasted to a stop at the end. "Do you know where we're going?" she asked.

Loaded question. She'd meant it literally, though, and he took it that way. "I've got a pretty good idea. The *Sentinel* covers plenty of Metairie news. I've been out this way more than a few times."

He cruised past a boring landscape of strip malls and gas stations, heading north along the Bonnabel Canal toward Lake Pontchartrain. Eventually he found the

street he was looking for, and the address: a two-story
apartment building of gray stucco facing its twin across
a courtyard parking lot. A few brave shrubs tried to
make a go of it along the edge of the courtyard; a magnolia in its death throes hovered on one side of the lot,
its brown leaves heaped in a circle around the gray
trunk.

The courtyard was illuminated by the fading dusk and
a few evenly spaced light fixtures fastened to the walls
of the two buildings. A group of children glided along
the pavement on bikes and Rollerblades, weaving
among the parked cars. Two women sat on a porch
stoop drinking iced tea and keeping a sporadic eye on
the children. Near one of the other light fixtures, a man
hunched beneath the open hood of his car, examining
the engine in the narrow beam of a flashlight.

Even in the encroaching darkness, Cody was able to
identify him. He'd studied the man's photograph long
and hard over the past couple of days; he recognized the
tall, slightly pudgy build, the short-cropped silver hair,
the face that seemed incomplete somehow, as if it had
forgotten to age. Reverend Bob looked like an image in
the wrong lens. No matter how well you focused, he just
looked soft.

"We're in luck," Cody said, pulling to a stop at the
curb near the driveway into the courtyard.

Jane traced the line of Cody's vision to the man tin-
kering with his car. "That's Stanhope?"

"The one and only." He glanced at Jane. "So what's
the plan? How are we going to do this?"

He loved the way she looked when she was thinking:
her eyes lit from within, her lips pressed into an unintentionally sexy pout, half the distance to a kiss. "I
think we should try reason."

"As opposed to violence?"

"Cody, I really think you ought to keep your temper in check. I know you're furious with him, but—"

"I won't resort to brutality unless it's absolutely necessary," he deadpanned.

Jane studied him, uncertain whether he was kidding. He wasn't so sure, himself. "I think you should keep your mouth shut and let me handle it."

"Spoken like a true lawyer." He turned from her to scrutinize Stanhope in the context of his automobile engine. The guy was zapping his flashlight here and there, looking totally inept. "I think there might be another way to approach this."

"You're going to sabotage his car?"

"I'm going to save his car, and his ass. And then he'll be putty in our hands."

"How do you know his car can be saved? For that matter, how do you know there's anything wrong with it? Maybe he's just looking for a serial number or something."

Cody choked on a laugh. He knew better than to question Jane's expertise when it came to the law. Surely she ought to know better than to question his expertise when it came to cars. Cody had instincts about all things mechanical, and his instincts were telling him that the scuzz-bucket pastor had an automotive problem that Cody could solve. Leverage presented itself.

"We'll start with the car and work our way to violence from there," he said, killing the engine of his own car and rolling up the window. Jane looked dubious, but she got out when he did. Her lips still pursed and her scarf fluttering in the hot breeze, she followed Cody up the driveway into the parking lot.

"Got a problem?" Cody called to the minister.

Stanhope straightened up, angling his head to avoid whacking himself with the hood. He was Cody's height but probably weighed a good twenty pounds more. In a loose-fitting green polo shirt and baggy khakis, he looked too clean-cut to consort with ladies of the night.

"I know cars," Cody told him.

Stanhope blinked, his eyes darting from Cody to Jane and back to Cody. They were brown, but the whites had a pink cast to them, as if he were suffering from hay fever. The pink eyes, combined with his pale skin and his pale hair, reminded Cody of a white rabbit.

"So," he persevered, "what's the problem? Engine won't turn over?"

Stanhope stared at him one minute longer, leaving Cody to wonder whether the minister recognized him from that day, weeks ago, when he'd inadvertently wandered into Cody's camera range on Esplanade Avenue. Evidently his need for mechanical assistance was stronger than any vague memory he might have of Cody, because he said, "I don't rightly know what the problem is. A red light flashed on the dashboard while I was driving home."

Cody nudged Stanhope aside and studied the engine. Buicks were not known for cryptic engines. He could psyche this one out easily enough. "Which red light?" he asked.

"I believe the water-level indicator." He pointed to a well less than half full of fluid.

"That's your windshield-washer tank," Cody told him evenly, doing his best not to ridicule him. Maybe lots of people didn't know their windshield-washer tanks from their radiators. "Your windshield fluid is a bit low; you can buy that stuff in any supermarket and top it off. If you've got a water-level problem, though, that'd be around here." He squinted at the water tank, then reached for Stanhope's flashlight. Stanhope handed it over like a nurse in an operating room, assisting the head surgeon.

"Uh-huh. See this hose here?" He pointed to the hose that connected the water tank to the radiator. "Your clamp is loose. Your hose is actually beginning to crack around the edge. See that?" He pointed out the damaged hose to Stanhope. "You're leaking water because the hose is corroded."

"Well, I'll be," he drawled, impressed.

"It happens over time. It's no big thing to fix. You should get the hose replaced, but in the meantime, I can trim that ragged edge and tighten the clamp for you. That would put an end to your leak."

"Well . . . I'd be mighty obliged."

Obliged enough to get out of my life? Cody wanted to ask. But he only dug his pocketknife out of the deep front pocket of his jeans, snapped open the screwdriver blade and loosened the clamp. He used a knife blade to cut away the crumbling edge of the hose, then wedged it back into place and tightened the clamp.

"I'm beside myself," Stanhope said, his pink eyes round with astonishment. "I'm afraid I'm all thumbs when it comes to cars."

Are you all thumbs when it comes to the doggie position? Cody wondered. But he obeyed his lawyer and kept his cool, giving the clamp a final tightening before he folded his knife shut and slid it back into his pocket. "Next time you've got the car in for a tune-up, tell them to replace that hose. It'll hold for a while, but not forever. And you'll need to add some water to the tank."

"I'll do that right now," Stanhope said, pivoting on his heel and starting toward a screen door. Cody tossed a quick look toward Jane, who motioned with her head that they should follow him in.

Sometimes, Cody thought, luck could be with a man. Reverend Bob was clearly so taken with Cody's generous spirit, he unquestioningly held the screen door open to let Cody and Jane into his apartment.

The guy must be a few cards shy of a full deck. Here he was, just a couple of miles from one of the most crime-ridden cities in America, admitting to his home two strangers, one of whom had already revealed that he had a knife on his person. The Reverend Robert Stanhope was some kind of idiot.

But then, Cody already knew that. Who but an idiot would have sacrificed his career, his wife and his children for the transient pleasures of a French Quarter hooker?

Cody let Jane step ahead of him as they trailed Stanhope through a depressingly barren front room furnished with a couple of Salvation Army chairs and a table constructed of orange crates with a strip of plywood across them. Passing through an arched door, they arrived in an equally dismal kitchen furnished with a small round table, obsolete appliances, scuffed linoleum flooring and a curtainless window, all of it painfully visible in the glare of a circular fluorescent ceiling light.

Stanhope lifted an empty milk bottle from the counter and turned toward the chipped porcelain sink, ready to fill it with water. "Mr. Stanhope," Jane said, "we have to talk."

The bottle went flying. Fortunately, it was plastic, so it only made a hollow rattle when it hit the floor. Stanhope backed against the counter, his complexion growing pasty as the blood drained from his face. "How do you know my name?"

"We're here on business," she said.

"But—but my car—"

"Just add some water," Cody said helpfully. "You won't see that red light on the dashboard anymore."

Stanhope rubbed his hands together, as if to stimulate the circulation in them. In the bright light his hair looked less silver than drab gray. He had freckles, too. The paler he became, the more vividly they showed themselves across the bridge of his nose.

"My name is Jane Thayer," Jane said. "I'm a lawyer."

"Oh, Christ," Stanhope muttered, sounding very unlike a man of the cloth.

"This—" Jane gestured toward Cody "—is Cody Sinclair."

The name seemed to ring a bell. He frowned, running his pallid fingers through his hair. "Cody Sinclair," he repeated, rummaging through his memory.

"Of the *New Orleans Sentinel.*"

"Oh, Christ," Stanhope groaned, then pulled himself together and said, with as much authority as he could muster, "I'm sorry, but you'll have to speak to my attorney."

"We don't want to speak to your attorney," Jane insisted, firm but kind, like a kindergarten teacher. "We want to speak to you."

Evidently, firm but kind kindergarten teachers made Stanhope panic. He turned his pink eyes on Cody. "What did you do to my car? You broke it, didn't you. You planted a bomb. It's going to explode when I turn the key!"

"Give me a break," Cody erupted. "I fixed your damned hose. Put a lid on it, Bob. Or is it Stanley? I understand you go by the name Stanley Roberts these days."

"Oh, Christ," Stanhope murmured. This time it sounded like a genuine prayer, one born of desperation.

"Our business is simple," Jane declared, luring Stanhope's attention back to her. Her voice was crisp, her hair sleek and silky despite the heat. The only nonlawyerly thing about her was the scarf. It was the most colorful item in the room. Something about the contrast between her professional poise and that splash of turquoise turned Cody on. It seemed to sum up who Jane was: the class brain all grown up, except for a flash of wild color, a flash of rebellious spirit, usually well buried—until someone like Cody came along and eroded her self control.

She might be wearing the scarf, but she probably resented Cody for giving it to her. Control was at the top of her list, after all. She'd left Cody twelve years ago because he made her lose control.

Well, she couldn't possibly be more in control than she was right now, even with the scarf. Stanhope looked like he was about to wet his pants, and Cody was still toying with a few violent ideas regarding the man—an ignition-triggered car bomb was a tempting notion. But Jane was the queen of control, speaking with cool intelligence, as if she were making a presentation before the Supreme Court. "You've brought suit against Mr. Sinclair's newspaper," she said, "and we want that suit dropped. As you can see, Mr. Sinclair is a good man. He's fixed your car for you. He means you no harm. He just wants this lawsuit dropped."

"That good man—" Stanhope pointed a trembling finger at Cody "—cost me my parish."

"Actually, Mr. Stanhope, that's not what happened," Jane argued, her voice steady, her eyes level on him. "Your indiscretion cost you your parish."

"God forgives me my weakness. God forgives all his children. It's only human beings who won't forgive me."

"Then you ought to direct your energies toward winning back their forgiveness."

"I've got nothing! I'm cut off from my income, from my children—and it's all because he put that blasphemous photograph in the *Sentinel*—"

"My pictures aren't blasphemous," Cody snapped. "Just a slice of reality, bud. And the reality there was that you and your playmate of the month were standing on a public street. Dumb move, Stanhope. You can't blame me for that."

"I can blame you for taking that picture and publishing it in the *Sentinel*. You and that newspaper of yours. The Satanic *Sentinel*. It's thanks to you I'm out of work. I've got no income. I'm living in this hellhole. My wife won't let me see the children." He puffed his flaccid chest up a bit. "I've got every right in the world to sue you. It's the American way."

"Sure, and it's the American way for a married man to go messing around with a twenty-dollar tart on Bourbon Street. That doesn't make it right."

"She—she was Satan in disguise. God tests his servants. He loves us even if we fail the test. And he lets us avenge our reputations—"

"If you sue the *Sentinel*," Jane pointed out as the two men seethed on either side of her, "your picture is going to be in the papers again. So is Suzie's picture.

The news reports will include all the details of what you and Suzie do. If there's a trial, you'll be subject to terrible, embarrassing publicity." She smiled with deceptive compassion. "You don't want that, Mr. Stanhope. It would be worse than what you've already endured. You'll never find a parish to hire you once the details come out in a public trial."

"But—but I'll get money from the *Sentinel*. My lawyer says we're not going to trial. The newspaper is going to settle, and they're going to pay for the trouble they've caused me."

"Your lawyer is charging you by the hour, isn't he?" Jane said. "He'll make money whether or not you win. But no amount of money will be able to buy back your reputation if you subject yourself to more publicity."

"He said he could clear my name. And he said it's never going to reach the courts. I know how these things work," he boasted, glaring at Cody. "You negotiate privately. You wind up with a settlement and nobody talks about it afterward."

"I'm sorry, Mr. Stanhope," Jane persevered, "but it doesn't always work that way. It only works that way if both parties are willing to negotiate. The *Sentinel* isn't."

"My lawyer told me—"

"Perhaps he misrepresented the situation. If he told you the truth, you wouldn't pursue the case, and he'd be out all those billable hours," Jane explained. "He wants to make money, Mr. Stanhope, and the only way he can do that is by keeping you active in the suit. But there's no way it will ever be settled privately."

"He swore to me it would be."

"He lied," Jane said, lying herself. Cody's violent impulses toward Stanhope faded. Physical revenge had its satisfactions, but...man, she was good. And she was winning.

"My lawyer said the newspaper—"

"Has deep pockets," she guessed. "But you're going to have quite a time convincing a judge and jury that you deserve any compensation. That photograph of you and the lady is pretty incriminating, and it was taken on a public street. And I'll tell you something else, Mr. Stanhope—the newspaper is just irritated enough that they'll drag the case out. They'll make it last as long as they can, and your lawyer won't fight them on it because the longer the case lasts, the more money he'll make. You'll be going through all sorts of public humiliation, your lawyer will be getting rich, and because of the publicity, you'll never find another congregation willing to hire you. This is the sort of case that will hit the national magazines. It will be dissected on tabloid TV. You'll be ruined forever."

She was better than good, Cody realized, awed by her charming malice, her devious way of convincing Stanhope that she had his best interests at heart.

"Oh, God. Oh, sweet God." His voice was tremulous. "I've sinned, I know I've sinned—it's human to sin. I shouldn't have to be ruined forever. God forgives me."

"Mr. Stanhope," she said, her voice dropping to a sensuous purr, "forget the suit. Nothing good will come of it. You know that as well as I do." She patted him on the arm, and he closed his eyes and issued a faint, sobbing sound. "It's your church you ought to be negotiating with, your congregation you need to settle with. Give up your lady friend and put your life back together. Don't prolong this tawdry episode."

"God save me," he whimpered. "You're right. You're absolutely right. If I can't get money for my troubles, there's no point in it. No point in making my lawyer rich and ruining myself."

"Just sign here," Jane said, producing several folded sheets of paper from her purse. They reminded Cody of the papers she wanted him to sign.

Unlike him, Reverend Bob was willing to pen his name on the dotted line. Or, in this case, lines. Without even bothering to read the documents first, he signed all three copies she placed before him.

"Please . . ." Stanhope moaned. "It's done now. Spare me any more of this. Please, just go."

Jane folded the papers and tucked them back into her purse. Cody tried not to grin. "Thank you," she said. "Take care, now."

Stanhope crumpled against the counter, seeming several inches shorter than when Cody and Jane had arrived. Cody would have felt sorry for him, except that he'd brought all his problems on himself and he really was a first-class jerk.

But he refrained from calling the guy a jerk. He refrained from mentioning that Stanhope had caused him a few sleepless nights and a lot of bad karma with his boss. He refrained from making the observation that any kind of minister who would cheat on his wife with a prostitute wasn't worth two cents in Cody's book, or God's.

All he said, as he ushered Jane to the doorway and out, was, "Don't forget to add some water to the engine."

CHAPTER ELEVEN

GUSSIE'S WAS AS SHE remembered it: stuffy, gloomy and noisy. But she was in a festive mood. Even the smoke didn't bother her.

"Give me a pitcher, Gus," Cody said to the butch-looking woman behind the bar. Then he thought to check with Jane. "Would you rather have wine? Or something else?"

She smiled and shook her head. She'd already tried Gussie's vintage Chablis, and it wasn't an experience worth repeating. "Beer is fine," she said.

Gussie grabbed a plastic pitcher from a shelf and positioned it under a tap. "Y'all look like you just got some good news," she said, clamping her cigarette between her teeth so she'd have both hands free to fill the pitcher. The movement of her mouth as she spoke scattered a shower of ashes onto the bar. Jane hoped none of those ashes fell into the pitcher.

"I did get good news," Cody confirmed, then wrapped his arm around Jane's shoulders and gave her a squeeze. "How did you know to have those papers on hand?" he asked her quietly. She could barely hear him over the wail of a guitar blasting from the jukebox.

"I'm a lawyer," she reminded him. "Lawyers know the importance of having the right papers on hand at all times."

"But . . . it's not like you've got a staff down here or anything."

"I don't need a staff to type up a statement. All I need is a keyboard and some paper. I asked the concierge if I could borrow a computer and printer this afternoon, and the hotel was able to accommodate me."

"But how did you know what to write? What if Reverend Bob had decided he wanted to read the papers before he signed them?"

She smiled. "To tell the truth, I didn't expect him to sign them. I figured they were just a starting point. His lawyer is going to have conniptions when he finds out what his client signed."

"Maybe his lawyer will say they were signed—what's the expression? Under duress. Maybe he'll say they aren't valid or something."

Jane let out a laugh. It was unlike Cody to worry about the details—and peering into his sparkling blue eyes, she realized he wasn't really worried. His questions were just his way of paying homage to her professional skills.

"We've already damaged the relationship between Stanhope and his counsel," she explained. "The trust isn't there. Stanhope won't listen to anything his attorney has to say at this point. Besides, there's nothing arguable in the document. All it says is that Stanhope agrees to drop all claims against the newspaper and promises not to bring suit again. He signed the statement in triplicate: one copy for you, one for your newspaper and one for his lawyer. How can anyone contest it? We got his signature, fair and square."

Cody's eyes narrowed on her, their intensity contradicting his relaxed grin. "Oh, come on, Janey. You weren't playing fair with him."

"I wasn't?" That was news to her. She knew everything there was to know about legal ethics, and she was
sure she hadn't crossed the line. "What did I do that
was unfair?"

"You looked at him. You used your voice. The way
you talked, the way you moved ... Hell, I don't know.
All I know is, I would have signed my soul to the devil
if you'd asked me."

He might have signed his soul to the devil for a lot of
reasons, Jane thought, few of which had anything to do
with her professional prowess. But right now, that
didn't matter. She and Cody were celebrating.

Gussie passed Cody the full pitcher and two glasses
still damp from a recent washing. "We'll need more
glasses than that," Cody told her. "Who's in the back
room?"

"The usual suspects," Gussie grunted, adding a few
more glasses to a tray and shoving it toward Jane. Table service clearly wasn't part of the deal at Gussie's.

As soon as Cody paid for the beer, he lifted the
pitcher and started toward the rear of the barroom.
Jane followed him with the tray, winding a path among
the tables to the poolroom where she'd first seen him a
few days ago. He held the door open for her, and she
blinked for a moment, waiting for her eyes to adjust to
the glare.

Three men, vaguely familiar looking, were lounging
around the billiard table, arguing about something in
muted, honey-thick drawls. When she crossed the
threshold they turned in unison to see who had invaded
their turf. One of them shouted, "Well, look who's
here! The Yank and his little lady."

"It's Mrs. Yank!" hooted one of the other men.
"But hey, who's all that beer for?"

"It's for anyone who treats me with the proper respect," Cody said sternly, though his voice was edged with laughter.

"I respect you," a beefy fellow swore, helping himself to a glass from Jane's tray before she could put it down on one of the side tables. "Matter of fact, I'll respect you even more in the morning."

That the men already had drinks didn't deter them from helping themselves to Cody's beer. They were a burly crew, all of them dressed in work clothes. Jane couldn't have imagined having a drink in the company of men like these back home in Boston. But here in New Orleans, with Cody at her side and a successful resolution to his problem under her belt, she warmed to the robust, good-natured specimens of Southern manhood who occupied the poolroom.

As each one took a freshly filled glass of beer from Cody, the specimens separated into individuals. "This is Claude," Cody introduced the first fellow. "If he gets fresh, let me know and I'll deck him."

"Oh, I never get fresh with ladies as pretty as you," Claude flirted. "Only with bowsers."

"He's a sexist pig," Jane observed pleasantly.

"No. I just happen to like bowsers. Thanks for the brew, Sinclair."

"Now, this twerp," Cody continued, introducing another friend, "is Darryl. If you ever want to place a bet on the pool table, don't wager on him. He's still trying to figure out which end of the stick you're supposed to hit the ball with."

"Least I know what balls is," Darryl retorted, winking at Jane. "There's folks still wonderin' whether Sinclair has a clue when it comes to balls."

"Keep it clean, Darryl," Claude scolded. "There's a lady in the room."

"And if she's Cody's wife, she may not know much 'bout balls, either," Darryl needled Cody. "Would I be correct if I suspected that this sudden largess with the beer is to get us sloshed so you can pick our pockets?"

"I don't have to get you sloshed for that, Darryl," Cody joked, evidently considering Darryl's anatomical critique unworthy of response. "I just have to place a bet on the table. You guys owe me from a few nights ago, don't you."

"We don't owe you nothin'," the third man piped up. "A man walks away from the table before the last ball goes down, he loses whatever money he's put up."

"He didn't just walk away," Claude reminded the others. "He was answering the summons of his lovely wife." He was laying on the palaver so thick. Jane wondered whether deep in his heart he considered her a bowser.

"Yeah, well, whatever, he don't get that money back," the third man insisted.

Cody shrugged, unflappable. "Whatever you say, Billy. Rack 'em up, would you? Let's ante up and get a game going."

"Why don't you let the wife play?" Darryl challenged.

"Oh, no!" Laughing, Jane held up her hands in mock surrender. "I don't know how to play pool."

"She don't know how? Where'd you find her, Cody? In a convent?"

"In Brookline High School, which is probably even more sacred. Come on, Janey—give it a try. I'll help you."

"No, Cody. I don't want you losing on my account."

But her protest was futile. All the men in the room were whistling and stomping their feet, cheering and waving her over to the broad green-felt table.

"Cody, really—I don't know how to do this."

He gave her a boyish grin, the same heart-melting grin he used to give her when their paths crossed in the long, echoing corridors of their school. "Don't worry about a thing," he assured her, his hand planted firmly at the small of her waist so she couldn't back away from the table.

"You're going to lose money—"

"I think we've talked enough about money tonight," he murmured.

His words reminded her of the confidences they'd shared in his car, the confessions and revelations. For a moment, the hullabaloo in the poolroom receded and a memory of those quiet, soul-baring minutes in his car took over her consciousness. She felt the rush of sultry air through the open window behind him, the closeness of the car's interior, Cody's tenderness as he reached across the gear stick and lifted a loose hair from her cheek. She saw him smile, not the pensive smile she'd seen earlier but a smile brimming with confidence—the smile he'd given her one dewy morning twelve years ago when she'd raced down her parents' driveway to elope with him.

"I trusted you with the sinister minister, Janey," he pointed out, hoisting a stick from a wall rack and chalking the end. "Now it's your turn to trust me."

She turned from him to the table, where Billy was racking the balls into a neat triangle. All she knew about pool was what she'd picked up from watching *The*

Hustler at a film festival a few years ago. How could she trust Cody when he was making a huge mistake? How could she trust him when she knew damned well she was going to make a fool of herself attempting to play pool?

She could trust him because he'd asked her to, and right now that seemed to be enough. Swallowing her panic, she surveyed the long green table. "I'm supposed to hit the balls into the holes, right?"

"That's the general idea," Darryl told her, chalking the tip of his stick and smirking with glee.

Cody urged her to the end of the table. "You don't have to hit all the balls into the holes, just some of them. And never the cue ball."

"The cue ball. That's this white one here?"

"That's right. See? You're a fast learner. Anyone want to bet against Janey?" he invited his pals.

"Now, Yank, we're gentlemen here," Claude declared. "We don't bet against a woman."

"Especially when you know you're going to lose."

Darryl rose to the occasion. "Here's five bucks says I won't."

"I knew I could count on you." Cody pulled five dollars out of his wallet and placed it on top of Darryl's on the table's rim.

"Cody." She sighed. She'd always admired his stubbornness, but it could be mighty exasperating at times. Like now, for instance. "Don't throw your money away."

"Okay, I won't throw it away. Win for me."

"I don't know how to play!" she nearly shrieked.

"If you'd stuck around twelve years ago, I would have taught you. It's about time you learned."

"I'm sure there are people who have lived very successful lives without ever learning pool."

"But you're not going to be one of them," he declared, his eyes glowing with laughter. "Loosen up, lady. We're partying tonight."

With that, he brought his arms around her so he could guide her hands. His chest pressed warmly against her back. His hands were strong on hers, manipulating her fingers around the stick. "Make a wedge with your thumb, like this . . ." He positioned her left hand on the felt. "And you're just going to move the stick, nice and easy." He covered her right hand with his at the thick end of the stick and showed her how to slide it to and fro against her left thumb.

Maybe it was the metaphor of the long, hard stick and the balls, and the back-and-forth motion in the bend of her hand. Maybe it was nothing more complicated than the fact that Cody was half wrapped around her, his arms paralleling hers, his thighs brushing against her bottom. Maybe it was the exhilaration of the day's triumph, the fact that Cody *had* trusted her with Stanhope, and she'd lived up to his trust, and now he wanted her to trust him.

Whatever it was, it stirred delicious, inappropriate sensations deep inside her, sensations that made her wish they weren't in a pool hall with Cody's buddies looking on. Sensations that made her glad she'd come clean with him in the car—and with herself that afternoon, when she'd concluded that once she divorced Cody she wasn't going to marry anyone until she got her head straightened out. Tonight was not the time to straighten out her head. It was simply the time to do whatever she could to keep Cody from losing the five dollars he'd wagered on her.

He slid the stick a couple of times against the notch formed by her left thumb, then tightened his clasp of her right hand and thrust the stick hard against the cue ball. It shot down the table, shattering the triangle and sending the balls in all directions. One of the balls dropped into a pocket. "Oh, Cody!" she exclaimed, giving a small, joyful jump. The bet went forgotten; the emotional talk they'd had earlier dropped into a storage compartment of her brain. A ball had gone into the pocket, and she was ecstatic. "Look! I got one in!"

"Uh-oh. Sinclair's got a secret weapon," Claude teased. "The lady can break—with a little help from her friends. Who knows what else she can do?"

"The lady can do just about anything she sets her mind to," Cody boasted, relaxing his hold on her only enough so that they could circle the table, searching for the best shot. "It just so happens that she's very graceful, too," he added, mostly for Jane's benefit. And indeed, she wasn't feeling the least bit clumsy at the moment. "Okay, Jane—you dropped the ten. That means you're going after the balls with the stripes on them. If you drop a solid-colored ball—the ones numbered one through seven—it's a scratch."

"A scratch," she repeated, her enthusiasm ebbing as she realized how little she knew about the game. "That's bad?"

"That's bad. Now, that's probably your best shot there—the fourteen in that corner pocket."

She traced a line with her eye from the cue ball to the ball numbered fourteen, and from that ball to the pocket. Angles were involved, but Jane had aced honors geometry and physics in high school. She knew about force and counter-force. "I've got to clip it on the side," she analyzed.

"Just a light kiss'll do it."

She didn't allow herself to respond to his mention of kisses. The two five-dollar bills were in her line of vision, and since she'd already cost Cody twenty dollars that evening, she wasn't going to cost him any more if she could help it. She traced the invisible line again, bowed over the table and tried to remember how Cody had arranged her left hand.

"Like this," he reminded her, reaching around her and adjusting her thumb. His hand was warm and firm, his fingers deft. But when she began to feel her confidence return, he stepped back, leaving her to take the shot on her own.

She eyed the staked money and ordered herself not to be a wimp. Pretending she was facing not a table full of hard, brightly colored balls but a philandering clergyman, she slid the stick back and then forward until it hit the cue ball.

When Cody had guided the stick, it had connected with the ball in a smooth, hard jab. But when she did it on her own, the stick barely nudged the ball. She straightened to watch as the white ball rolled down the table at the speed of molasses. The other men in the room chuckled. One of them recited the Lord's Prayer in the time it took the ball to travel down the table. It barely touched the fourteen-ball, but the slow-motion contact was enough to start that ball on an even more leisurely course toward the corner pocket.

"I think I hear my wife callin' me," Billy taunted. "Maybe I could run on home and come back and still catch that ball dropping."

"It ain't gonna drop," Darryl predicted.

"It's on the right path."

"It's moving too slow. I seen dead rats move faster than that."

"He's worrying about his five bucks," Claude guessed.

"It's stopped moving," Darryl announced, bending over the ball.

"Don't touch it," Cody warned. "It's got some action in it."

"Meanwhile, I've aged five years," Billy groaned.

The fourteen-ball plopped into the pocket.

Cody beamed. "She's hot, friends. She's got the right stuff."

"Beginner's luck is what she's got," Darryl groused.

Jane agreed silently. Beginner's luck was all it was. Even so, she couldn't suppress a giddy thrill at having gotten the fourteen-ball into the hole all by herself. She had spent her entire life accomplishing what was expected of her—and avoiding those areas where she doubted her abilities. She was not programmed for failure, and she would have especially hated to fail at this game with Cody's friends witnessing her ineptitude and Cody's money riding on the outcome.

She shot him a quick, dubious look. "What do I do now?"

"Find another striped ball near a pocket," he coached her.

That was it, then. He was abandoning her to play the rest of the game on her own. Once again, he was placing all his trust in her.

Determined not to let him down, she strolled around the table, assessing the angles and keeping her mind on the principles of physics. "I can't go for that red ball, can I?" she asked.

Cody shook his head. "Any ball from nine up."

"Okay." She studied the position of the eleven-ball and decided that if she banked it at just the precise angle, she could send it into the pocket across the table. She bent over, remembered to position her left thumb properly and tapped the cue ball.

"Another lightning strike by Miz Sinclair," Claude announced as the cue ball crawled at a tortoise pace across the green felt.

"Putting a little power into your stroke helps," Cody advised.

"I'm doing the best I can," she snapped, wondering whether blowing on the cue ball to speed it along would be considered cheating.

"You're doing great," he assured her.

An eternity passed, and the cue ball bumped the eleven, which followed the trajectory she envisioned, bouncing against the cushioned edge and setting off toward the pocket across the way one millimeter at a time.

"Wake me when it's over," Billy groaned, then faked a loud yawn.

"The suspense is just about killing me," Claude chimed in.

The eleven inched hesitantly toward the pocket, teetered on the lip of the hole—and stopped.

"Sneeze at it," Claude suggested. "It might drop."

"Don't help her. This is my big chance!" Darryl grabbed his stick and stormed the table. It took him less than five seconds to pick his shot and slam the stick into the cue ball. Balls scattered everywhere. The vibrations were enough to send the eleven into the pocket.

"That," Cody announced, "is a scratch." He gathered Jane in a playful hug and spun her around. "You're winning, Janey. Time to clean up."

"Clean up?"

"Just drop the rest of those striped balls without getting any of the solid ones."

His faith in her ability touched her. He seemed even more confident in her pool playing than in her legal expertise. Maybe he thought she could "clean up" because she'd had the foresight to prepare a statement in triplicate for Stanhope to sign.

She might have argued that there was no known correlation between doing good work as an attorney and dropping striped balls into pool table pockets. But Cody's optimism was contagious. She wasn't going to let him down, not if she could help it.

Darryl's shot had rearranged the entire table. She scrutinized it, picking out the striped balls, drawing mental angles and lines across the table. Then she decided on a shot, arranged her left thumb, slid the stick and tapped the cue ball.

It moved so slowly, a passing contact with the eight-ball was enough to halt it in its tracks.

"That's okay," Cody reassured her when none of her balls dropped. "You didn't really have a shot. He left you set up with nothing."

"Oh, so you admit I know what I'm doing here?" Darryl snorted, tossing down the cube of blue chalk and advancing on the table. "Tell your little lady there that she's about to get slaughtered."

He dropped three solid-colored balls in succession. At first, Jane's dismay was based on the prospect of Cody's losing his money. But then she realized she was more riled by the prospect of losing the match. When at last it was her turn to shoot again, she approached the table prepared to slaughter Darryl back, just for spite. She analyzed her best shot, and when she struck the cue ball she did it with enough force to send the white ball rolling at least two miles per week.

Billy issued more raucous yawns. The cue ball struck the fifteen and sent it toward a side pocket. Claude refilled his glass with beer and downed half of it. The fifteen dropped into the pocket.

She glanced at Cody. His smile sent a hot shiver down her spine.

For heaven's sake, why was this silly game turning her on? Why was Cody's approval so important to her? Why did she care?

The why's weren't important. She *did* care. She wanted to win for him. For herself, too. For both of them.

With the taut resolution she used when she entered into tricky negotiations or prepped for a tough court battle, she appraised the table, picked her next shot and hit the cue ball. It occurred to her that she hadn't chalked her stick in several plays, but things seemed to be going well enough without the chalk. When the ten-ball dropped into a pocket, she forgot about everything—the chalk, the money wagered, even Cody's seductive grin. The only thing that existed for her was the opportunity to succeed at something she'd never done before, to excel in a field no one would have ever expected of her.

She experienced a heady thrill not unlike the thrill she'd felt when she'd run away with Cody. She'd been crazy in love with him, of course, but she'd also been elated by the sheer freedom of shattering everyone's preconceptions. She'd felt frightened, riddled with doubt—and more alive than she'd ever felt before. Or since. Imagine her teachers, her parents, her associates at the firm, watching her shoot pool in a grungy, smoke-filled tavern. Imagine Jane Thayer, alumna of Wellesley and Harvard Law School, playing with the panache of Minnesota Fats. She wasn't just the straight-A student, the bookworm, the goody-two-shoes. She was a lady shooting pool in a dive in New Orleans. The very notion intoxicated her.

The nine didn't drop, and she stepped back from the table. Darryl was grumbling. Billy and Claude were mocking him. Cody was sipping his beer, his eyes on Jane, his smile gone.

What was he thinking? That she wasn't going to live up to his high hopes for her as a pool shark? That he'd gotten everything he wanted from her, give or take a five-dollar wager?

Or that maybe she wasn't the opposite of him, after all? Maybe she had a lust for winning as strong as his, and an ability to focus, to shut out the world and do the job. Maybe, despite her upper-crust pedigree, she could chug beer and wield a cue stick with a group of good ol' Southern boys. She could be worth betting on.

The room was hot—not just from Cody's steamy gaze and Jane's overabundance of adrenaline, but because it was small and the men were big and in June in New Orleans no amount of air-conditioning was sufficient. Jane tied the turquoise scarf in a loose knot around her neck and fingered the silk, trying to steady her nerves. Darryl sank another ball before missing a shot and turning the table back to her.

"He left you with less than nothin', sugar," Claude commented.

"Take a look at her," Billy refuted him. "This is a lady who can do a lot with less than nothing."

Jane tuned out their chatter. Her mind filled with a fleeting picture of Cody ignoring the hubbub around him as he shot photos of the wayward Jeep in the flooded street earlier that day. She, too, ignored the hubbub and figured out her best shot.

Angles. Lines. Trajectories. She hit the cue ball, which rolled sluggishly down the table. Cody's friends chatted among themselves to pass the time until the cue ball tapped the fifteen into a pocket. She took aim and struck again. Down went the twelve. "Cody?" she said. "There aren't any more striped balls on the table."

"Now go for the eight," he told her. "You've got to call the pocket, too."

"You mean—I have to guess which pocket it's going to go in?"

"That's right."

She studied the table. If she hit the eight-ball straight ahead, it might have a chance of falling into a corner pocket at the other end of the table. But to succeed, she would have to hit the cue ball hard, and while she could handle geometry, she hadn't mastered velocity. She decided to try brushing the eight-ball sideways into a side pocket instead.

Just a light kiss, she thought, shifting a few steps to the left. "That side one, over there," she announced.

"Oh, no—don't do it that way," Billy cautioned her. "You're never gonna get it in that way. Go for the left corner."

She smiled. "I'm going for the side pocket," she repeated, permitting herself a quick, uncertain glimpse of Cody.

He was smiling—not a broad smile, not a sexy one, not a confident one, but a smile of trust, of encouragement. A smile that said, *Take a chance, Janey. Follow your instincts.*

"Just a light kiss," she murmured under her breath, then hit the cue ball.

Hours passed. Centuries. Eons. At least a minute—and then the white ball kissed the black, lightly. The seconds ticked off in silence. No one dared to breathe until, with a loud kerplunk, the black ball dropped into the side pocket.

Jane felt her spine go limp. She sagged against the table, oblivious to the hooting and hollering of the men around her. Even Darryl was laughing. Claude slapped her so hard on the back he might have cracked a few of her ribs, but she was too gloriously numb to feel any pain.

But not too numb to feel a gentle hand on her shoulder, Cody's hand. "You amaze me, Janey," he whispered, sending another searing shiver down her spine.

"I thought..." She craned her neck until she could view his face. Once again he was smiling, but it was an enigmatic smile, a wistful one. "I thought you were sure I was going to win," she said.

"I wasn't sure of anything," he admitted, his smile widening enough to cut a dimple into his cheek. "I wasn't going to let you know that, though. Put enough faith in a person, and sometimes they live up to it."

Perhaps she should have been insulted, but she was too delighted about winning her very first game of pool. "I could use some fresh air," she said. "Look at me—I'm soaked." It was true; a drop of perspiration rolled from her hairline down to her chin, gliding over her skin with more speed than any of the balls she'd propelled across the pool table during the game.

"Sure." He pried the stick from her hand—she hadn't realized she'd been gripping it so tightly—and slid it into place on the wall rack. Then he helped himself to the two five-dollar bills. "It's been fun, boys. The Union scores another victory."

"The South shall rise again," Darryl warned, although he was still laughing, gracious in defeat. He extended his right hand to Jane. "I mighta thought you were trying to con me, all that stuff about you never playin' this before. But you played so strange. Nobody who knew how to play pool would play it the way you did."

"Thanks, I think," Jane said, shaking his hand. "You were right, though—it really was just beginner's luck."

"Cody's luck, I reckon. He got you and he got my money. I ought to know better than to tangle with him, but I'll never learn." He jabbed an index finger at Cody. "I'll win next time, Sinclair, and that's a promise."

"Yeah, sure," Cody teased. "I'll bring my wallet if you bring yours. Finish up that beer, boys." He slung his arm loosely around Jane's shoulders and escorted her out of the back room.

She wanted to skip. She wanted to dance. She was drained, she was sweating, she was utterly fatigued—and she wanted to yank off her sandals and climb on a table and boogie. Which really wasn't like her at all.

Suppressing the urge to kick up her heels, she let Cody usher her through the smoky front room and out into the dark, hot evening. Only when they were safely outdoors did she let out a whoop. "I won, Cody! I won!"

"I always knew you were a winner," he said, releasing her so she could spin in an exuberant little victory dance.

"I've never even played before! I can't believe I did it! I didn't care about the bet, Cody—I did it for my ego!" *And your trust,* she wanted to add.

He beamed like a proud papa as she hooked her hand around a lamppost and swung around it in a circle. "God, I hate the thought of getting into a car right now," she said, filling her lungs with the steamy night air. "I'm too keyed up. This is a night for a motorcycle."

"We could take a spin on the Harley," Cody suggested.

She halted in midrotation and let go of the lamppost. "You still own it?" she blurted out in astonishment. "My God—it must be an antique. How old is it? You bought it used, and that was more than twelve years ago."

Once again his smile transformed itself. She detected a glimmer of mischief in it, a glimmer of amusement, and a whole lot of something else. "You want to see it?"

She would love to. But then, she would love to turn back the clock, to be the kind of woman who could have made a real marriage with Cody, who could have driven that motorcycle instead of being only a passenger on it, who could have marched into pool halls and won games with skill and flair rather than with luck and honors physics.

"Where is it?" she asked carefully, afraid to admit to Cody how much she longed to see the vehicle that had carried her to an impetuous, passionate, ultimately doomed freedom so many years ago.

"If you really want to see it, I'll take you there," he said, his voice low and husky, laden with a warning.

She should have declined. But she was beyond should-haves. Tonight she'd triumphed over Robert Stanhope and she'd triumphed over Darryl at pool. Tonight she'd confessed why she left Cody, and he'd confessed why he hadn't wanted her to leave. Tonight, everything was different.

"I really want to see it," she said.

CHAPTER TWELVE

CLARISSA SAT IN HER living room. Actually, *sat* didn't quite describe it. She was curled up into a tight round knot on her couch, her knees drawn to her chest and her arms hugging her shins.

What was she going to do?

What she *ought* to be doing was sleeping, but it was getting on toward midnight and she was still wide-awake. Energy simmered inside her. She'd gone to bed twice and sprung out of bed twice, unable to lie still without being inundated by panic. How could a person sleep when her whole life was about to implode?

She knew too much. She'd said too much. Mark had to think she was a ninny, and Jane would fire her if she didn't do Jane the courtesy of quitting first. Her career was in a shambles, her ambitions swept away like a sand castle on the Cape at high tide. And she couldn't depend on modeling to pay the rent. She'd have to move back in with her parents, or else relocate to a city with a lower cost of living.

And on top of all that, someone was pounding on her door.

Probably a mugger, or a robber. Who else but a troublemaker would be banging on a single woman's door at such a late hour?

She tightened the sash on her bathrobe and tiptoed to the door, promising to herself that the next apartment she lived in would be in a doorman building instead of a walk-up, where lazy neighbors were always admitting strangers through the locked front door. The next apartment she lived in would probably be in Ypsilanti, anyway, or Paducah. She had no future in Boston.

She peeked through the spy hole in the door and saw a tiny Mark Dennison, shrunk by the lens to the size of a button.

Her heart thumped. What was he doing here at this hour? She'd thought he was a gentleman. Gentlemen telephoned first, didn't they? And they rapped gently on a door. They didn't pummel it with their fists.

But she couldn't let him stand out in the narrow hall, raising a racket. And really, she had nothing to fear from him. She'd already made a complete fool of herself in his company. Things couldn't possibly get any worse.

She slid back the chain lock, opened the door—and gasped. The person on the other side of the threshold was Mark Dennison, all right, but he was Mark as she'd never seen him before. His elegant silk tie hung askew, his dark hair was mussed, his shirttails hung out of his pleated trousers, and his jacket lay crooked across his shoulders. She was astounded to realize how messy such a magnificent suit could look.

For that matter, she was even more astounded to realize how messy such an impeccable man could look.

His eyes were glazed, yet they zeroed in on her upturned face. "Are you going to invite me in?" he asked, exerting himself to pronounce each syllable with precision.

"You're drunk," she declared.

"Now, now, now." He gave her a crooked smile. "Let us choose our words with care, Clarissa. I am inebriated. Not drunk."

He seemed tranquil, and his complexion lacked the ghastly green undertone of someone about to puke—although if he did puke, it might cure her of her infatuation with him. Jane was the sturdy sort of can-do woman who would know what to do with a sloshed suitor. Clarissa, on the other hand, was the squeamish sort who fell swiftly out of love with anyone guilty of committing a disgusting act.

So far, Mark hadn't done anything disgusting. Drunk—or inebriated—she could handle him, as long as she didn't have to clean up after him.

She stepped away from the door, and he entered the small, neatly decorated living room of her apartment, closing the door behind him. His movements were almost too deliberate, as if he were sending robotic messages from his brain to his hand: *Push the door shut. Do not stop pushing until you hear the latch click. Once you hear it, let your hand drop to your side.*

"I'll make some coffee," she said.

"Be my guest."

"I can't be your guest," she objected, wishing he'd do something gross so she'd have an excuse to kick him out and get over him. "This is my home. You're my guest."

"Oh. Well, then, don't go to any trouble for me. I don't want any coffee."

"Mark. You're drunk."

"I am not drunk. I've been drinking. There's a difference, Clarissa. Do you know what *in vino veritas* means?"

Her fingers itched to straighten his tie, to brush his hair back from his high, square brow. She shoved them into the deep pockets of her robe and tried to hang on to her exasperation. "It's the Harvard University motto, isn't it?"

He chuckled. "Oh, you dear, amusing girl. I'm convinced of it now. I'm in love with you."

"No, you're not. You're just drunk."

He ignored her and prowled around the small room. He fingered the fabric of her draperies, then lifted them and peered out her window, which overlooked the street. He lifted a little Buddha statue—"This must be Vietnamese," he guessed—and she didn't have the heart to tell him she'd bought it at Pier One. He studied the framed print hanging on the wall above the sofa— "Monet in his late period," he pontificated—although it wasn't. "What a lovely home this is," he concluded before settling on the sofa. She'd bought it for her own comfort, and his large frame dwarfed the cushions. "The Harvard motto is *Veritas,* love. That means 'truth.' *In vino veritas* means 'in wine is truth.'"

"In wine is truth," she repeated, perplexed.

"We drink of the grape and see the world as it truly is."

"I don't think you're seeing anything at all," she murmured, too agitated to sit. She moved to the window and fussed with the curtains until they lay straight. Then she started toward the kitchen, trying to recall the article she'd read in the *Globe* a few years ago, which said either that coffee did sober a person up or it didn't. She couldn't remember which.

"I'm really not drunk," he insisted, although one glance at his eyes convinced her otherwise. "I'm just . . . besotted."

"If it quacks like a duck," she muttered, glowering at him.

He gazed up at her, looking oddly boyish—an oversized, well-dressed Huck Finn. "I beg your pardon?"

"You drink of the grape," she explained, folding her arms over her chest and doing her best to look stern. She remembered a few occasions when her father came home loaded after a union meeting or a night at Fenway Park with his buddies. Her mother used to make him sleep it off on the couch in the living room, as Clarissa recalled. And in the morning they'd be lovey-dovey, as if nothing had happened.

"Nothing does happen," her mother had explained to her. "Some men are mean drunks. Your daddy is never a mean drunk."

Mark wasn't a mean drunk, either. Clarissa supposed she could put him up on the couch...except that she'd have to cut off his legs at the knees to get him to fit. Besides, if he slept on her couch, he'd be on her couch in the morning, rumpled, handsome, wealthy and hung over, wondering what the hell he was doing in her apartment. And she'd be twice as embarrassed as she'd been a few hours ago when she'd blurted out her feelings for him.

"I think I'll make some coffee," she repeated.

"No, don't do that. I came here to see you, Clarissa. But now that I'm sitting, I don't think I'd like to stand. So if you walk out of this room, I won't be able to see you anymore." He shook his head in apparent bewilderment. "Quite a predicament I'm in."

"Are you going to throw up?"

"It's a thought." He sighed, closed his eyes and leaned back until his head hit the wall, since the sofa's back wasn't tall enough for him. "Clarissa...sweetheart... you see, the *veritas* in the *vino* is that I can't marry Jane."

"What are you, crazy? Of course you can marry her!" Bad enough that Clarissa had fallen for Mark. If she thought she was in some way responsible for breaking them up... It was almost as bad as being a home-wrecker.

"Don't you see? Marrying Jane would be like...like marrying myself. We're exactly alike, other than a few genitals."

"You're not making any sense. You need coffee."

Mark snapped to attention and wagged a threatening finger at her. "If you make me drink coffee, I swear to you with all my heart that I'll throw up."

"Okay, okay. No coffee." She settled into a chair and scrutinized his complexion. It remained a reasonably healthy pink, but she wasn't going to take anything for granted.

"Well, I'm glad we worked that out," he said, then smiled placidly.

The silence that ensued told Clarissa they had no chance of ever working anything else out. She listened to the whisper of the air conditioner in her bedroom and wished she were there. She wished she could be there with Mark—only Mark sober, Mark making sense and behaving like a gentleman.

"I could take very good care of you," he said.

She blushed just thinking about it. "This conversation is going nowhere," she announced.

"You're right. It's staying right here, with us." He looked marginally more alert. "So, what do you say?"

"I don't know what we're talking about."

"We're talking about you and me. My parents won't be thrilled—I'll warn you right off the top. They're very stuffy, narrow-minded folks. I love them dearly, but they're truly insufferable at times. And the fact of the matter, Clarissa, is that you aren't quite...Caucasian."

"I'm not Caucasian at all," she snapped, in no mood to discuss racism in America with a stewed suitor.

"In all my life," he went on, "I have never really taken a chance. I've always chosen the safe route. Jane's exactly the same way, you know. She always, *always*, does what's expected of her. I don't know whether we love each other. I don't know that love ever had anything to do with it. It was just so...reasonable, our getting together. Love was never a part of it...."

"That's just the booze talking."

"That's the *veritas* talking, my dear. Let me put this simply." His eyes seemed to grow clearer, sharper. "You turn me on."

"I can't believe this!" she exploded. "You came here stinking drunk and you've got the nerve to hint that you're looking for a roll in the hay! What are you, crazy?" Because she was small and delicate-looking, people never expected her to show her temper. But in fact, her temper was in reverse proportion to her size. And right now it was radioactive.

Just because Jane had run off to Louisiana, just because she was apparently married to someone else, just because Clarissa had a wicked crush on Mark and had made the major mistake of letting him know about it didn't mean she was going to put up with this nonsense. "You can leave right now, Mr. Dennison. We have nothing more to say to each other."

"But..." He sighed and his smile grew wider. "I can't leave."

"You sure as hell can, buster."

"I can't stand up," he explained.

"I'll help you." She sprang from her chair and stormed across the room. She wasn't sure how a ninety-eight-pound weakling like her was going to haul a big lug like him off the sofa, but if there was anything more offensive than a potted guy, it was a potted, rich, white, sex-crazed guy. She wrapped her hands around his wrists, planted her feet on the rug and pulled.

And fell unceremoniously into his lap.

Yelping, she recoiled from him. "Get out!" she shrieked. "Get out! Get out! Get out!"

"First—" he gave her a plaintive smile "—I would greatly appreciate it if you would show me where the lavatory is."

"I want you out of here—"

"Your wish is my command. But I sense an imminent stomach disturbance."

"Oh, God. Here," she said, grabbing his wrists once more and lifting him off the cushions with hardly any effort. She supposed it was like those miracle cases where an ordinary mother could lift a car off her child to save the child's life. Desperation enabled Clarissa to do the impossible—propel a six foot tall, hundred-eighty pound jerk with an imminent stomach disturbance through her apartment to the bathroom in record time.

He stumbled into the small room, and she slammed the door behind him. Then she sank against the wall and let out a shaky breath.

What was she going to do? He'd gotten drunk because of her, and he was here because of her, and he was now driving the white porcelain bus because of her.

As furious as she was, she couldn't really hate him. His voice emerged through the closed door, echoing oddly as if he were still leaning over the bowl. "Clarissa?"

"Yes," she said, softening slightly.

"This is what turns me on."

She scowled. "Being sick to your stomach turns you on?"

"Living in doubt. Not knowing what tomorrow may bring. Taking a walk on the wild side. Jane would never walk on the wild side, Clarissa. I want to walk on the wild side with you."

"In your condition, you aren't going to walk anywhere, with me or without me."

"I understand that." His voice echoed more deeply; his head must have been drooping. "In my condition, I'm on my knees."

"I know."

"So it seems the appropriate time to ask, Will you marry me?"

She wanted to scream. She wanted to cry. She wanted to kick the door down and then kick him in the butt. She wanted to call him every name she could think of, in English and Vietnamese, and maybe Latin, too, while the *vino* was *veritas*-ing. She wanted to tell him to clear out of her life.

But she also wanted to walk on the wild side with him. Even if at the moment he was infuriating. She wanted to know that tomorrow could bring anything, and it could bring happiness. It could bring love. It could bring Mark.

She hoped she wouldn't hate herself for not refusing him flat out. "Let me think about it, okay?"

He said nothing. Bracing herself for whatever she might find, she inched the door open.

Mark was lying on the bath mat, smiling sweetly, sound asleep.

THE MOTORCYCLE WAS IN Cody's bedroom.

Various thoughts passed through Jane's mind: Why would anyone keep a motorcycle in the bedroom? Had Cody parked it there hoping to use it as bait to get Jane into his bed? Had he planned this entire evening so that, at some point, she would ask to see the old Hog?

No. For one thing, he couldn't have had any idea how things would work out with Stanhope. For another, he'd been pretty straightforward about wanting to make love to Jane. He didn't have to resort to convoluted schemes to get her to his bedroom. Indeed, she was sure that if she turned and marched out of his bedroom right now, he wouldn't push the issue. He hadn't pushed it with her before tonight. He'd never pushed it with her.

He'd never had to.

As bachelor pads went, his was better than the stereotype. His living room was small but relatively tidy. He had a few outdated *Sports Illustrated* magazines lying around, and a light veneer of dust layered the tables, but the framed posters on the walls were tasteful, and the rug matched the curtains. When he'd escorted her inside, they'd passed a door which, he'd said, led to the kitchen—and he'd made no move to show her that room, so she assumed that was where he kept the mess.

His bedroom, though... She wasn't certain she'd been prepared to enter this room. She'd wanted to. Lord, she'd wanted to since the day she had arrived in New Orleans and seen the man who'd once stolen her heart, and who had secretly held on to a small piece of it when she'd wrested it back from him.

The bedroom was smaller than the living room, and more cluttered. The closet door was ajar, revealing a glimpse of crookedly hung shirts, workboots and sneakers jumbled on the floor, a terry-cloth bathrobe hanging from a hook, a basketball stashed on an upper shelf and a jockstrap dangling from the inner door-knob.

Jane hastily looked away. Her gaze journeyed across the full-size bed, which had been made but not made well: beneath the slightly crooked comforter she could see wrinkles and lumps from the rumpled sheets. The bed was flanked by matching night tables, one of which held a clock radio and the other a paperback novel and a telephone. Two of the dresser's drawers were slightly open, and the top surface was crammed with grooming items, newspaper clippings, pens and a couple of dusty glass beer mugs with the names of bars etched onto them.

The mirror above the dresser threw a reflection of the room back at her—as well as a reflection of the motor-cycle, which stood in the corner behind the door, invisible to her when she'd first entered.

She closed the door so she could see the bike. Nostalgia buffeted her, a bittersweet kaleidoscope of memories. The chrome bore a few more scratches and nicks than she'd remembered, and the seat had a few more cracks in the leather surface. But she remembered that seat. She remembered perching on it, her arms wrapped snugly around Cody's lean waist. She remembered the sun bouncing off the chrome and into her eyes. She remembered the arching windshield, the mirrors, the array of dials and gauges that had always seemed more complicated than a space-shuttle cockpit to her.

She had been afraid of Cody's motorcycle the first time she'd seen it. Even more afraid the first time she'd ridden it. But by the time she'd walked out on him, one of her numerous regrets about leaving him was that she would never learn how to drive the thing.

"Why is it in here?" she asked.

"Theft," Cody told her.

She frowned at him. He was lounging against the dresser, his arms crossed and his smile crooked. "I used to keep it parked in the tenant lot, but then somebody ripped it off. Stealing a bike isn't so hard. You just lift it into the back of a pickup and take off."

"That's terrible." More terrible than if someone had stolen his Datsun, she thought. More terrible even than if someone back in Boston had stolen her BMW. The motorcycle was a relic of her youth, as precious as a museum piece. How dare anyone touch it, let alone steal it?

"It turned up the next morning near the Tulane campus. Whoever took it couldn't figure out how to hot-wire it, so they just left it in an alley. They'd snapped off all the mirrors, though, and dinged up the chrome. It took me a long time to get it back into shape. It's still got some dings," he noted, pushing away from the dresser and pointing out a gouge on one of the exhaust pipes.

"So you keep it here?"

"It's safer. I had it out in the living room for a while, but it just seemed kind of weird. I'd have some buddies over to watch a game on the tube, and they'd all want to sit on the bike. It's an old thing, you know? It can't be treated like a trampoline."

"Of course not. That would be sacrilegious."

He shot her an amused look. "I wouldn't go that far. It's a bike. Not a shrine."

But to her it *was* a shrine. Hesitantly, exercising the proper respect, she crossed the bedroom and ran her hand lightly along one of the long, graceful handlebars. She recalled the way Cody's hands had fisted around them, the way he'd leaned forward, as if daring the road to defy him. She recalled being as awed by him as she'd been by the bike.

Probably every teenage girl, at one time or another, thought a guy looked sexy on a motorcycle. But when Cody rode, Jane had considered him not just sexy but free. There had been times she was convinced that running away had been more liberating for him than for her. She'd been running away from everyone's plans for her and assumptions about her. But he'd been running away from a home that wasn't a home, a mother who wasn't a mother, an existence that wasn't anywhere near as good as he deserved.

Or maybe he hadn't really been running away, at all. Maybe he'd been running *toward* something: His life. His future. His manhood.

She moved her hand from the handlebar to the seat. The cushion was worn, the front half more deeply indented than the back. Was that shallower dent the shape of her bottom? she wondered. How many other women had sat behind Cody on the bike, snuggled up to him, clinging to him as he drove? How many had pressed their cheeks to the strong arch of his back, and closed their eyes against the biting wind, and felt the engine tremble between their thighs?

She would never ask.

"It was strange, always riding in back," she admitted.

"What do you mean, strange?"

She laughed, oddly embarrassed that she was so absorbed by her memories of her jaunts to the park with Cody, and their long, long cross-country trek on the bike. "I could never see where we were going," she explained. "I couldn't see our destination. All I could see was you."

His smile grew pensive, as if he knew why she was embarrassed, as if he was as stirred by the memories as she was. He studied her, his eyes as blue and limitless as the sky over the continent they'd crossed on the bike. Then he turned back to the bike and relaxed. "Why don't you get on?"

"I'm not going to ride this thing around your apartment," she said with a laugh.

"No, but you could sit in the front seat and see what you were missing. I should have let you take the front sometimes."

"I couldn't take the front. I didn't know how to drive a motorcycle."

"I should have taught you. Go ahead, get on."

An inner voice warned her that she shouldn't, that she was taking a huge risk. But she'd already taken too many risks with Cody. She had been taking risks with him since she'd first met him.

And risks weren't so bad. He had risked his money on her at Gussie's and won, hadn't he?

She had to shove up her skirt a couple of inches to straddle the bike. Her rear end settled into the curve of the seat and she gripped the handlebars. "Don't you dare touch that kickstand," she warned, picturing the bike toppling over with her on it.

"I wouldn't dream of it. Now...see, this is how you shift gears," he explained. "That's the gas gauge, that's the speedometer, that's the tach—"

"The tach?"

"Tachometer. Tells you how fast your engine is turning over. You drive an automatic, huh."

"I'm afraid so."

"Well, some of them have tachs on them, too. Okay... that's the engine temperature, that's the directional signals, that's the headlight. When you're riding a bike, it's a good idea to keep your headlight on all the time, even during the day. Motorcycles have to do whatever they can to make themselves visible."

She nodded, amused at how seriously Cody was taking this lesson—and surprised at the power she felt simply by hunching forward and gripping the handlebars the way he had when he'd driven it. It wasn't like a steering wheel, where the driver couldn't actually see the connection between her hands and the tires. Here the connection was obvious. She controlled that front tire. If she turned the handlebars, she would be able to watch the tire turn.

"This is neat," she said, chuckling inwardly when she thought about what her colleagues at Baker, Dunn would say if they saw her tooling about on a monster bike like Cody's Hog. "I feel like Peter Fonda in *Easy Rider.*"

Cody laughed. "Peter Fonda in *Easy Rider* wound up dead. Don't feel like him." Abruptly, he removed his jacket and tossed it onto the bed, then swung one leg over the bike and squeezed onto the seat behind her. She felt the firm warmth of his chest against her back, the iron-hard muscles of his thighs against her hips.

"Cody, what are you doing?" she asked, suddenly breathless.

"You never sat in front. I never sat in back." He curved his hands gently around her waist. "I want to see what it feels like to see you instead of my destination."

She could tell him what it felt like: scary, but powerful. Erotic. Very dangerous. More dangerous than when they'd necked in the hall at the *Sentinel* building, more dangerous than when he'd kissed her outside her hotel, more dangerous than when he'd gambled on her, and she'd won, and he'd acted as if he'd known all along that she would win because she was his wife, a part of him, someone he knew the way a man knew his woman.

He moved his hands forward, over the jutting bones of her pelvis to her thighs.

"Cody?" she said in a small voice.

"Lean into it," he murmured. "Get a feel for it." His fingers flexed against her skirt and he touched his lips to her shoulder.

Her skin broke out in goose bumps. "Cody, I'm not sure I..." Her words dissolved into a sigh as he inched her skirt higher.

"The thing about riding a bike," he explained, his breath floating through her hair, "is, you've got to trust your instincts. You can learn this and that, but in the end it's all a matter of trusting your instincts." He shifted his head, using his chin to push her hair back from her face, and nipped the edge of her earlobe.

She shuddered. Her instincts told her to travel this road, to run this route to its end. There might be freedom there, or heartbreak—or both. But her instincts told her to take this ride.

Cody slid her skirt as high as her hips. Her legs moved restlessly, anxiously, awaiting his touch. But he thwarted her expectations by gliding up to her blouse and pulling it out of the skirt's waistband. He slid one hand under the blouse to caress her midriff.

She felt heat where his palm covered her skin, heat that spread down to her hips and up to her breasts, heat that swelled to fill her soul. She thought of the bed, just a few quick steps away. "Cody, maybe we should—"

"Stay with it," he murmured, sliding his hand higher, until he reached her bra. "You're doing great." He found the clasp and snapped it open, then brought both hands under her blouse and cupped them around her breasts.

She sank against him, unable to sit straight. The trembling between her thighs came not from the motorcycle but from inside her, from the promise of where he was taking her.

He kissed her neck, grazing along the edge of her scarf. "You're a natural at this, you know?" he whispered.

She laughed, but it came out a gasp. She could feel his hardness against the small of her back. Had he been as aware of her against him when he drove? she wondered. If so, it was nothing short of a miracle that he hadn't driven off the road.

He found her nipples and rolled them between his thumbs and forefingers, squeezing. She flinched and bit her lip. What he was doing felt too good to hurt. She recalled what he'd said that first night at Gussie's, that the sex they'd had as a married couple had been phenomenal.

They were still a married couple, she reminded herself.

He urged her forward with his chest, bringing his hands out from under her blouse and down across her wrinkled skirt to the hem. When his hands made contact with her legs, she sighed, and when he shoved the skirt up to her waist and wedged his fingers under the elastic of her panties, she whimpered.

"Shh. We're shifting gears, now." His voice was a low rumble. He raised her just far enough above the seat to ease the panties off her, slithering them out from under her and down her legs.

"Cody, I think . . . the bed . . ."

"You don't like the bike?"

"I . . ." Her mind misted over as he found the dampness between her legs, the soft, yearning flesh. Her body clenched, opened and closed and burned for him. How could he do this to her? How could he take Jane Thayer, a proper blue-blood attorney, and have her writhing and moaning on a motorbike?

She didn't know. She only knew that Cody had always been able to make her insane with desire. Like no one else she'd ever met, he'd been able to turn her from everything she was supposed to be into someone else, someone guided only by her senses, by need and hunger and love.

"I want you," he said, sliding his fingers over her, into her, making her moan again.

"I want you, too," she breathed.

"On the bike."

"On the bike."

He pulled away, and she cried out in protest. But when she twisted around, she saw that he had stood only to tear off his clothes. He moved swiftly, graceful despite his eagerness. His shirt sailed across the room, his jeans dropped to the floor at his feet, he dove across the bed to yank open a night table drawer, and returned carrying a condom.

She gaped at him, astonished not just by his speed but by his body. He was bigger than she'd remembered, his shoulders broader, his torso more densely muscled. His chest was still smooth and sleek, but more substantial somehow. His hips were taut, his legs long and athletic. His erection . . .

She blushed a deep scarlet. He was definitely bigger than she'd remembered.

He gathered her into his arms and lifted her off the bike opening his mouth over hers as he set her on her feet. She trembled; her legs could barely hold her up as he devoured her with a kiss. She clung to him, vaguely aware that he was tugging her skirt down. He dragged his hands up along her legs, over her hips and up further, snagging the bottom edge of her blouse along the way. He had to tear his mouth from hers to pull the blouse and bra over her head, but as soon as she was naked his mouth came down on hers again, his tongue lunging, his groan mingling with hers. It wasn't until he hoisted her onto the bike once more, still in the driver's seat but this time facing backward, that she realized he'd left the turquoise silk scarf in place, dangling like a loosely knotted necklace around her throat.

He boarded the rear seat, facing her. He reached around her head to grab the handlebars on either side of her shoulders. "Is this thing going to collapse?" she asked.

"Not if you don't make any wild moves." He drew his legs forward, propping his feet on the foot rests below the handlebars.

"This whole thing is a wild—" she began, but he cut her off with another greedy kiss. She felt her body tumbling backward until her head came to rest on his forearms. Her soul was tumbling, too, tumbling down into the dark, passionate world she had never found without Cody—had never sought without him. He was bringing her there once more, and she could only hope that once he was done, she would be able to find her way back home, the way she had twelve years ago.

She raised her hands to his shoulders, partly for balance and partly because she wanted to feel him. His skin was smooth and hot. When she stroked down his chest, he held his breath; when she scraped her fingers over his nipples, they tightened into points and he moaned.

That she could turn him on the way he turned her on had always amazed her. She had thought herself plain and brainy—a double turnoff for most boys. But for some reason, Cody responded to her, responded with a craving that turned her on even more.

Let the bike tip over. Let it collapse. She didn't care.

She settled lower, the seat supporting her back and Cody's arms cushioning her head. She skimmed her hands down over his abdomen to his groin. "Oh, Janey...Janey..." He rocked against the curve of her palms, kissed her throat, contorted himself until he could suckle one of her breasts.

Her body arched to him. He rearranged himself once more, rising higher, using one hand to lift her legs around him. And then he plunged into her, hard, strong, filling her completely.

She was afraid to move, afraid to throw off their precarious balance. She was probably unable to move, anyway. Cody had taken over; he was the one steering, shifting gears, accelerating into the climb. All she seemed capable of was receiving him, absorbing him, feeling the length of him as he surged inside her, touching her in ways she couldn't name.

His thrusts grew fiercer, quicker. Her body clutched, tensed as they scaled the steep path. They reached the top, Jane in front as Cody had promised, seeing her destination as it loomed just ahead of her, as they raced toward it.

She opened her eyes and gazed up into his beautiful face, his sensuous lips and his luminous blue eyes. And she realized, in the instant she peaked, that her destination had been Cody all along.

CHAPTER THIRTEEN

HE WAS GETTING TOO OLD for this.

It took an eternity for him to come around to full consciousness. Once he did, he felt cramps in his thigh muscles, an ache in his back and the weight of Jane's head on his forearms, jamming his elbows against the hard chrome of the handlebars. If he moved too fast, he would topple the bike. But if he didn't move, if he stayed wrapped around her, buried deep inside her, he . . .

He would die happy, that was what.

The thought made him laugh. He peered down at Jane and found her looking stunned, her lips dewy from his kisses, her cheeks rosy and her eyes unfocused. "Hey, Janey," he whispered.

She closed her eyes and sighed. "I can't believe we did this."

"It's a first for me," he admitted. "Hang on." Slowly, carefully, he eased out of her. She let out a small moan of protest, and then a loud cry of alarm when the bike began to wobble. "It's all right—I'll get us off," he said to calm her, reaching with his foot for the floor. His leg had fallen asleep, and it nearly buckled under him, but he clung to the bike with one hand and kept the other under Jane's head so she wouldn't bang her skull on the dash. Gently, he lifted her up until she was sitting.

Her hair was a tangle of brown, her eyes were glassy, and her back shaped a beautiful curve as she hunched, bowing her head and breathing deeply. His gaze drifted to her lovely breasts, as round and firm as they'd been the first time he'd seen her naked. Her belly was still flat, her thighs as sleek as a dancer's. His attention was drawn to the seat where she straddled it. He saw the curls of hair between her legs and remembered the way she'd felt, the way she'd responded when he was inside her.

He was getting hard again.

Would she be interested in going another round with him? Or were her downcast face, her bewildered expression and the slump of her shoulders indications that she was regretting the last few minutes?

If she was, he wasn't going to apologize. Regrets were her problem, not his. He wasn't going to indulge in second thoughts or futile hopes. He'd invested way too much emotion in her last time, and he'd wound up a basket case. He wasn't going to make that mistake again. When she walked out on him this time—and it was only a matter of hours or days until she did—he wasn't going to let himself feel anything.

On the other hand, he wanted her. Call it maturity or practicality or the natural aging process, but he wanted to make love with her on his bed, with a mattress and pillows and room to move. He wanted her on top of him. Under him. All around him. Hell, he just *wanted* her. He wanted the smart, rich princess to groan and clutch at his back and come until she couldn't stand it anymore. He wanted her hot and wet and his, all his, only his.

She still hadn't moved from the bike. "Are you okay?" he asked, sliding his hand along her arm to her shoulder and savoring the softness of her skin, the rigid slenderness of the bone in her shoulder.

She lifted her face to stare at him. "How do you do this to me, Cody? What is it about you that gets me to do these things?"

"My irresistible sex appeal," he answered, grinning.

She seemed to take his reply seriously. "It doesn't make sense. We're so wrong for each other. I can't find the logic in it."

"Sex isn't logical. It isn't supposed to be."

"It ought to be logical. Here I am, thinking. I'm sure you're thinking, too. We ought to be able to figure out why this kind of thing happens when we have sex."

She was so true to form, he thought with a grin: trying to ace the written part of the test on sex. "There's nothing to figure out," he argued, blowing the written exam but raring to move on to the orals. "Animals do it. Insects do it. Plants do it."

"They don't do it on motorcycles."

"I'm sure if it occurred to them, they would."

"No, they wouldn't," she said, straightening her back and letting Cody help her off the bike. She seemed shaky on her feet. "If plants had any brains at all, they'd know better than to do what we just did."

"Admit it—you had fun."

She glared at him. Her scowl slowly dissolved into a sheepish smile. "You're bad for me, Cody."

"I know." He pulled her into his arms and kissed her. Standing face-to-face and toe-to-toe with her, he could caress her without worrying about crashing to the floor. He could run his hands up and down her smooth, graceful back and draw her so close her breasts were crushed against his chest. He could curve his hands over the soft roundness of her bottom and sense the changes in her, her hands tensing where they rested on his shoulders, her lips softening against his, her belly flexing against him as he grew harder. If this was being bad for Jane, bad was terrific.

Without breaking the kiss, they stumbled over to the bed. He shoved his jacket to the floor and dragged her up across the blanket until her head rested on the pillows. Then he rose onto her, as old-fashioned a position as there was, and conquered her mouth with his tongue.

He tried to imagine her with another man, but he couldn't. It wasn't arrogance on his part—well, maybe it was, but he couldn't imagine her digging her fingers into another man's back, wedging her knee between another man's legs, skimming her hands down another man's sides to his waist and then forward. He couldn't imagine her gasping the way she was now, or moaning, or sweetly, softly pleading with anyone but Cody to kiss her, touch her, take her breast with his mouth and suckle it. He simply couldn't imagine that she could respond to any other man the way she responded to him, because he had never responded to any other woman the way he responded to her.

She raked her fingers through his hair as he teased one breast and then the other with his tongue, as he tugged one swollen nipple and then the other with his lips. She murmured his name as he nuzzled the hollow between her breasts, as he nibbled a path down her midriff, as he dipped his tongue into her navel. She groaned as he kissed her lower, and lurched as he spread her legs and brushed his tongue against her.

She squirmed, and he clamped his hands on her hips and held her motionless as he slid his tongue deeper. He wanted to make her as crazy for him now as she'd been twelve years ago. He wanted her to think of this when she left him, when she walked down the aisle in some fancy church to marry Mark the Banker. He wanted her to think of it when Mark the Banker took her to bed. Whenever she slept with her new husband, Cody wanted her to think of her old husband, her first husband, the one who'd taught her how to love. The one who was bad for her.

Fighting his grip, she arched her hips and twined her fingers convulsively into his hair. She shook, cried out, and then unwound, settling back down onto the mattress. He could feel her pulsing against his mouth.

He let out a long, ragged breath. He had expected to savor some sort of triumph that he'd left his mark on her this way, but he felt only a strange, uneasy sadness. No matter what she thought about on her wedding night, that wedding night wasn't going to include Cody. No matter how well he loved her tonight, she was still going to leave him tomorrow.

This time, at least, he knew what was coming. He was no longer the idealistic adolescent who thought dreams really could come true and he could win the love of the princess. She would leave, and he would remember that he was better off without her. He'd never been a prince; he couldn't imagine trying to act like one, let alone become one. He could turn off all the heavy emotions and enjoy tonight, because tonight was all he was going to have with her, all he really wanted from her.

He lifted himself onto her and took her with his body, and she came again, throbbing around him, sighing helplessly as he surged inside her. All he wanted was this: Jane Thayer shattering with passion in his arms for just one night.

"THERE'S A NOTARY at the *Sentinel*," he said.

They were seated in his kitchen, drinking coffee. Jane wore one of his old shirts, the sleeves rolled to her elbows and the tails dangling to her knees. In spite of that suggestive attire, in spite of her tousled hair and her flushed cheeks and the whisker burns along the tender skin of her throat, she sat demurely, her knees pressed together and her pinkie crooked as she lifted her cup to her lips. When Cody studied her from his post, leaning against the counter and waiting for the English muffins to toast, he saw exactly what Jane was—a prim, proper Bostonian with a lusty streak that she tried to pretend wasn't there.

He knew it was there. All night long, he'd tapped into it. If their little romp on the Harley hadn't made him sore, the rest of the evening's activities sure would have. He hadn't gone at it with a woman that way since he was a kid.

With Jane, he was a kid again. A fierce, headstrong eighteen-year-old determined to take what life owed him, because life sure as hell wasn't going to deliver it on a silver platter.

So last night he'd taken, and given, and been a kid. And this morning, before any dangerous emotions had a chance to creep in and ruin everything, he was going to be an adult.

She peered at him over the rim of her cup, her eyes dark and unreadable. "A notary," she repeated.

"Maybe more than one. But I know for sure there's a lady in human resources who's a notary. We can go sign the papers if you want."

He watched her carefully, measuring her reaction. She lowered the cup and pursed her lips. Her nostrils narrowed as she took a deep breath. "That would be fine," she said. She seemed on the verge of saying something more, but she only sipped her coffee.

"I don't suppose you have the papers with you," he said, trying to keep the conversation alive.

She looked pinched, the color fading from her cheeks and her knuckles bloodless when she set down her cup and folded her hands on the table. "The papers," she said in a brittle voice, "are at the hotel."

"Then I suppose we'll have to stop off there to pick them up."

"I suppose we'll have to."

Silence. He watched specks of dust dance in the morning sunlight that slanted in from the window behind her. He didn't want to delay the inevitable, but after last night... Maybe he could convince her to stay another day or two in New Orleans before she picked up her papers and got them notarized. Sure, they'd reached nirvana on the bike, and more than a few times in bed, but they hadn't done it in the shower, or on the floor, or on the kitchen counter next to the toaster. They hadn't done it under the stars or on the couch. They still had worlds to conquer.

But she had a wedding to plan in Boston. And he had to come to terms with reality, something he'd been very good at doing in every aspect of his life except one: Jane Thayer.

The rattle and click of the toaster spewing out the English muffins tore his attention from her. He arranged the muffins on a plate and carried them to the table. Jane stared at them but kept her hands knotted together next to her cup. "I'm not hungry," she said.

Just one more day. Where was the harm? She'd still get home in plenty of time to be the fanciest bride in Massachusetts.

He flopped onto the chair across from her. He had thrown on a pair of jeans and a shirt, but he hadn't bothered to do up the buttons on the shirt, and the fabric fell open. He was glad; even with the air-conditioning on, the kitchen always got hot. "I could call in sick today," he said, trying to keep his tone casual so he wouldn't scare her out of considering the possibilities.

It wasn't until she dragged her eyes from his chest that he realized she'd been ogling him. Her cheeks grew pink again, and she shook her head. "No, Cody. I think we may as well get it over with."

"Whatever you say." He refused to take it personally. She was right, of course. There was no point in prolonging things. No point other than some mutual pleasure. They didn't love each other. They shouldn't stay married.

He decided he wasn't hungry, either. He slugged down what was left of his coffee and shoved away from the table, suddenly eager to sign her goddamn papers. He honestly didn't want to spend any more time with the slim, exquisite woman at his table, with her plain brown hair and her far-from-voluptuous figure, her shadowed gray eyes and her lawyer mind and her upper-class genes. He didn't want to spend a minute more than necessary with the woman in his shirt, her slender legs extending out from the drooping tails, her narrow wrists reminding him of a journey his mouth had taken along her arm last night, the hollow of her collarbone reminding him of the honeyed scent of her skin, the fullness of her lips reminding him of the way she'd kissed his chest, and his stomach, and his thighs and...

Damn it to hell. If she was going to clear out of his life, he wanted it done, already. He wanted her gone.

SHE WAS ABLE TO GET a seat on a late-afternoon flight out of New Orleans. By the time she'd caught her connection in Cincinnati, daylight was fading from the sky. She clicked off the overhead reading light, turned her back on the two businessmen sharing the row with her, and stared at the ghostly reflection of herself in the window. The jet flew east, leaving the sunset behind and carrying Jane into the night.

The divorce decree, signed and notarized, sat folded inside her purse. She could have packed it into her suitcase, but if she had, given the whimsies of fate, the airline would probably have lost her luggage. Airlines always advised passengers to keep the essentials with them on flights: medication, toiletries, expensive jewelry. The papers inside her purse qualified as essential.

Signing them in front of the cheerful notary in the *Sentinel*'s personnel office had been nothing more than a mechanical act. Cody hadn't even bothered to read the papers. He was as bad as Robert Stanhope. It was people like them who kept lawyers like her in business, she thought grimly.

Watching Cody scrawl his signature with such nonchalance told her not to view the signing as anything remotely ceremonial. It was just two signatures and the embossing of a notary's seal. Nothing profound. Nothing significant.

She was divorced—almost. The papers still had to be filed with the state of Massachusetts. Not that there was any rush to enter them into the record. She wasn't going to be getting married any time soon.

She tried to concentrate on what she would say to Mark when she saw him—tomorrow, she hoped. The sooner she saw him, the sooner she got her life, and his, straightened out, the better. She would be tactful and gentle; she would place the blame fully on her shoulders, where it belonged. It wasn't Mark's fault that her trip to New Orleans had opened her eyes, and she hated to hurt him.

But after seeing Cody, she was finally coming to understand what she wanted in a husband: not just the stability Mark offered, and not just the passion Cody offered, but both. It was probably too much to ask for, but if Jane had learned anything, it was that she wasn't willing to settle for stability alone.

She closed her eyes, and the ghostly outline of her face was replaced by an all too vivid vision of Cody. His shaggy black hair. His ice-blue eyes. His mouth, his tongue, his body...

An involuntary sigh escaped her. Maybe she should have settled for passion alone.

But of course that had never been an option. After making glorious love to her all night long, Cody had awakened with the blunt announcement that they could sign the divorce decree that morning. Not once had he said—or even hinted—that he loved her; not once had he suggested that their divorce was an even greater mistake than their marriage.

All he'd wanted last night was sex. And all he'd wanted the following morning was for Jane to clear out of his life.

She'd known what he wanted from her, and what he didn't want. She couldn't plead ignorance. The only surprise was that the aftermath had left her wounded and wistful, longing for things to be different, wishing that instead of the young executive tapping away on his lap top, a scruffy newspaper photographer who refused to call himself a photojournalist was sitting next to her right now, traveling back to Boston with her, swearing he was ready to renew his vows and his commitment to her.

She sighed again. A chill settled over her as the last of New Orleans' sultry weather drained from her soul. She rubbed her hands together to warm them. The two-carat diamond Mark had given her was missing from her hand. She'd packed it in her suitcase. Unlike the divorce decree, it was no longer essential.

Her hand didn't look naked without the ring. She hadn't had it that long, and she'd never really gotten used to wearing it. She still had the wedding ring Cody had given her, a cheap gold band barely thicker than a strand of hair. That was all they'd been able to afford at the time. She'd considered it the most beautiful ring in the world.

After the divorce, she'd set it back in its satinet box and tucked it into a storage trunk that was now in the basement storeroom of her condominium. She hadn't looked at it since the day she'd stashed it in there, years ago.

She really ought to get rid of it. She was sure he'd gotten rid of his.

She exhaled wearily and let her hands fall to her lap. Glimpsing her palm, she recalled something Cody had said in the lounge at the *Sentinel* just yesterday afternoon. Something about her having a long, unbroken marriage line.

She flicked on the overhead light and lifted her hand. There it was, the line he'd traced for her, the marriage line. Long and unbroken.

Just as she'd always suspected: palmistry was a load of bunk.

THE AIR IN GUSSIE'S was thick with clouds of blue smoke. Cody inhaled the familiar scent and let it sear his throat. The wail of B. B. King's guitar rose from the jukebox in the corner and coiled around him like a boa constrictor. Gussie spotted him hovering in the door and waved. "The usual?" she asked, reaching for an empty beer mug.

The usual. Taking pictures, hanging out, shooting pool. Dating here and there. A life with few demands and even fewer risks.

Pathetic.

Once, when he'd been too young to know better, he'd taken a risk and wound up, however briefly, with Jane. Less than a week ago, she'd reappeared in his life and suddenly he'd started taking risks again, fighting for his freedom at work, betting on Jane to win at pool, taking her into his home and allowing himself a taste of what he'd gone without for way too long. Like the alcoholic who takes one sip after spending years on the wagon, Cody was hooked. Weak. Thirsty for more.

But she was gone.

"Where's your sweetie?" Gussie asked.

He remained in the door. The front room was more crowded than normal. It must be a big night for lonely guys looking to lose.

His gaze circled the dim, stuffy room. The voices on the TV above the bar seemed to be coming from another universe. The screen was full of garish color. He couldn't bear to look at it. Couldn't bear to listen to the greatest blues guitarist in the world. Couldn't bear to shoot a round of pool with Darryl and Claude and Billy. Couldn't bear to spend the evening in a bar, consuming enough booze to convince himself he wasn't hurting as bad as he thought he was.

He couldn't do it. Not tonight.

"I gotta go," he called to Gussie, then pivoted on his heel and left the bar, exiting into the muggy downtown night.

He'd get over Jane, he promised himself. He'd stop hurting soon. This time was different, after all. This time he'd checked his feelings at the door before he'd gone in. She'd saved his butt at the *Sentinel,* they'd had a few kicks, and she'd said goodbye, and in his pocket he still had the money he'd won last night to remind him of her.

An unexpected chuckle slipped past his lips as he remembered her pool-playing technique. Those slow-rolling balls, those mathematical calculations—he'd practically heard the gears whirring in her head as she'd figured out her shots. But she'd won. That was the way Jane did things: not with flash, not with cocky self-assurance, but with persistence and brainpower, luck and hard work. She had always been the good girl, the quiet girl, the one most guys overlooked—yet in her own quiet, well-behaved way, she always managed to sneak past the competition and win the game.

He would get over her. He swore to himself that he would.

He crossed to his car, got in and slumped behind the wheel. More memories assaulted him, memories of her sitting next to him, apologizing—the most genuine, from-the-heart apology he'd ever heard—and prying from him the truth of what had been going on behind his own cocky self-assurance all those years ago. No woman had ever gotten to him that way. None ever would again.

With a miserable groan, he turned on the engine and pointed the Datsun for home. It wasn't an evening for

a car, he decided. The night was closing in on him,
smothering him, isolating him from everything bright
and joyous. The atmosphere felt as thick as syrup,
dragging on him, sucking down his spirit.

He got home, parked and took the stairs two at a time
until he reached his apartment. Lugging the Harley
down to the street wasn't easy, but he'd done it before,
and if ever he had to do it again, it was now. The bike
would cure him. He would get on and rev the engine
until it roared, and then he would tear down the highway. He would ride all night if necessary, from here to
there, from the past through the present and right into
the future. He would ride as far as he had to, as long as
he had to, until he'd ridden Jane out of his system for
good.

He grabbed the keys, grabbed his helmet and grabbed
the bike, refusing to dwell on what had happened the
last time he'd been on it. That was then. This was now.
He wasn't looking for sex this time. He was looking to
save his sanity, his freedom, his soul.

CHAPTER FOURTEEN

THE OFFICE SEEMED ALTERED when she entered Monday morning.

Of course, everything seemed altered. Everything *was* altered. Most of all, Jane was altered.

From the time she'd unlocked her apartment door late Friday night, fatigued from her connecting flights, her passage through a time zone and the emotional upheaval that had preceded her return to Boston, she hadn't felt like herself. She'd felt like a different Jane Thayer, the Jane Thayer who had once been daring enough to listen to her heart. She'd been reunited with that other Jane Thayer during the past week. She'd played pool, she'd outtalked and outmaneuvered a sleazy ex-minister, she'd worn a turquoise silk scarf and ridden a motorcycle in ways the designers and engineers at Harley-Davidson couldn't possibly have imagined. She had remembered what loving Cody Sinclair could be like.

Returning home to her tidy, tasteful condominium had been anticlimactic. Wandering through the pristine rooms with their expensive furnishings had made her want to replace her sofas and chairs with motorcycles. She didn't want to be a straight-A good girl anymore. She wanted to be wicked and wild.

But it wasn't easy to change course without a map. She had no idea where she was going. All she knew was that it couldn't be in the same direction she'd been traveling up to now.

And it couldn't include Cody. He might have pointed out the road to her, but he didn't want to accompany her down it. He'd made that plain enough when, the morning after they'd made love, he had hurried to the nearest notary to sign the divorce papers.

She couldn't think about him anymore. She couldn't let herself. Wherever she was headed, she would have to go without him.

And without Mark. Ending things with him—as tactfully and painlessly as possible—was her first order of business. She didn't want to leave him wounded and hating her. She reassured herself with the thought that it would be even crueler *not* to end things with him now. They had never been a match made in heaven. She suspected he knew that as well as she did. And until she'd experienced a recent taste of heaven with Cody, she hadn't minded.

She minded now. And she had to tell Mark.

But she couldn't reach him. She tried to telephone him repeatedly throughout the weekend, without success. By Sunday evening she'd left six messages on his machine. She'd even gone to his Harborside penthouse and asked the doorman to summon him. The doorman had buzzed upstairs on the intercom, but Mark hadn't been home.

His mysterious disappearance perplexed more than angered Jane. She deserved it: she had left Boston without any explanation, so Mark was entitled to leave town without any explanation, too. But she really had to see him. The sooner she could convince him that their marriage would be a dreadful mistake, the better.

At least she doubted that she'd break his heart. One broken heart was plenty.

Her heart wasn't really broken, she tried to console herself. It was just bruised—and she had no one but herself to blame for that. She had botched everything, twelve years ago and now. All her scholastic brilliance might have helped her through a billiards game, but she'd forgotten to learn how to calculate the angles and trajectories of love.

Monday morning, restless and out of sorts, she arrived at Baker, Dunn at nine-thirty. Everett Baker was chatting with one of the summer interns near the entry; he beamed when he saw Jane. "Well, well! The prodigal lawyer returns!" he bellowed.

She managed a weak smile. The prodigal lawyer was exactly what she felt like. "I understand you want me in the second chair for the Gaylord case."

"We can work that out later," he said, his aristocratic gaze running the length of her, from her neatly combed hair to her beige silk suit to her brown leather pumps, and then back up past the straight skirt to the loosely shaped blazer... to the bright turquoise scarf she'd looped around her throat. "Nice touch of color, there. Is that new?" he asked.

Her cheeks cramped from her attempt to keep her smile looking natural. Here, at this strictly conservative law firm, a colorful scarf was considered noteworthy. "Yes," she admitted, wondering what reckless impulse had made her add it to her otherwise tailored outfit.

"A touch of color in your cheeks, too. I do believe a week away from the drudgery did you good."

"Well, I'm glad to see the firm didn't collapse in my absence. If you'll excuse me, Everett, I'm sure I've got a ton of messages to plow through."

"I'm sure you do. Welcome back," he said.

She nodded at the intern and strode past them to her office. She was surprised to discover that Clarissa wasn't in yet. Promptness was one of Clarissa's assets. But her sleek L-shaped desk stood vacant before the door to Jane's private office, her computer silent, the dust cover still draped over the monitor.

The muted sounds of Baker, Dunn's suite of offices offered a profound contrast to the bustle of the *Sentinel*'s newsroom and the rabble-filled streets of the French Quarter. No doubt somewhere in the greater Boston area, a toddler was getting into trouble or a fire hydrant was spouting water and flooding a street, but one would never guess it from the cool, decorous atmosphere of this elite law firm.

Sighing, she glanced at the turquoise silk fluttering between her breasts. She wanted to believe the scarf could give her the courage she'd need to get through the day—and the rest of her life.

She unlocked her door and found her inner office clean and apparently untouched. The bud vase was empty, the windowsill dusted. A neat computer print-out on her desk listed all her messages for the week.

Clarissa had gotten that much done. So where was she?

Maybe she'd called in sick. Jane set her leather brief-case down on the carpeted floor beside her desk and pressed the buttons on her telephone console to review her phone mail. The tape was blank. Clarissa must have collected and included those messages in the printout.

She'd done her job last week. But none of the messages gave a clue as to where she was today.

Frowning, Jane dropped onto her chair and phoned the receptionist's desk. "Sally? It's Jane Thayer. Is Clarissa Bonnert in today?"

The receptionist hesitated before answering. "Um . . . yes, I think she's in the bathroom."

"Oh." Jane's frown deepened. If Clarissa was in the bathroom, why hadn't she stopped at her desk to set up her computer first? Had she been stricken just as she entered the reception area? "Is she all right?"

"Well, um..." The receptionist giggled. "'All right' doesn't do her justice. I see her coming out of the ladies' room. She's on her way."

Before Jane could say another word, the receptionist disconnected the line.

Jane's scowl cramped different muscles than her fake smile had. She struggled to relax her face, and struggled even more to make sense of why the receptionist had sounded so evasive in talking about Clarissa. Maybe it was just a coincidence that Mark had vanished and things at the office seemed slightly off kilter. Or else maybe it was simply a matter of Jane's perspective. Maybe her week with Cody had rearranged her perception of the world, and everything was actually in order, except for her.

How long had it taken her to recover from Cody last time? Years, at least. This time—in spite of the fact that she was older and wiser—it was going to take longer. This time she'd been old enough to understand the ramifications of making love with Cody. But she'd done it, anyway.

So much for being wiser. All Jane was was older.

A light tap on her door distracted her from her gloomy ruminations. "Yes?"

The door inched open and a young woman peeked around the side. It took Jane a full minute to realize that the woman was Clarissa.

She looked beautiful. Breathtaking. Without her owlish eyeglasses, with her hair hanging free, she had the exotic allure of an orchid, both delicate and sensuous. She was wearing a pair of seersucker shorts and a baggy Hard Rock Café T-shirt. And here Jane had thought she was testing the limits of Baker, Dunn's dress code by accessorizing her suit with a flamboyant silk scarf.

"Clarissa? Is that really you?"

Clarissa nodded meekly. "I wasn't sure you'd be in today," she explained, tiptoeing into the office as if she were a cat burglar. She glanced over her shoulder, then closed the door behind her and leaned against it. A shiver wrenched her shoulders, and no wonder. Her summer-weekend outfit offered little protection from the office building's high-powered air-conditioning. "You didn't call in on Friday, so I didn't know when you were coming back."

"I flew home Friday," Jane explained, remembering why she hadn't phoned the office Friday morning. She'd been naked in Cody's bed, that was why. "But Clarissa—my God. What's happened to you? You look so... different."

"Well, I didn't dress like this for work, Jane. And you can see I took care of your messages, and I helped some of the other secretaries, and I caught up on all your back files, and..." Clarissa smiled feebly. "So you've been in Boston all weekend, huh."

"Yes." A headache blossomed behind Jane's eyes. She pressed her fingertips against her temples, wishing she could rub away the pain. She lacked the strength to deal with Clarissa's astonishing appearance and her puzzling behavior. Too much else was crowding her brain; all she wanted was for this one aspect of her life—the Baker, Dunn part—to be normal. "Where are your eyeglasses, Clarissa?"

"You were in Boston all weekend?" Clarissa asked again, her smile contradicted by the frantic glint in her eyes. "Did you stay home? I mean, did you . . . did you call anyone?"

No one other than Mark, but that had nothing to do with Clarissa. Indeed, Clarissa's questions were out of line, and terribly uncharacteristic of her. One of the things Jane admired most about Clarissa's work was her unstinting professionalism. Interrogating Jane about where she'd spent her weekend was inappropriate.

Studying the lovely young woman standing before her, Jane sensed that her life had truly jumped the tracks. Everything was off. Everything was weird. Clarissa's behavior was just one more example of how totally derailed Jane was.

"It's a quarter to ten, Clarissa," she said, too weary and bewildered to become angry. "Why aren't you at your desk? Why are you dressed like that?" She waved at the seersucker shorts.

Clarissa let out a tiny groan. "Oh, Jane—I'm so sorry, but . . . I'm quitting."

"You're quitting?" Jane gripped the edges of her desk, doing her best to anchor herself. She had the feeling that if she let go she would simply float away, leaving reality behind. Her panic made her erupt. "Why in the world are you quitting? I thought you were happy

here! I've tried to be a good boss. We pay you well, and
the firm is covering the tuition for your paralegal
classes. I thought you had ambitions, Clarissa. I
thought you were taking the long view..." Running out
of steam, she petered off.

"I was going to write you a letter," Clarissa said,
lowering her gaze to the carpet. "I was just going to
write something and leave it on your desk, but...I didn't
know you were going to be here, and..."

"You wanted to sneak away? That makes absolutely
no sense. At the very least, you might have given me
some warning. Two weeks' notice at the minimum. Beyond that, though, if it's something we can work out,
if you've got some problem with your job here—"

Clarissa shook her head. "No. It's me. I just can't
work for you anymore." Her voice broke and her eyes
filled with tears.

Jane considered rising from her chair and giving
Clarissa a hug. But she'd never been a touchy-feely type
of boss. She and Clarissa had worked well together because they'd respected each other, and they'd kept their
relationship friendly but impersonal. If Clarissa was
going to start blubbering, Jane wasn't sure she could
handle it—not when she herself was so emotionally
precarious. "Are you upset about something I did?"
she asked cautiously.

"Yes. No." Clarissa wrung her hands, her white nails
glinting in the light of the desk lamp. "It doesn't matter. I just have to—"

"Don't do it, Clarissa!" a familiar male voice roared
through the closed door. It flew open, and Mark Dennison stormed into Jane's office.

If she had been startled by Clarissa's appearance, she
was floored by Mark's. Not once in all the time she'd

known him had she ever seen him in blue jeans. They were very clean, crisp jeans, so new they were starch-stiff, but they were blue denim and had double-seams and rivets at the pockets, just like the jeans regular salt-of-the-earth people wore. Mark was also wearing a cotton knit shirt with a polo player embossed on the breast pocket. He could have passed for a prep school alumnus at a reunion.

It dawned on Jane that he had scarcely acknowl-edged her. His gaze locked onto Clarissa, who had to tilt her head back almost ninety degrees to view his face. Her eyes were still glistening with tears. "It's better this way, Mark."

"No. No, it's not better. Jane," he said, at last turn-ing to her, "this whole thing has been my fault. Don't take it out on Clarissa."

"*What's* your fault?" she asked, too intrigued to be troubled by the bizarre scene unraveling before her. There stood her secretary and her fiancé, dressed for a Cape Cod vacation and talking to each other as if they were intimate companions. Jane didn't know what to make of it—except that perhaps the two of them had been replaced by aliens while she'd been away.

Or perhaps, as she'd suspected, she was so turned around she no longer recognized the universe she used to live in. Maybe Mark and Clarissa were acting nor-mally, and Jane was viewing them through a lens of de-mentia. Cody Sinclair could do that to a woman.

"Jane, I want you to believe this—nothing hap-pened," Clarissa declared.

"Clarissa and I are lovers," Mark said at the same time.

Jane *had* to be insane. There was no other possible
way to make sense of this. "Lovers?" she exclaimed,
then burst into laughter.

"That's not true," Clarissa insisted. "Mark, nothing happened. I know we spent the weekend together,
but you were drunk that first night, and—"

"Drunk?" Jane was laughing so hard her headache
vanished. The image of prim, priggish Mark Dennison
three sheets to the wind was hilarious. But Clarissa and
Mark looked so distraught, she wrestled with her gig-
gles, swallowing a final hiccup. "I'm sorry, but Mark...
Drunk? *You?*"

Clarissa launched into a desperate explanation. "See,
that was the thing. I couldn't let him leave my place because he was crocked. But I swear, nothing happened
that night. Given his condition, nothing could have
possibly—"

"My condition was excellent," he protested.

"Your condition," Clarissa retorted, "was curled up
in a fetal position on the floor of my bathroom!"

Jane clamped her hand over her mouth, but she
couldn't hold back another gale of laughter. Mark
Dennison, the scion of one of Boston's finest families,
spending the night on Clarissa's bathroom floor?

She did her best to compose herself. Clarissa and
Mark were going at each other like two opponents at a
deposition. Jane realized the necessity of defusing the
situation so that she, the only lawyer present, could get
to the bottom of the case.

She held up her hands to silence them. "Mark, sit
over there," she said, gesturing toward one of the chairs
that faced her desk. "Clarissa, you sit there." She
pointed to the love seat near the window. "Now. Ev-

eryone take a deep breath, and let's see what we have here. Clarissa, are you and Mark lovers?"

"No," she said vehemently.

Jane turned expectantly to Mark. "I'm afraid we're in love," he confessed.

Clarissa flared. "You were drunk. We really didn't do anything except buy you some real clothes and spend the weekend pumping aspirin and Pepto-Bismol into you."

"But it was done with love," he insisted. "Admit it, Clarissa. You were the first person to use that word. Even if I was a physical wreck, there was great affection in the wreckage."

"Well, maybe." She scowled.

Mark had the good taste to look abashed as he said, "Jane, I'm afraid something rather unseemly has happened. While you were away this past week, Clarissa and I had occasion to...well, to talk."

"If you wound up in a fetal position on her bathroom floor, I'd say it was more than just talk," Jane observed.

He plowed ahead. "Your absence seems to have brought us together. There's no rationale for it, no excuse. It happened, that's all."

"I understand," she said, keenly aware of how two people could fall for each other in spite of logic, in spite of everything.

"I've asked Clarissa to marry me. I know I should have discussed this with you first, but—"

"That's all right," she said. He was obviously bewildered by her equanimity, but she held up her hand to hush him before he could question her. She wanted to remain in control of the moment. "Do you think you and Clarissa would make a successful marriage?'' she asked reasonably. "Do you really love her?''

"No!'' Clarissa shouted from the love seat.

"Yes!'' Mark outshouted her. He leaned forward earnestly. "Jane, this wasn't how I wanted you to find out. But Clarissa has this absurd idea that she had to quit her job here at Baker, Dunn before she could feel free to let me court her properly.''

"I see. And you felt you had to... what? Curl up on the floor in a fetal position?''

"I had to break things off with you,'' he said contritely. His brown eyes were warm and sad, like a puppy's. "However, I believe I'm failing to do that. We've made a terrible hash of things in your absence.''

"She's made a hash of things, too,'' Clarissa snapped.

True enough, but how would Clarissa have known that? Jane eyed her secretary with growing suspicion.

"It's just a bachelor party,'' Mark said. "Surely she can cancel the contracts.''

"What bachelor party?'' Jane blurted out. "What contracts?''

"Isn't that what you were doing in New Orleans? Planning a surprise bachelor party for me? But you know how I hate those things. Surprises appall me.''

"Luckily they don't appall me. I'm pretty surprised,'' Jane said, gazing at Clarissa. "What sort of hash have I made of things?'' she asked.

Clarissa began to wring her hands once more. Her eyes glistened with tears. "I really have to quit this job.''

"Why?''

"Well...I was trying to...to find something...'' She darted a quick look at Mark, then turned bravely, if tearily, back to Jane. "I was trying to find information about the bachelor party."

"What bachelor party?" Jane asked once more.

"Well, Mark wanted to know what you were doing in New Orleans so he wouldn't be surprised. Surprises appall him."

"So he's said," Jane muttered, impatience gnawing at her.

"Well," Clarissa continued miserably, "I was trying to figure out what was going on, and—and I went into your desk. And I found some papers in there."

"Oh." Jane sat straighter, regarding her secretary with displeasure. She could figure out what papers Clarissa had found: the documents she'd assembled from her mishandled first divorce and the private investigator's report on Cody. "Those papers were in an envelope, Clarissa."

"It wasn't sealed." Clarissa's fingers were in such a frenzy Jane feared she would dislocate one of her knuckles. "I'm sorry, Jane. I didn't mean to see those papers. I was only...trying to find something about the bachelor party," she concluded lamely.

Jane checked herself before asking *What bachelor party?* for the third time.

"You searched through my desk at Mark's behest?" Jane turned to glare at Mark.

"No!" he protested.

"Yes!" Clarissa countered.

"I have no idea what she's talking about, Jane. What papers were in an unsealed envelope?"

Jane sighed. If everyone else was going to be honest, she decided she ought to be, too. "Mark, while planning our wedding, I discovered that..." She took a deep breath for fortitude. "I discovered I was already married."

"You were *what?*" Now it was his turn to be flabbergasted.

"I was married for two months when I was eighteen. It was a terrible mistake," she explained, unsure whether she was straying from the truth in calling it that. Yes, the marriage *had* been a mistake. Loving Cody had been an even bigger mistake. None of what had occurred in the past week changed that. "I discovered that the divorce had never been entered into the record. Technically, I was still married. So I went to New Orleans to complete the paperwork with my...my husband." She'd meant to refer to Cody as her *former* husband, but he wasn't. Until she took the notarized papers, which were currently sitting in the drawer of her night table at home, and filed them with the court, Cody remained her husband.

"Why didn't you tell me this?" Mark asked, frowning.

It amused her that he had the nerve to be indignant after the hanky-panky he and Clarissa had engaged in while Jane was gone! "I was embarrassed," she admitted. "The marriage had been a youthful fling. Once it was over, no one in my family ever talked about it again. It was all but forgotten."

"Not by you, apparently."

"Well, I remembered it enough to make sure all the papers were in order before our wedding plans got too far along. Unfortunately, I found that the papers were *not* in order. So I went to New Orleans to straighten things out."

"For a week?" Mark grilled her. "Surely you didn't have to go at all. You could have express-mailed the papers to the fellow—"

"I didn't think it was the sort of thing I could do long-distance. I was running the risk of opening old wounds." Cody's and hers, both.

"So, you could have flown down, done the paperwork and flown back. It shouldn't have taken a week."

Indeed, it shouldn't have. If Cody hadn't chosen to blackmail her into helping him with the former Reverend Stanhope, Jane would have been back in Boston before Mark had gotten drunk and wound up on Clarissa's bathroom floor.

She was suddenly *very* grateful to Cody for pressuring her as he had. "It didn't take a whole week," she quibbled. "And anyway, if I hadn't been gone, you and Clarissa would never have learned that you were made for each other." She gazed from one to the other, the two of them in their casual attire, their eyes wide and fierce, and their chins thrust forward pugnaciously. Bizarre as it seemed, they did make a good match. Certainly as good a match as Jane and Cody.

But Jane and Cody were a horrible match, she reminded herself—phenomenal sex notwithstanding. By the time the sun had risen and she'd acknowledged that she loved him again—actually, that she'd never really stopped loving him—he couldn't wait to tie up the loose ends of their divorce.

At least one happy couple should emerge from this mess. And it wasn't going to be Jane and Cody. "Don't quit on me, Clarissa," Jane pleaded. "If you and Mark decide to get married and you want to be a stay-at-home wife, okay—but please, don't quit now. At least stick around long enough to help me find someone to replace you.''

"You—you would still want me to work for you?'' Clarissa asked, incredulous. "After *this?*'' She gestured toward Mark.

"As long as you'd still be willing to work for me.''

Clarissa looked stunned but pleased. "If you're really sure... Okay. I'll stay.''

"And Mark,'' Jane continued, reaching into her purse and pulling out a small velvet box, "here's the ring you gave me. It's a lovely ring, but for obvious reasons, I can't keep it.'' She extended it toward him. He gave her a poignant smile as he took the box from her. "As for the reservations we made at the Ritz Carlton for the wedding, I'm sure we can cancel them. Unless, of course, you and Clarissa want to take advantage of what we've already booked.''

"Oh, I don't know.'' Mark sent Clarissa a dopily sentimental smile, then turned back to Jane. "I dread to think what my parents will say when I tell them I've chosen Clarissa as my wife. We may just choose to simplify things and elope. You probably think that's inexcusable.''

"Actually, I think it's very romantic. But you'll have to work out the details later. I need Clarissa today. Look at all these messages we have to go through.'' She lifted the printout and shuddered.

"I'm not dressed for work,'' Clarissa said, rising from the love seat.

"I don't care. Mark, leave me with my secretary. I've got a lot of catching up to do.''

He stood, his smile now tenuous. He turned the velvet box over and over in his hand. "You're taking this whole thing very well, Jane,'' he said hesitantly.

She smiled, although she no longer felt particularly amused. "I've come to learn that even though I'm pretty smart in most areas, I'm a complete ignoramus when it comes to love. But I do know there's a world of difference between fondness and desire. I'm very fond of you, Mark—but when the world is offering you a choice between the two, you ought to choose desire."

"I think you're smarter than you realize," Mark said, leaning over Jane's desk and kissing her cheek. "You're a dear, Jane. I wish you happiness. That's a gorgeous scarf, by the way." He straightened up, gave Clarissa a small, private wave, and strode out of the office.

Jane let out her breath. She was satisfied to have brought Clarissa and Mark together, however inadvertently. She liked them both, and, despite their heated argument, it was obvious that they loved each other. If she was entitled to any of the credit for their happy ending, she would take it. Given how cheerfully Cody had signed the divorce papers, a gorgeous scarf might be as close to a happy ending as she herself would ever get.

CHAPTER FIFTEEN

HE HADN'T BEEN BACK to Brookline in twelve years.

Around five years ago, his mother had dropped him a line saying she and her current boyfriend were moving to Florida, having had their fill of New England winters. She'd since broken up with the guy, but the past few Christmas cards Cody had gotten from her were all postmarked Tampa, so he figured she was still down there. Even if she were living in Brookline, though, he wasn't sure he would pay her a call. Exchanging Christmas cards was about the extent of their relationship.

He sat on his motorcycle, his helmet causing his head to sweat, and stared at the three-decker in which he'd grown up. It sat among a crowded row of equally shabby three-deckers on a busy street near the Brighton line. The place hadn't changed much. Twelve years ago, it had been a dive. Today, it was a dive. The clapboards were shedding their gray paint in sheets, the front porch sagged, and two of the windows were missing screens. From one open window, rap music blasted from a boom box. A rusty, crooked basketball hoop without a net occupied the far end of the alley that separated Cody's old home from the building next door.

His back was sore, his butt cramped, his knuckles chafed from three days' worth of wind and sun. He should have been exhausted, but he was too wired to be sleepy. He'd caught a few hours of shut-eye in Atlanta, a few more in D.C. That had been enough to get him here.

The Hog had handled well, considering. It could use a tune-up, and once he'd found his way back to sanity, he would give the bike some tender loving care. But he wasn't ready to be sane, not quite yet.

Not until he'd seen Jane one more time.

A group of kids careered down the street on Rollerblades. They were dressed in a present-day version of the way Cody used to dress, in grungy shorts and oversized shirts. They looked as if they were trying hard to appear tough, but their sweet, young faces gave them away. They were on the cusp of adolescence, certainly no more than fourteen years old.

Cody recalled how hard he'd tried to look tough when he'd been their age. Looking tough could get you through a lot in the less genteel neighborhoods of town. It could hide your disappointment when your mother didn't come home all night. It could scare off would-be pests and thugs. It could sometimes save your life.

Looking tough was something Jane would never have to know about. But until last week, Cody had never realized how tough Jane could be inside, even if she appeared as innocent and untouched as the girl he'd fallen in love with in high school.

The kids slowed as they neared Cody's bike. "Cool wheels, man," one of them remarked.

"Hey, check it out!" one of the other kids called from the rear of the bike. "A Louisiana plate!"

"Wow, man. You ride this thing all the way from Louisiana?" the first boy asked.

"Yeah."

"That's a long way."

Apparently the public schools were still teaching geography. "Yeah, it's a long way."

"Whaddya doin' up here?"

God only knew. He'd climbed onto the bike last Friday night, thinking he was only going to cruise back and forth on the interstate until he'd burned off some steam. But the night had been mild, and the truckers sharing the highway with him had given him room, and the next thing he'd known, he was crossing the state line into Mississippi. He'd tanked up on coffee in Mobile, Alabama, and he'd just kept going from there.

A man could learn a lot on a cross-country motorcycle trip. Like love. A man could learn a lot about love.

"I'm here to find a woman," Cody told the kids.

"Oh, man, there's lotsa women around here. You know Commonwealth Avenue?"

Cody grinned and shook his head. "I'm looking for a particular woman."

"Oh, yeah? Who?" As if the kid would actually happen to know Jane Thayer.

"My wife," Cody said, then revved his engine and released the brake.

"Sounds intense, man. Good luck!"

Cody waved and pulled away from the curb. Jane lived in Boston, but he wasn't done with his hometown tour yet. First he had to visit her old house, just to remind himself of who she was and what he was up against.

He headed south and west, into the more graceful neighborhoods of Brookline. Three-deckers gave way to well-kept brick apartment buildings, which gave way to charming city houses, which gave way to sprawling lawns and stately brick mansions. Years of living far from Brookline hadn't dulled his memory; he could have found Jane's old address with his eyes closed.

He knew her parents weren't living there anymore, but when he reached the end of the long curving drive-way, he felt his gut twist reflexively into a noose-shaped knot. He could almost picture the old man stepping out onto the pillared porch at the peak of the driveway, grinning proudly at the manicured grounds, the grand oaks and blooming azaleas . . . and then losing his smile as he saw a flaw in the perfect scene: Cody. A scruffy punk on a motorbike, mooning for his daughter. Cody could almost hear the old man's voice calling him a piece of dirt and ordering him off the property.

It had happened so long ago. But like an old war wound, the right conditions could bring the pain back to life.

Cody sighed. The sun was sliding down through the sky. He checked his watch. A few minutes past five.

He had no idea where Jane worked, but her home address had appeared on the divorce documents, and for reasons he hadn't bothered to analyze, Cody had made a note of the information: a block in the Back Bay neighborhood, a section of Boston as ritzy as this sec-tion of Brookline was.

Turning his back on the majestic brick mansion where she'd grown up, the mansion from which he'd convinced her to run away, he kicked the engine into gear and roared down the street toward the city, to-ward the woman he'd married, the woman who had probably spent the day filing all her legal documents so she could be rid of Cody for good.

He'd forgotten what rush hour in Boston was like— or, more precisely, rush hour with Boston drivers. The city had been designed for horses, not cars, and its mo-

torists were famous for driving like homicidal maniacs.
Cody stayed in third gear, hugging the curbs when he
could, feeling the heat of the sun-baked parked cars
penetrating through his jeans to his right leg. Every
traffic light he came to was red. Every intersection was
gridlocked. If the traffic was an omen, he'd made a big
mistake in coming to Boston.

But it couldn't be a mistake if he hadn't even thought
about what he was doing, could it? He'd been on auto-
pilot for the past few days, tearing along the highways
because he'd had to, because fate had called to him,
because he couldn't sit still, couldn't find peace,
couldn't bear not to come. It wasn't until he'd hit the
outer limits of Washington that he'd realized he was on
his way to Boston. It wasn't until he'd survived the
worst of the New Jersey Turnpike that he'd admitted to
himself that he was going to hunt Jane down once he
got there. If he'd permitted himself to think about what
he was doing, his ego would have gotten in the way. It
would have reminded him that he'd gotten along just
fine during the past twelve years without her, that she'd
walked out on him before, that now that he was over her
he should keep his distance.

The only problem was, he wasn't over her. One interlude with her on the Harley, and he doubted he
would ever be over her.

He refused to consider the possibility that once he did
find her, she would tell him to drop dead. He just kept
inching along the congested city streets, ignoring the
too-familiar sights and sounds and smells, the crush of
pedestrians with their flat Yankee accents, the *latte*
parlors and bookstores, graduate students and street
people. He ignored the smells of summer asphalt,
steaming hot dogs, auto exhausts and the tang of the

Charles River. He focused only on the road ahead of him, just as he had when he'd left New Orleans last Friday night. At a time like this, if you let yourself think, you were lost.

Her address belonged to a charming brownstone overlooking the river. He'd bet good money it was just as charming inside as out. He parked the bike perpendicular to the curb between two parked cars, dismounted and yanked off his helmet. The hot river wind tangled through his hair.

Boston, he thought. A city where a kid like him wasn't worth spit—except to one beautiful girl who'd taken a chance on him, tried to make things work out. He'd wanted her to meet him on his level, and she'd done her best. She'd put on a helmet, climbed onto his bike, and set out with him to find a new home, a new life.

Maybe this time, instead of forcing her to meet him on his level, he ought to try to meet her on hers. He could dress a little better—a quick glance at his worn jeans and his protective leather jacket layered in highway dust indicated that he needed to learn a thing or two about fashion. He could try drinking wine instead of beer and doing cultural things instead of playing pool. He could call himself a photojournalist. He could meet Jane halfway.

He pulled his backpack from the bike and climbed the steps to the building lobby, a cozy anteroom behind the leaded-glass outer door. A panel of buttons linked the lobby with the apartments upstairs. The building contained only six apartments, so each one must be pretty big.

He found the button labeled J. Thayer and pressed it. No response.

He pressed it again. Nothing. She must not be home.

Cripes. What if she was with Mark the Banker right now? Cody would really be making an ass of himself if she was.

All right. She might have been with Mark the Banker in mind last week, but she'd been with Cody in body. He had managed to distract her from thoughts about her fiancé for a few precious hours. If Jane decided she would rather have money and security than Cody, then Cody would give up and go back to New Orleans. But as long as there was a chance, as long as he had his memory of the night they'd spent together—and the nights they'd spent together twelve years ago—to inspire him, he'd fight for her, even if it meant making an ass of himself.

He pressed her intercom button one last time, then shoved the leaded-glass door open and exited the building. From the top step, he surveyed the silver-gray river and the green riverside park of Cambridge on the other shore. He studied the hazy evening sky, the cars streaming along Storrow Drive and the cars parked along curb, sandwiching in his bike. Halfway down the block a woman strolled toward the building, her gait brisk despite the muggy air. She had on a conservative beige suit—below-the-knee skirt and tailored blazer. Her clipped brown hair glittered with reddish highlights in the sun, and her eyes reminded him of a fire—dark as smoke but illuminated by an inner heat. Her cheeks were peach-pink, her lips tawny. A turquoise scarf circled her neck with jaunty color.

He continued to watch her as his pulse accelerated, as the muscles in his neck tensed up, as his fingers curled against his palms. He watched as she slowed her pace and stared at the motorcycle. Was she remembering what it had felt like to lie naked on her back on the leather seat, with Cody above her, inside her, carrying her off the way he'd carried her off twelve years ago? Was she remembering the slickness of their skin, their groans, their sighs, the velvet-hot throbbing where their bodies were joined?

He wished he wasn't remembering. His jeans suddenly felt way too tight.

She came to a complete halt and frowned at the bike, her right hand planted on her hip and her left hand clasping her leather briefcase. He could barely see her face—and then she spun around and confronted him.

He came down the steps slowly, afraid that if he raced to her he might scare her away. She held her ground, refusing to shrink from him. Her eyes widened, growing smokier and brighter at the same time as she watched his descent. He reached the sidewalk but she didn't move, didn't speak. Her expression was unreadable, her gaze impenetrable. She didn't smile. She didn't dive into his arms and cover him with kisses. She simply stared at him.

She was as much in her element as he was out of his. She looked like a Boston lawyer, and the strange quirk of her mouth told him she wasn't exactly thrilled to see him.

She wasn't wearing that obscene engagement ring, though. And she was wearing the scarf Cody had given her.

Maybe, just maybe, coming here wasn't the biggest mistake he'd ever made.

He'd certainly traveled too far just to turn around and leave. He would see this thing through, one way or another. Jane was his goal, the lure that had drawn his motorcycle along the interstates, east and north to a place he'd sworn never to return to again. Jane was his reason. His wife. His lover. The Crown Princess of Brookline, the only woman who had ever made him feel noble, the only woman who had ever made him feel whole. And even though she wasn't opening her arms to him, even though she wasn't weeping for joy—or even smiling—he understood why he'd come.

"Run away with me," he said.

THE SHEETS WERE COOL. His body was hot. Jane couldn't stop touching him, even now, when her heart was finally beginning to slow down. She ran her fingers down the center of his chest, watching with fascination as his muscles flexed, his breath caught and his groin showed the definite stirrings of renewed interest. "Don't." He laughed, closing his hand over hers before she could reach his reviving manhood.

"Why not?"

"I've been on the road for three days, Janey. I'm tired."

"You didn't seem very tired a few minutes ago."

"Those few minutes did me in." Yet he had enough energy to lift his head from the pillow, roll onto his side and urge her onto her back. He peered down at her, his eyes sleepy yet bright, bluer than a morning sky. Slowly, tenderly, he bowed to kiss her. "I didn't know what I was going to find when I got here," he murmured.

"You were going to find me," Jane said. It seemed so clear to her now. Cody's palm-reading neighbor was right. Jane had one straight, unbroken marriage line, and it led her to Cody as plainly as Cody's motorcycle had led him to Boston, to her.

He kissed the edge of her jaw, then settled his head next to hers on the pillow. "Somewhere around New

Jersey, when I started thinking, I realized I might just arrive in time to find you getting fitted for a wedding gown or something."

She closed her eyes and laughed, the full impact of her overloaded day hitting her. "I'm not marrying Mark. He's planning to marry my secretary," she told Cody.

"Yeah?"

Despite his alleged exhaustion, he couldn't seem to lie still. His hand traced the curve of her earlobe, the crease behind it, the silky strands of her hair and her neck, and then it wandered down to her collarbone, to her breast. He circled her nipple, making it swell and tingle, kindling deeper responses between her legs, in her soul. "It seems they fell in love while my back was turned."

"Well, aren't *they* trustworthy," Cody snorted.

She laughed again, then sighed as he roamed to her other breast, curving his palm around it. "I almost wouldn't have known them this morning. They've changed." He massaged her breast more firmly and her hips twitched, growing uncomfortably warm. "Love changes people, I guess," she said.

"Mmm." He skimmed his hand down her belly and between her legs, making her moan. "Wanna try doggie-style?"

She opened her eyes, about to protest, but when she saw the laughter in his gaze, she relaxed against the soft bed linens. His hand delved between her thighs again, sliding over her. "I want you," she pleaded as his strokes grew more daring, more insistent.

"Sorry," he teased. "I'm all used up."

She could see perfectly well that he was far from used up. He was full and hard, and when she tightened her hand around him he gasped and thrust against her fingers. With obvious reluctance, he peeled her fingers away.

"You're right about love changing people," he said. His smile faded. "I want to marry you, Jane."

She dragged herself out of her blissful daze and commanded her mind to remain lucid. Cody wasn't discussing youthful rebellion, running away from home, pretending to be grown-ups for the thrill of sex. He wasn't discussing unshackling herself from the expectations of her parents and teachers.

He was a thirty-year-old man asking a thirty-year-old woman to get married. This wasn't a game.

"Why?" she asked, as serious as he was. "You seemed awfully eager to divorce me just a few days ago."

"I thought that was what you wanted."

"I'd just spent the night with you, Cody!"

"And I'd spent the night with you, too. I thought all you wanted from me was a farewell—"

"We made love," she said. "It wasn't what you were going to call it. What we did was make love."

He brought his hand back up to her face, caressing the sharp angle of her chin, the hollows of her cheeks. "You walked out on me last time," he finally said, his voice faltering but his eyes steady as he gazed down at her. "This time I wanted to be ready for the inevitable. I wanted to be the one walking."

She fell silent, aware of what it had cost him to reveal so much. With Cody, the message lay between the lines. She'd hurt him, and he hadn't wanted to be hurt again.

"I thought you were glad to be rid of me," she told him. "The way you acted Friday morning, I figured it was just as you said—a farewell . . . well, you know."

"I don't want any more farewells," he said. "I didn't realize where I was heading until I was almost here, Janey. I mean, *Boston*. God. This is a town that chews up people like me and spits them out."

"Any city can chew people up. It's what people make of the place, Cody, not what the place makes of the people."

"Well, that's the thing of it. I got to talking with some kids in my old neighborhood, and they were cool. And I survived the crazy drivers. And all the red brick, and the street life, and... The river is beautiful—you know? It's cleaner than I remembered it."

"Yes. They've done a good job of restoring the Charles. It *is* beautiful," she said, his words giving her hope. Boston had become an even more beautiful city the moment she'd seen Cody in it.

"I realized I could survive this place. It's not so bad. New Orleans isn't my home any more than Los Angeles was, or Denver, or any of the other places I lived after you left me. I could live in Boston if I had to."

"You don't *have* to," she argued.

"If you're here, I do."

The romance in his words stunned her. The commitment in them moved her to tears. She clasped his shoulders and pulled him down to kiss her. "You don't have to marry me, Cody," she whispered.

"I want to."

"We're already married. I still haven't filed the papers."

His eyebrows shot up. "You haven't?"

She reached behind her to tug open the night table drawer, and pulled out the notarized divorce decree. "I haven't entered our divorce into the record," she said. "Until I do, we're still married."

He took the papers from her, skimmed them, and then tore them in half, and in half again, and again, and again, until they were tiny shreds of paper. He tossed them into the air, and they fluttered back down onto the bed like confetti. "I guess we're still married, then."

Grinning, she pulled a tiny white fleck of paper from his hair. "I guess we are."

"I can't buy you one of those million-dollar rings," he warned.

"I don't need a ring. I still have the one you gave me twelve years ago."

"You do?" A smile lit his face, then vanished. "I got rid of mine. It reminded me too much of you. Having it around depressed me, so I got rid of it."

His honesty touched her. "It doesn't matter. We'll buy new rings."

"Yeah. Fourteen-karat gold this time. Like grown-ups."

"Solid rings that will last," she said.

"Like our marriage." He shook his head and laughed. "We really are married, aren't we."

"We really are." Still smiling, she rolled into his arms.

"What are you going to tell your parents? They probably still hate me."

"I'm of legal age," she reminded him. "They don't pick my friends for me. Or my lovers. Or my husbands." She nudged him until he was on his back once more, and she was sprawled out on top of him, their bodies and their hearts aligned. "Maybe I'll just ask them how they'd feel about becoming grandparents."

Cody's eyes grew brighter, his smile warming them, warming her. "Yeah," he murmured, pulling her down to him for a kiss. His tongue slipped past her teeth and deep into her mouth, and his body arched up against her. "Let's make them grandparents right now," he whispered. "We've been married twelve years. It's time we did something about making a real family."

"Yes," Jane agreed, welcoming him into her body, into her life forever. "It's definitely time."

BRIDE'S BAY RESORT

UNLOCK THE DOOR TO GREAT ROMANCE AT BRIDE'S BAY RESORT

Join Harlequin's new across-the-lines series, set in an exclusive hotel on an island off the coast of South Carolina.

Seven of your favorite authors will bring you exciting stories about fascinating heroes and heroines discovering love at Bride's Bay Resort.

Look for these fabulous stories coming to a store near you beginning in January 1996.

Harlequin American Romance #613 in January
Matchmaking Baby by Cathy Gillen Thacker

Harlequin Presents #1794 in February
Indiscretions by Robyn Donald

Harlequin Intrigue #362 in March
Love and Lies by Dawn Stewardson

Harlequin Romance #3404 in April
Make Believe Engagement by Day Leclaire

Harlequin Temptation #588 in May
Stranger in the Night by Roseanne Williams

Harlequin Superromance #695 in June
Married to a Stranger by Connie Bennett

Harlequin Historicals #324 in July
Dulcie's Gift by Ruth Langan

Visit Bride's Bay Resort each month wherever Harlequin books are sold.

HARLEQUIN ®

BBAYG

Fall in love all over again with

This Time... MARRIAGE

In this collection of original short stories, three brides get a unique chance for a return engagement!

- Being kidnapped from your bridal shower by a one-time love can really put a crimp in your wedding plans! *The Borrowed Bride*— by **Susan Wiggs**, *Romantic Times* Career Achievement Award-winning author.

- After fifteen years a couple reunites for the sake of their child—this time will it end in marriage? *The Forgotten Bride*—by **Janice Kaiser**.

- It's tough to make a good divorce stick—especially when you're thrown together with your ex in a magazine wedding shoot! *The Bygone Bride*— by **Muriel Jensen**.

Don't miss THIS TIME...MARRIAGE, available in April wherever Harlequin books are sold.

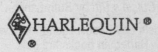

HARLEQUIN ®

BRIDE96